NGDOM

NORBURY

KAIZIA

GOLDEN CITY

ISLAND OF
SEVERED KE

THE
LEGIONNAIRE

SAMANTHA TRAUNFELD

INIMITABLE
BOOKS
UNFORGETTABLE STORIES

Published by Inimitable Books, LLC
www.inimitablebooksllc.com

Library of Congress Cataloguing-in-Publication Data is available.

First edition, 2023
Cover design by Keylin Rivers

ISBN 978-1-958607-18-3 (hardcover)
10 9 8 7 6 7 6 5 4 3 2 1

To everyone alive and dead who made this dream a possibility, but especially my mom, you have my gratitude.

Not all monsters look like monsters. There are some that carry their monstrosity inside.

-My Grandmother Asked Me to Tell You She's Sorry by
Fredrik Backman

TRIGGER WARNING

Graphic depiction of violence and self-harm, mention of infanticide, acts of religious fanatacism

1
SAIDEN

S aiden punched the tree in front of her, ignoring her already-shredded knuckles. She couldn't feel the pain of it, anyway. The moon over Norbury was just a sliver that night. It was dark enough that the stain of her blood on the tree bark seemed like just another shadow. She could barely see anything around her. She didn't mind. If she couldn't see in the darkness, at least no one would find where she was hiding.

She let the rhythm of each thud soothe her soul. This was her form of penance, a way to make up for her failure.

Their mission was to take out one lord. No other casualties.

Images popped through her head of the terrified little girl, sitting surrounded by blood, huddled against the floor. Saiden knew all too well how that blood would stain the little girl forever and couldn't help but think she would have been better off dead.

They had had a mission, and she had fulfilled it. The little girl would be taken somewhere new and given a new home. New people to raise her. And maybe, in time, she would forget the horrible genesis of her childhood and live a happy life.

She swung another fist at the tree.

She knew staying out late would get her in trouble tomorrow. She had left her partner, Mozare, to go over the details of their mission without her. At the moment, she didn't care.

She struck the tree again. The bark cracked underneath her knuckles, sending small pieces of it falling to the ground at her feet. She was sure she would have splinters, but that didn't bother her either.

Flashes of another girl—a younger one—watching her parents being taken away, her father's blood spilled in front of her. Crying out that she hadn't meant to leave the house. She pushed the image from her mind. Dwelling in the past would do her no good.

Saiden struck out at the tree again. The muscles in her arms were getting tired, and her hands shook from the exertion. She hit it one last time before she slumped against the tree and was pulled unwillingly into the land of sleep.

The first thing Saiden noticed when she woke up was the sun, hanging bright in the sky, the trees around her doing little to protect her eyes from it. If the plant life was sentient, she imagined the trees would resent her assault on one of their friends. She doubted they would have wanted to shield her.

Quickly after, she felt the stinging consequences. She had expected it and to see the damage, but she had not expected wounds where she could see down to the bone. Her hands shook, this time from pain. She held them close to her and resigned herself to the fact that she was going to have to go find a healer. Wrapping them and letting them heal by themselves would take too long and would add insult to injury when General Nakti finally came to speak to her.

She squinted against the sun and felt something sticky on her forehead. She touched it and knew without having to look at her fingertips that she was marked with blood. How perfect, she thought to herself, marked as Blood-Cursed in one more way.

She tore a strip off her ripped uniform shirt and spat on it, using it to wipe away the worst of the blood from her hairline. She couldn't do anything to change her blood-red mane from showing everyone who she was, but she refused to walk around with blood painted on her face.

THE LEGIONNAIRE

She pulled herself up from the ground, careful not to apply too much pressure to either of her hands. She was mostly sure that she hadn't broken any of her fingers, but she was worried that she wouldn't even notice if she had. It was one of the side effects of being in the Legion. She had acquired a very high tolerance for pain.

She had picked a spot on the outskirts of the forest, but close enough that she could run to the barracks within a few minutes. Saiden could feel the fatigue of yesterday's battle weighing heavily on her, mixed with her poor night's sleep, making her return take her a little longer. If she were honest with herself, she would admit to making it slower. The healers would not be happy to see her like this, and she wasn't quite ready to deal with them yet.

Not that many people ever enjoyed seeing the Blood-Cursed girl. When she first came to the Legion, they had tried to strip her of her name, as most of them did not go by the names they were given at birth. They called her shadow girl, death-bringer, Blood-Cursed, and world-ender.

But she didn't listen when they called her. She held onto the only present her parents had given her, though she could not hold it in her hands. It was the only thing she had left of them. She would not give it up for anyone.

But she had grown used to the names and the infamy that they granted her. She could terrify people without even once showing her face, and that was a great power in itself. It was the reason she had been allowed to stay with the Legion despite the fact that neither side of her Gifts had manifested. She was not like Mozare, Gifted by the goddess of death, or the healers, granted powers by the god of life. She was a fighter, strong in her own right, but the Gifts that gave her the Blood-Cursed title had not shown themselves.

Too soon, the barracks were in view.

She knew it would be better to present herself to the healers in clean clothing—save herself at least a little of their judgment—but she was not sure she could bend her fingers enough to even take her gear jacket off. She would let them heal her first, and then she would shower and change, just in time to meet her partner for breakfast.

They all stared at her as she walked through the double doors, not a single one surprised that she was coming to visit. She sat on one of the clean white-sheeted beds and waited for Kasand to come over. They were the kindest of the healers and, at this point, the only one willing to risk touching her.

She had been right about the splinters. They needed to be pulled before the healer could use their Gifts. Otherwise, they would fester under the skin and cause an infection.

Saiden sat there, not flinching or showing any outward sign of pain, while she waited for the torture to be over.

2
MOZARE

Mozare pulled himself up until his chin hit the bar secured to his wall. He had a few extra minutes before breakfast this morning since Saiden hadn't slept in the barracks last night. She was always like that after a bad mission, worried about how the world would see her as the monster she was, and determined to rid herself of the restless energy. He wasn't exactly concerned for her safety—anyone who tried to attack Saiden was a damned fool—but he was worried about what she might have done to herself. He made his way to the mess hall, hoping to find her waiting for him at their regular table.

He'd been surprised when he had first arrived at the Legion that no one would sit with her. Mozare couldn't understand why they didn't see the greatness the gods had given her. How could they not want to be near it? But then he had heard them talking about her. But he had walked in his first day and sat right next to her, not even leaving a single empty chair between the two of them. He smiled at the memory, remembering the shocked and confused look on her small face. She had pushed him away at first, but he was too stubborn to sit somewhere else. No matter how many warnings she had tried to give him, he had never changed his mind about being close to her. He could tell, maybe from his upbringing or plain intuition, that she was close to the gods, and he had known he was meant to be with her.

In the temple where he had basically grown up, the gods were revered, and those with Gifts were seen as doing their will on earth. It was why his parents had given up their only son to the Legion as soon as he had started manifesting his.

He opened the door to the mess hall, relieved to see her four red buns gathered at the nape of her neck. He half-ran, half-galloped, evoking laughs from many of the others.

He went to speak once he reached her, but she beat him to it.

"One of these days, you are going to get a blade to the gut, Moze."

He laughed at the threat. "It's not really sneaking up on ya if you knew it was me, anyway."

"Who else would it be?" she asked, turning with her tray full of food—a bowl of porridge surrounded by fruits—and made her way to their table. He grabbed a tray, piled it with random foods without really paying attention to what he was grabbing, and followed after her.

"So, where were you last night?" he asked, trying to keep his tone casual. This was how they behaved. Him worrying after her without trying, and Saiden telling him he didn't have to.

She raised one of her hands, showing off a new set of bandages.

He knew she hadn't been injured in the raid, so whatever had required the bandages was clearly new and of her own choice.

"Should I be adding time to my schedule to stack firewood?" he joked.

She looked at him, the beginning of a smile tugging at the corner of her lips. Before she could respond, General Nakti slammed her hands against the opposite side of their table. He felt Saiden stiffen next to him.

"Didn't we say no collateral?" the General asked, staring at Saiden.

His partner had followed the mission to the letter. *He* was the one who had dispatched the guards, and only because they had been trying to protect the target. But the General would always put the responsibility on Saiden since she ranked higher than him. But he was frustrated that Saiden was always the one who received the bad side of things. She was the best of them.

She bowed her head. "Yes, General."

"Then why are there extra bodies to be buried?"

Mozare tried to speak, but Nakti gave him a hard look. He knew that speaking would only make it worse for his partner. He saw the grief in Saiden's eyes, though he doubted anyone else would see her expression as anything besides rage. No one else would have been able to tell how much this conversation hurt Saiden, how heavy those extra deaths weighed on her shoulders. But *he* knew she didn't take it lightly.

He tried to keep himself from saying anything that would further aggravate their superior. These questions were just a way to keep Saiden in her place.

"You'll have recruits today," the General said, picking an apple off Saiden's tray. She took a bite out of it before replacing it. "Report to the training hall directly after breakfast." And she left without waiting for Saiden to reply because she knew she, of all her soldiers, would never disobey direct orders.

Once she was gone, Saiden stood and threw out her breakfast, everything untouched except for a single bite from the shiny red fruit.

3
LORALEI

"Your Majesty?" one of her advisors called out.

Queen Loralei had been lost in her thoughts, staring at the profiles of trained guards that had been placed before her. Her mind kept going over the recent attack, people flooding out from the streets and trying to hurt her. She hadn't thought there existed that kind of hatred in her country until she had witnessed it first hand.

She was lucky that the family she had been visiting was willing to harbor her in their home until her guards could come and run the rebels out of the streets. And now, she was being forced to pick a special Queen's Guard from the elite fighters at the Legion to protect her at the upcoming parade.

Her advisors had considered canceling it, but the seven of them had ultimately decided that the tradition was too important to abandon. Everything else Loralei deemed important—her charity days, visits to the prison, walks in the garden, and free time—had been taken away from her.

There was a servant girl standing next to her, a pot of hot water for tea shaking slightly in her hands. She went to smile at her but remembered that her advisors were likely staring at them, ready with a lecture on why servants do not make appropriate friends. So, she turned her face away and simply pushed her teacup closer to the edge of the table.

There were eighteen files in front of her, soldiers that the Legion's General considered strong fighters, skilled enough otherwise to defend her. Though her advisors had given them to her, Loralei doubted she would get much of a choice in who actually served in her new Queen's Guard.

When her tea was poured, she turned to face the men who had served as advisors to the previous king and now to her. She should be grateful, but as her coronation day grew nearer, she wondered more and more what her life would have been like had she not been selected twelve years ago.

She remembered her Choosing Day so vividly. The way the temple priest and priestess had paraded through the streets in a trance, looking for her. The next gods-Chosen monarch. She'd been playing with other children in the street, grubby fingerprints leaving mud spots on her face and clothes. They had singled her out and brought her to the palace. She only saw her aunt once since, and she had never cried as much as that day.

"I've picked six," she said, trying to remember to add authority to her voice. Her advisors often made her feel small, someone to be controlled instead of someone who would one day rule one of the most prosperous kingdoms in the known world. She handed them the papers and waited as they passed them around the table.

"Absolutely not," one of them said, passing the files to his right. "That Blood-Cursed soldier should never have been on the list in the first place."

Loralei knew they were talking about Nakti's adopted daughter. A girl meant to die as an infant but had somehow lived to become one of the country's best soldiers. No matter how often she had tried to put it aside, Loralei was stuck looking at it, thinking about what her life must be like and how the legionnaire became so good at what she did.

The Blood-Cursed girl's partner also seemed an impressive fighter, one they gave no argument to.

"She is the best at what she does. Rebels tried to kill me in the streets. If they attack at this parade, it's going to be important to have soldiers who we know are strong and loyal to me."

They bowed their heads, though she could see that they disagreed with her.

9

She doubted her controversial choice would be sent to the General, but she at least tried. Silence hung heavy in the air for a while.

"Your Majesty," Oscan interrupted her thinking again, "we were wondering who you would prefer to lead the parade this year."

"Who will be giving the speech?" she asked in return.

"Alastair, madam."

"Then let him lead." It was incredibly foolish that they needed her here at all. They made all the important decisions themselves, anyway. She wished for fresh air more than anything and didn't understand why these meetings couldn't be held in the garden. They were still well within the palace walls, but her advisors saw it as improper.

"Please excuse me." They moved to stand with her, and she quickly waved a hand at them. "Please, continue working. I'll be gone only a few moments." She knew none of them really wanted to join her.

They all quickly took their seats, turning away from her and talking in quiet voices about different arrangements. She knew her predecessor would have had them flogged for turning their backs to her, but at the moment, she let their disrespect go in favor of leaving sooner.

Loralei had been secretly blessed by the god of life, but those who found out rarely lived long enough to share the information. Chosen monarchs were not meant to be Gifted for fear they would be too partial to one side of the world and disrupt the balance. But she had been too old when her powers had appeared, too beloved by her people that to have her killed or exiled would likely have caused a rebellion.

But it was why she was barefoot now. Why the castle felt more like a prison to her than a home. The gardens were her favorite place, full of flowers and brimming with life. She took in a deep breath of the fresh air and turned, opening her arms wide.

She heard another pair of footsteps behind her. The serving girl, Cara, flew into her arms, leaving trails of kisses across her cheeks.

THE LEGIONNAIRE

Loralei smiled this time, knowing that there was no one to stop her from doing so or to reprimand her for being with a lowly castle attendant. She was not required to produce an heir. There would be another choosing ceremony when it was time for another monarch-elect, but her advisors would expect her to find a suitable husband. Another thing for her to loathe about the life she was given.

She picked Cara up, feeling a brief reprieve from the tension of ceremony planning as she swirled her lover in her arms and kissed her, taking her time to show how sorry she was for how she had acted in the hall. Loralei knew the girl understood why she had to be so cold with her in front of others, but it didn't make Loralei feel any better about it.

Still tangled in each other, they sat down at a bench Loralei had requested be moved in front of her favorite peonies. They were beautiful flowers, and the light pinks made Cara's skin glow. She rested her forehead against hers, both breathing heavily, though neither of them minded. They would get only a few moments together, and neither wanted to waste them.

She smiled again, free in her garden to do as she wished, and pulled Cara closer to her. "Will you come to my room tonight?" she asked, holding her breath as she waited for the answer.

Cara kissed her, soft lips moving over her own. "I have to prepare for the parade," she spoke, her words soft. "I will not be able to get away tonight."

Loralei had expected as much, but it still stung.

Cara ran a thumb across her cheek. "I will come the night after, though. Do not worry."

Loralei grabbed her hand and squeezed. She knew they would be expecting her back any minute. If she waited too long, they would certainly send someone after her. It would only result in punishments for Cara, which Loralei could not bear.

"Goodbye, my love," she said, kissing Cara once more on the lips, then on the forehead as she curled her bare toes into the grass at her feet.

"Until I see you again," Cara said, looking down at her lap and smiling, a blush creeping onto her cheekbones. Cara would go down to the kitchen for a few minutes, so she could attribute her rouge to the fire and not make anyone suspicious.

But Loralei knew she had brought on the blush. For now, that was enough.

4
SAIDEN

S aiden hated training recruits, which is surely why Nakti had assigned her and
Mozare the task today. They were always scared of her. Of the Blood-Cursed
rumors told as bedtime stories to frighten small children into doing as they were told.
They looked at her and were terrified before she even pulled a weapon. She hated seeing the horror on their faces.

Resigned to her new morning tasks, Saiden strapped the hilt for her kindjal
around her waist. They were her favorite weapon, though she was a good fighter with most of the weapons kept in the Legion's arsenal. The two blades, when
holstered, sat against her back where her spine met her hips. They were always
easy for her to reach, and she could sit while armed with them.

Training had been the way she had spent her days those first few years before Mozare had arrived. She had spent countless hours teaching herself new
moves, pushing her body further and further until she was one of the best
fighters in the entire kingdom. Training was one of the only things that quieted
her mind, something she had needed when she was younger, back when she
had no one.

Saiden was not in full gear. She would not need it with a bunch of new
recruits, and her body was still chafing from sleeping in it last night. She could
have asked for a salve but the healers were upset enough about having to fix her
hands that she hadn't been willing to push it.

Moze came in several minutes after her, axes already clipped into a harness on his back. He nudged her with his shoulder as he passed. Next, he shed his other weapons, leaving them in a small pile at the side of the room. She doubted either of them would use their chosen weapons today. The recruits they were going to be working with wouldn't be using bladed weapons for another few months, but she knew Mozare also felt more comfortable with weapons strapped to their bodies. The weight of having them kept her centered. Something she desperately needed at that moment.

Her partner came to stand next to her, posture slouched. Mozare was trying too hard to look calm and laid back, and she knew it was just for her. Still, she appreciated him being there. Otherwise, she doubted she could have forced herself to walk into the training hall.

"What do you say we whip these young recruits into shape?" he asked, putting both his hands on his hips.

Recruits started to join them, rubbing at their eyes as if they had just woken up.

"It looks like they are going to need it," she replied. Recruits often took a few days to get used to the early morning wake-ups. They ranged from age nine, one of the youngest ever besides her, to around fourteen, which was old enough to be exhibiting Gifts. The Legion took in everyone brought to them, and with coronation day approaching, they would need the extra hands.

As the last of them came into the room, she looked at Mozare, who stepped in front of her.

"Oldest recruits in front, youngest towards the back," he commanded. The recruits had no rank as of yet. That would come after training, when their individual skills could be judged.

Saiden kept an eye on the older kids who watched her with a mixture of hatred and fear. The smaller children looked like they were shivering, though she knew they weren't cold. She pulled her hood off so they could get a good look at her. They would stare for a while. Next, they would hate her without the fear.

Only then could she go back to her shadows.

Moze wove his way through the rows, kicking at ankles until the lines were straight. "Stance is the most important thing you will learn in training. Without a good foundation, it will be all too simple for someone to knock you off your feet." He moved to stand behind one of the oldest in line.

Saiden had noticed a special rage in her eyes.

Her partner swept a foot out, easily knocking the recruit onto the ground.

Saiden let him finish the lecture and small acts of intimidation as she picked out fourteen bo staffs, doing her best to get appropriate lengths for all the recruits.

When it was finally her turn to speak, she took a deep breath before building the walls in her mind that would separate her feelings from her training. "The bo is one of the most important weapons to train with. Even without a blade, it can do a lot of damage. If you find yourself in a fight without weapons, you can often find something in your surrounding that will have the same feel. Your fists are the only weapons you can count on having, so you must be able to rely on your brain during tough situations."

She went around passing out the staffs, ignoring the scowls and glares cast in her direction.

"If a bo is such a great weapon, maybe you'll do us the honor of a show, *world-ender*." It was the same girl Mozare had already knocked to the ground.

Saiden glanced at her partner quickly and saw he looked like he was ready to do much worse. She turned back to the stocky recruit. It would make her slow.

"Step forward, recruit." She watched the color melt from the girl's face. "If you want to fight, grab a weapon. Otherwise, you would do well to learn who your superiors are and keep your mouth shut." Saiden had tried to explain to her partner not everything needed to be solved with violence, and this was an opportunity to demonstrate it.

The recruit stepped back into line, her eyes tracing the cracks in the training room's floor.

Moze came back to stand next to Saiden, two nicer bo staffs in his hand. "It might not be a bad thing to show them what you're capable of," he said quietly, leaning into her so she could easily hear him.

"Most of them are terrified enough already," she whispered back.

She looked at him and knew what he was going to say next. They had this argument plenty of times. He was of the firm belief that if people continued to be afraid of her, she was protected from their wrath.

But she knew how easily fear became anger.

Despite knowing how this would play out, she gave him a slight nod and prepared herself to fight.

5
MOZARE

"On the walls." Mozare's voice didn't allow for an argument. Most of the recruits moved carefully at his words, walking around the others and helping the smallest among them carry and perch their weapons against the wall.

He remembered what training had been like for him when he had arrived at the Legion eight years ago. Mozare had been a scrawny young boy, all skin and bones, after the fasting rituals his parents had often required of him. He had never been in a fight and had only manifested the first sparks of his powers a few days before arriving.

His parents had not even come into the barracks with him, choosing instead to leave him to find the General on his own to explain where he had come from.

His first training session had taken place the day after, and he had barely been able to lift the bo because his arms were so weak. He relished how far he had grown, how far behind he had left the scared little temple boy.

"When you train, it's important to be aware of your opponent's weaknesses," he said, starting the main part of the lesson. "However, it's even more important to be aware of your own. We all have our shortcomings. In order to become stronger fighters, you need to work on fixing your mistakes." He shifted the bo in his hands. "Learning these basics, no matter how trivial you think they are, could be the thing that saves your life one day." They had saved both Saiden and himself a handful of times on various missions.

His partner tapped the end of her bo against the marble floor of the training room, regaining his attention. He turned to look at her, spreading his hands further on his bo.

Without warning, Saiden picked up the tip of her staff and slammed it behind his knee.

He felt the force of it pitch him forward. He stumbled and turned quickly to block the next strike.

They moved back and forth, switching seamlessly between the offensive and defensive, giving the students plenty of techniques to watch and later try to use themselves.

She launched herself against the wall to flip over Mozare, striking for his back.

He spun and moved to block her, but the strike made contact with his arm, and he hissed with pain. Saiden was much faster than he was. He dropped the bo, his functioning hand reaching up to grab at the bruise he knew was already forming under his shirt.

Saiden took advantage of the pause, swinging her bo to pull his legs out from under him. She placed the end of the weapon against his neck, waited a few seconds to see if he was going to try to fight back, and then reached down to offer him a hand up.

He accepted and knocked his shoulder against hers, smiling. When he turned back to the recruits, he saw that they now shared their scowls with him instead of saving them just for Saiden.

He sighed. "There is no shame in losing to someone who is better than you are. It doesn't matter who that opponent is." In fact, he would be nowhere near as good as he was now without the many beatings Saiden had given him. She was an amazing fighter, a weapon in the flesh, and he was glad to have her defeat him again.

His arm was sore, but feeling finally returned to his fingers as he told the recruits to get into partners.

Saiden went to get them both glasses of water.

Mozare turned his attention to one of the pairs, two younger girls of opposite Gifts.

The smaller of the two was a dark-haired girl Gifted by death. She was the only one who looked at Saiden with wonder in her eyes instead of fear. She had her hands spread to the correct spacing on her bo and stepped back, raising it as her opponent struck out, trying to overpower her. But the small girl was fast, and she defended herself before returning the strike, aiming at her opponent's fingers.

It was a dirty move, but he admired that she had gone with her instincts instead of following any misconception of rules. There weren't any when it came to staying alive in battle.

To the other girl's benefit, she took the hit with little complaint. Her only reaction was shaking her hand out and readjusting her grip on the bo.

They kept fighting, each swinging and blocking. He let them be and moved to other partners whose stance or grip he adjusted as needed.

When he could see that everyone, even the youngest among them, had worked up quite a heavy sweat, he called for lunch. From the corner of his eye, he saw Saiden nod and knew she agreed with his decision.

They stacked their staffs back up in the storage closet, briefly instructing them on the care of the bo, and they all filed out of the training room and moved towards the mess hall.

Two recruits needed the infirmary for broken bones. He knew the healers would have them ready to continue their training by later today. It was a kind of exercise in and of itself to know when you needed help, and seeking it out instead of needlessly suffering.

6

SAIDEN

The new recruits impressed Saiden, despite the unorthodox method of the training that morning. She was worried that a few of them had only joined the Legion to quench a deep-seated blood thirst. Two of them had already sent their sparring partners to the healers with broken bones. She made a note to keep a close eye on them.

She could feel her stomach rebelling against its emptiness and was glad when she and Mozare made their way to the mess hall for lunch. She was always hungry—perpetual training would do that to you—but she could feel the exhaustion in her muscles from effectively skipping the first meal despite having compiled a tray of food at breakfast.

"Give them a talk about proper diet while I get something to eat," she said to Mozare. Her mistake could at least serve as guidance to the recruits. She piled her tray high with food, sneaking around the corner to grab a few extra pieces of fruit since she had unceremoniously dumped hers into the trash that morning.

When he finished, he got himself his own tray and sat down next to her.

"I'm worried about those two," Saiden said, picking at her fingernails. It was a nervous habit that she'd had since coming to the Legion, and she doubted that her nails would ever grow because of it. Not that she really minded.

"The healers will have their arms fixed in no time," Mozare said, speaking through a mouth full of noodles and chicken.

"Not those two, Moze. I'm worried about the ones angry enough to break bones with a bo staff."

Her partner looked at her, thinking over what she had just said. "Well, you could beat them up. Put them in their place."

"That will terrify the rest of them." She had already seen enough of them flinching away from her. She didn't need to give them any actual reasons to fear her. Her chest tightened at the idea of it.

Mozare went to speak, but a tray slammed down on the table.

Saiden straightened her back, the mask of an obedient soldier sliding into place, assuming it was going to be the General come to tell her to clean the bathrooms or some other menial task she would do without argument. She couldn't hide her surprise to see that one recruit had sat at their normally solitary table.

"I'm Rhena," the girl said, looking pleased with herself. She took a sip of orange juice, closing her eyes as she swallowed.

Saiden looked at her, her own curiosity growing steadily. She glanced at Moze, but he was also just watching the recruit. A thousand thoughts raced through Saiden's mind. Saiden had seen that Rhena was a good fighter, her instincts already honed. She would have lots of good fortune in the Legion. But not if she sat with Saiden. It would soil her in the eyes of her fellow recruits.

"Go sit with the other recruits," Saiden said, her tone firm. She told herself she was doing the girl a favor, even if it hurt to push away the only other person who did not seem to be afraid of her. She had once tried to do the same with Mozare, but he had been too stubborn.

Rhena ignored her, something she hadn't expected from the recruit. "Your fighting skills are incredible," she said. "I was hoping I might get some private training with you." She looked around the hall, watching the others failing to covertly stare at her. The girl was already branding herself as a target.

Saiden knew it was a stain that would follow her, even if she were to leave the Legion. Fear burned through Saiden, panic for the young girl, and the trouble that might find her because of this choice. She turned to Mozare, who was smiling at her like he knew something she didn't. It was unnerving, sitting between the two of them, staring at her. She looked down at her plate. She was probably the fittest to be training others—the other senior legionnaires had grown old and rusted in their more official positions—but she knew she'd be damning the girl to the lonely existence she and Mozare shared.

"Those other recruits don't scare me," Rhena said, the words forcing Saiden to look back up at her. "I want to be good at what I'm doing. Like you are." She was confident, assured in a way that Saiden almost envied.

She already knew she would regret her next words, but she said them anyway. "You'd best be prepared for lots of early mornings."

Rhena fumbled her drink in excitement, placing it on the table and rushing around to grab her.

Saiden almost stabbed the recruit on instinct, shocked at unexpectedly being hugged. She didn't know what to do, so she sat there rigid until Rhena let go of her and took her tray to sit with the young girl she had been sparring with.

She looked at Mozare.

He smiled at her, bumping his shoulder against hers. "Looks like you have a fan," Moze said, taking another bite of his food.

She punched him in the stomach, and he spat it back onto his tray, laughing through the pain.

7

LORALEI

Loralei woke late that morning, alone in her bed with golden sunlight shining through her windows. She understood that Cara had duties to attend to, especially with the anniversary of her choosing day coming up in just a few days, but she hated it. She wished to elevate Cara to a position where she no longer had to work, but her advisors had voted against her. Until she was officially crowned, she had to do as they said. A sense of helplessness crept over her, filling her with dread. She was to be queen, yet there was so little she was allowed to change. She went about her routine alone, not bothering to call her ladies in waiting to help her dress. She was in a sour mood and knew that she would be cruel to anyone who came in, even if she didn't intend to be.

She sat at her mirror, a plate of untouched fruit in front of her, and gently ran a brush through her long locks of black hair. It was relaxing, and the repetitive motion centered her. When she was done, Loralei grabbed sections of it, twisting it back and pinning it behind her head. The braids were nothing as nice as Cara would have done for her, but she couldn't bear to have someone else doing it.

She dressed in a simple green gown, the sleeves and hems embroidered with flowers and gold stitching. It was long enough that the fabric covered her bare feet, so she skipped searching for the matching pair of slippers waiting at the bottom of her wardrobe.

As soon as she stepped into the hall outside their corridor, she was bombarded by three of her advisors. She wondered how long they had been waiting out there while she slept, dressed, and fretted about her purpose in this life.

"Your Majesty," Avestan spoke, bowing slightly. He didn't hesitate to throw himself into whatever matter was so important that they had waited outside her private chambers. "There are so many more decisions to be made about your Choosing Day parade, Your Majesty. Ribbon colors, light fixtures, dessert choices…"

She tuned him out as his list grew and grew with every step away from the peace of her solitude.

"Why don't you make the choices for me?" she asked, turning to him. "Like you do for everything else."

The stout man swallowed hard. Clearly, he was unsure if she was genuine in her rebuke.

She placed a gentle hand on his shoulder, and the others stopped around them. She did her best to hide her displeasure behind a pleasant mask. "I'm sure that you will decorate the palace and the city beautifully. I trust you will make excellent decisions." She smiled, internally cringing at how fake it felt. Luckily, her advisors didn't seem to notice her insincerity and bowed once more before quickly scurrying away.

Determined to finally feel useful in decisions about more important things than party decorations, Loralei realized there was a duty she had long neglected that she could tend to in the absence of company. It wasn't a task she enjoyed, but she knew it was important to care for every person under her rule. Prisoners were no exception to the standard she set for herself. Resolved, she moved her way through the palace until she reached the guarded doors that lead into the entrance of the prison.

"Your Majesty," the guards said, bending over at the waist.

"I'm here to visit the prisoners."

"Alone, Your Majesty?" one sentry asked without raising his eyes to look at her.

She didn't want an escort. Her advisors, whenever they deemed to come with her, often ushered her from the prison long before she was finished. There were cells in the deepest part of the prison that she had never even laid eyes on.

"I will shout if there is something wrong. The prisoners are behind bars. There is nothing they can do to me from inside their cells." Besides, she had her Gifts to protect her, and no one would hear the prisoners if they started raving about a Gifted queen. No one would listen, either.

She waited for the guards to move away from the door and stepped past them into the darkened stairway. She grabbed a torch from the wall with one hand and pulled her skirts up with the other. As the cold of the stone floor seeped into her soles, she suddenly wished she had worn slippers.

She skipped the prisoners at the beginning of the prison. She had visited them often and didn't have any time to waste. Who knew when another of her advisors would seek her out again and force her to leave the prison?

The floor beneath her feet eventually grew slick, and the darkness pressed in around her as she walked into the deepest part of her dungeon. She cringed at the smell of vomit and waste that bombarded her. Despite her orders to maintain a clean prison, these prisoners had been completely neglected.

She passed one cell and moved the flame closer to peer inside. There was a large man in the cell, his arms and legs all chained to the walls with thick iron chains. She could tell he used to be a bigger man. The memory of muscles hung to him even now. She stepped closer, trying to get a better look.

He surged forward, tugging against his restraints, rage in his eyes.

She almost reached for her Gift but paused to settle her nerves and move to the next cell. She understood why none of the guards or councilmen wanted her down here, but curiosity still bloomed in her despite her fear.

The next cell contained a lithe young man. A drastic difference from his neighbor. Even with the lack of muscle, he was still wearing heavy chains that pulled at his arms. The prisoner turned to watch her and bowed deeply. He moved closer, and she strained to stay where she was as he approached her. He started singing a weird song in a language she had never heard before, and she flinched as the sound broke the silence in the prison.

She walked on to the next cell, her nerves fighting to convince her to leave.

She had expected something horrible after the first two prisoners, and what she found in the third cell surprised her even more because of it.

Crouched in the corner of the cell, shivering and covered in dirt, was an old woman. Loralei stepped forward until she was flush with the bars of the cell, her torch light making the shadows in the cell dance. With a closer look, she didn't seem as old as Loralei first thought, but the prison had not been kind to the woman. The matted strands of her hair were a mix of silver gray and brown pieces.

"Why are you here?" Loralei asked.

The prisoner stayed silent, curling tighter into herself and turning away from her.

"My name is Loralei. I can help you."

Finally, the stranger's voice cracked as she spoke. "I've been locked down here for thirteen years." She coughed into her hands. "Leave me here to die and don't pester me with questions."

Loralei placed her torch into one of the holders on the wall outside the cell. "Please. It's clear you don't belong here," she tried again. "Why are you in prison?"

"They locked me up because I wanted to protect my daughter." Tears streaked paths in the dirt on her face. "They killed my husband, took my baby girl away from me, and locked me in here."

Loralei's heart broke at the words. At the truth she could feel radiating from them. "I will do everything I can to right this wrong," she said.

She swept up her skirts, grabbed her torch, and ran for the exit of the prison before she could start crying.

8

MOZARE

When afternoon training finally finished, even Mozare was tired. And he had been bruised pretty badly. He would have gone to see a healer, but he had dealt with worse. Besides, he had other matters to attend to. He went to his room, changed into darker clothing, and left a message on Saiden's door letting her know he would be spending the night drinking. It was lucky for him that Saiden had no taste for alcohol. Otherwise, his lie would never have held up to her scrutiny.

She would most likely spend the night going over her own training regime so the note wouldn't be seen until later, but they always left each other notes. They were partners. If he were to go missing without an explanation, she would surely come looking for him, which would end badly for everyone involved.

He pulled up his hood, glad that he had been born with dark hair. It made shadow bending easier since he didn't have to worry about any light blond poking through. He stepped outside the barrack doors, creeping along the edges of the building and slowly gathering darkness around him. Calling shadows was one of his greater strengths. He could also predict pregnancies and had some talent for communicating with the dead, though those weren't useful in the Legion. He had been raised to think they were doing the god's and goddess' will, so he was glad to be called to a higher purpose.

When he was clear of the building, he ran for the tree line, passing a blood-stained tree, realizing how Saiden had ruined her knuckles this time. He hid behind the trees and waited to see if he was being followed. If anyone were to see him running, they wouldn't recognize him, and he wouldn't be missing long enough for them to realize it was him. After he had been standing there for a few minutes, he turned back into the woods, slipping past the familiar landmarks that would bring him to his destination. He was glad it was getting dark outside. It would make slipping back into the barracks after curfew much easier.

Fully trained legionnaires were allowed to leave barracks whenever they wanted, though most at least requested a day of leave in advance. Mozare could not give his officers the same courtesy, seeing as where he was going would get him hung for treason.

When he passed the three berry bushes, he knelt in the grass, wiping away the pine needles and leaves he had used to cover the door. He rapped his knuckles against the barrier. First, once, then three times, then once again. He finished with four knocks. Footsteps approached, and the sound of locks clicking open before the door moved. Then he was being pulled inside. He was used to it. All outsiders were treated with hostility until they could be identified. And while nighttime was a good cover for him, the Giftless saw it as a better time to be ambushed and took extra precautions after sunset.

He spoke to the guard who brought him in, stating his name, rank, and business. When asked for the password, he quietly spoke the sentence he and Revon had agreed on last time he was there: "Let us bring to dawn the darkness."

The guard released him.

Now safely inside, Mozare pulled down his hood. Saiden liked to keep her head covered, her blood-red hair a clear sign of who she was, but it made him claustrophobic.

"Mozare, lad, come in." Revon walked through the door, dressed all in black, as usual. Surrounded by those without powers, he seemed to want to remind everyone that he had been Gifted. Only a few of the rebellion with higher clearance knew his Gifts weren't worth much. Mozare had found out the hard way after challenging the man to show his Gifts. He had gotten twenty-three lashes for it.

Revon walked in front of him, stopping every few steps to talk to someone. Mozare didn't listen to the specific words, but knew the conversations were likely asking about food delivery, different missions, or whatever other conversations the leader of a rebellion needed to have. It was Revon making himself look important, nothing deeper. When Revon finished his rounds, he led Mozare into the small room he had claimed for his office.

He was surprised to see him so relaxed after the attack they had planned failed. Their fighters couldn't even get to their target when she was without guards. Now, he doubted they would have the same access ever again.

The underground tunnels where the rebellion hid had once been home to the Legion. It'd been a few decades since the above-ground buildings were built, a show of strength by a king who should not have been wearing a crown. As pretentious as he might find Revon, he found the man to be a better leader than any Chosen monarch with their board of political advisors.

"What have you come to report?" Revon asked. He always started each of their meetings the same way.

Mozare went over their recent mission, pleasing Revon that they had killed some of the lord's guards instead of just their target. The rebellion's leader was very different from Nakti, who disliked unnecessary death. Revon valued death when he believed it would further the cause. Dead lords didn't come free, but their tenants likely wouldn't like to have their land transferred to new lords and would be more sympathetic to the rebellion's cause if they believed it would grant them reign over their own territory.

"Saiden and I were made to train recruits because of it."

"And how are the newest Legion members?"

"Strong. Each group comes in stronger and from farther away from the temples. I am sure Keir and Ilona are planning something." He bowed his head as he spoke the gods' names.

"That Blood-Cursed girl is sure to play some part in this all."

They had this conversation often, too. About why Saiden had been left alive when others with the same status were often killed in infancy. Mozare hated the way Revon talked about her and had tried many times to show Saiden was innocent, but his words had not changed Revon's mind. He doubted even the gods could change the man's path at this point.

When they were done debriefing, Revon took Mozare around, showing off his Legion deserter, another favorite pastime of his. If Mozare hadn't believed in the goodness of the people, in fighting a corrupt power that defied the gods' will, he never would have put up with it. But this was Revon's way of trying to show they had power on their side—and the righteousness of those above—so he went along with it.

Afterward, Revon walked him out, gave him a new code sentence, and sent him back to the barracks with orders to keep an eye on Saiden. Moze was always looking out for Saiden, even if that wasn't exactly what Revon meant.

When he finally fell asleep in his room, the sun was starting to move its way back up into the sky. Not that he was asleep very long since Saiden banged on his door what felt like only minutes later.

"We have to patrol the city today," she called.

He groaned, rubbing one of his hands across his face as he stepped down from his bed.

Sleepless nights were his punishment for partaking in the rebellion, and though Mozare believed the cause just, it was a price that made it hard for him to do more for them.

9
SAIDEN

The first thing she noticed was that Moze looked tired. Saiden imagined getting drunk wouldn't make for a good night's sleep. Or a peaceful wake-up. He still smelled like alcohol, but at least he was dressed.

That morning, she had strapped on her kindjal and slipped two stilettos blades into the sleeves of her gear jacket. She liked having them when they fought foreign armies. They were also good in a pinch, and since she kept them hidden, they were often a shock to her opponents when she hit them through small gaps in their armor.

She always felt better armed. People were perpetually threatened by her, and scared people were dangerous. Their fear often turned quickly to rage. She had more than a few scars to attest to that. Saiden pulled her hood tighter to hide her hair as they left the barracks.

Moze left her to go off to the kitchens for a late breakfast. He was lucky the cooks liked him enough to set aside a plate for him. Most of the Legion would have had to wait for lunch.

Saiden quickly reached the stables. They could walk to town, but she doubted her partner was up for the walk. She needed him alert in the town more than she needed to walk there. She liked the horses and had often been found in the stables when she was first brought to the Legion. It had been her only comfort before she started training. Now, she hardly made it there unless she was riding into the town.

She picked a black horse for Mozare. He would want that if he needed to call his shadows.

In contrast, she picked the brightest white horse for herself. She had secretly named him Sirius, after the brightest night star, though others felt there was no need to name animals. Especially horses in the Legion, who would be ridden until they died with no regret from their riders. Saiden did not agree. She saddled her horse while she waited for Moze to join her.

She did not put one on the other horse. Moze preferred riding bareback.

When he finally joined her, they took off, galloping through the forest as fast as the underbrush would allow them to. There was a road to town for carriages and shipments, but she and Mozare both preferred the cover of the forest. She let her hood fall while riding. She couldn't imagine there was much she could do to keep it up anyway, but as they reached the edge of the forest where it met the town, she slowed Sirius and tucked the loose strands of her hair back into her braided buns. Lastly, she pulled her hood back up to finish hiding the red locks.

They brought their horses to the first inn they reached, a small hovel in the stacks. They paid the innkeeper there to give the animals a quick bath, brushing, and some food before starting their walk through the town. Norbury was a strange one, though Saiden could only compare it to the few others that she had seen under the cover of darkness.

The city had originally been built a long time ago, and you could see the difference in the materials used to build the houses. When people had run out of room, they started squishing buildings between others or adding on top of existing houses. It made the town unique, though the levels and disarray of the construction made patrolling more challenging.

They passed a small tavern, and Mozare went in with a handful of coins to get them each a mug of cool well water. Most patrols kept to the street, but gossip stayed in the taverns. It had been her idea, on one of their first trips through the city, though she insisted Mozare go in alone. She had enough trouble with fights without adding alcohol to the mix.

In the meantime, she waited outside. There were children in the streets playing, and she watched them for a little, listening to their shrieking voices mixed with bird calls carried on the wind. She hoped none of them were sent to the Legion, where they would never be as free as those she saw in town. She heard a footstep behind her and quietly pulled one of her kindjal from its harness, retreating into the buildings' shadows.

She spotted a girl lurking and, before realizing who she was, pushed her back against one of the mismatched walls and placed the blade against her throat.

Rhena looked at her, eyes wide, and Saiden heard a blade fall from her hand and clatter against the cobblestoned street.

She pulled her own blade away, returning it to its sheath. She grabbed the recruit by her arm and dragged her out of the darkness where she could get a better look at her.

"What are you doing out here?" Saiden asked, her voice low. She didn't want people to pay her too much attention. Their gear already brought them enough of an unwanted audience. "You could've gotten yourself killed or sold into the den."

"I came for you. To learn from you."

"Well, then, lesson one: when you're following someone, you wear shoes that don't make a sound." She pointed a hand down at their feet, comparing her tightly laced boots to the shoes Rhena was wearing. She imagined the girl hadn't been given gear yet since her training had practically just started, and part of her wanted to lash out at Rhena for being so foolish. The Legion was a strong force in the town, but that didn't mean they were untouchable and that crime never happened.

She heard the bell over the tavern door ring behind them, and Mozare came out with a glass. He looked somewhat shocked to see her standing with the younger girl, though he quickly cleared his face of any expression.

"Brought a friend?" he asked, always joking.

Saiden scowled at him, face still partially hidden behind her hood. They needed to keep walking, or people would come out of the bar to investigate. She turned to Rhena. "Did you bring a horse?"

The girl shook her head. She was still staring at the two of them, her face pale, like she was wondering when the punishment was going to come. Recruits weren't supposed to leave the compound before completing training, and here she was in town. Caught by two higher-ranking members of the Legion.

But neither she nor Mozare would turn her in. She was only a child, and Moze would respect Saiden's wish if she asked him to skip reporting the incident. But they were going to have to bring her with them. There was no way Saiden would send her back alone, not knowing what danger might find her with no one there to protect her.

She addressed Rhena again. "You stay between me and Mozare. You will do exactly as we say, and when we say it. Do you understand?"

The girl nodded her head.

She was angry at her for coming, but beneath the anger, she feared for the girl's safety. Why would a young girl with such promise care so little for her reputation? Saiden would have given anything at her age, and likely still would now, to have been given a chance at being a normal soldier. To have her success and movements through the ranks celebrated instead of feared. She shook the thoughts out of her head. There was no time for pity or doubt now. They had to be vigilant. Saiden pulled a small, sheathed dagger from her waist and tucked it into the waistband of Rhena's jacket. She would not leave the girl unarmed. And this way, she would have a chance if something happened.

Together, they walked through the streets, twisting as they followed the rows of houses as the path grew steadily steeper. The town was built with the palace at its center, perched on high ground where it could be seen, if only slightly, from any point in the town. Before the stacks grew so tall, she imagined the path to the capital was easier to see, but the stacks gave the town character, which she enjoyed.

THE LEGIONNAIRE

They passed by the temple, and Saiden and Mozare both stopped to offer prayers to Keir and Ilona for blessing them. Saiden did not often feel blessed, but she believed that they had a higher plan for her, and so she endured in wait for the day when it would all make sense. As she stood, a piece of her hair slipped free from under her hood. She froze, hoping no one would see as she tucked it away.

An Enlightened, those who believed the gods would grant them divine favor in return for suffering, gasped and pointed at her. They turned and spoke to the others gathered in front of the temple.

Saiden could hear only one word of what they said, but it rang loudly in her ears: *Blood-Cursed.*

10
MOZARE

Mozare saw Saiden tense at the words and reach behind her to where he knew she stored her kindjal. He pushed Rhena behind them, slipping a small dagger out of his boot and reaching back to hand it to her. Saiden had already given her a blade, but it could never hurt to have another.

He returned his attention to his partner. Most people hated her for her curse, and that word was a strong reminder that people didn't see her as a person at all. Just a bad omen and warning from their higher powers.

The worst people were the Enlightened. They thought themselves to be the righteous seekers of the gods' true will, though none were Gifted. They stood in the streets and preached, broke mirrors to warn against vanity, forwent meals to bring them closer to the afterlife, and sacrificed each other to show their willingness to die to bring the gods closer to earth.

They made his stomach curl in on itself in disgust.

He felt a calm settle over him as his muscles tensed while he examined the group. Namely, how the tallest member inched backward, away from the fight. Mozare picked him as a target, seeing how he was trying to sneak around them. The one who had started the altercation with her outburst moved her fingers at her side, motioning two others forward.

They ran past their leader and attacked Saiden, reaching for her face with no weapons besides their broken fingernails.

Had Saiden been willing to kill them, the fight would have been immediately over with two swipes of her blades. But Saiden, contrary to what people believed about Blood-Cursed individuals, was always hesitant to take life. She saw everyone's lives as an extension of the planet and, therefore, of Ilona and Keir. Even those of people insane with the desire for power.

His partner swung out, connecting her fist with one's jaw and knocking them out cold. The second was stealthier, trying to get behind her. But Saiden was cleverer than some half-starved Enlightened.

And there was more at stake with Rhena behind her. He knew Saiden would protect the girl with her own life, even if she didn't understand the girl's fondness for her.

The individual he'd been watching moved towards him. Though he had tried to hide his gender as all Enlightened did, Mozare clearly recognized him to be male by his large size.

Despite the height difference, he didn't pull his blades. He didn't need them if they were only disarming and not taking lives. He called his shadows and wrapped them around the man, confusing him. A few of the Enlightened dropped to their knees at the sight of Ilona's Gift, and their blood wet the pavement where broken mirror shards dug into their knees, swirling through the cobblestones as it moved down the street.

The man, confused about his whereabouts, hit his head on the sign for a shop and passed out on the ground. He was sure to wake up with a headache, which he would probably enjoy. Just more suffering to bring him closer to the Almighty.

Saiden was fighting two more Enlightened. There had been only a few of them in front of the temple when the fight had broken out, but now they came out from the alleyways and from behind the temple, swarming them.

He could tell Saiden was trying to be careful, but the two she was fighting had a few cuts on their arms where Saiden had nicked them. Their blood joined the red already flowing through the streets.

Mozare, distracted by checking Saiden wasn't also bleeding, didn't see a small fanatic jumping on him with a shard of glass prepared to slice down his face. Mozare was too slow to block the blow and brought one of his hands up to press against the wound.

The assailant moved to cut him again, aiming for his upper arm, and the shard of glass ran through his skin.

He jerked away. The movement caused them both to fall into a heap on the ground. He groaned, and Saiden turned from her fight to look at him.

She paled at what he imagined was a lot of blood. He was lucky, though. The Enlightened had missed his eye, so while the cut might leave a scar, he wouldn't be permanently blind in that eye or need an eyepatch. He would never have gotten over letting the Enlightened get one over on him, especially with Revon.

He heard a whimper and looked up. Half of his vision was tinged red with blood, but he could see that one of the Enlightened both he and Saiden had assumed was passed out was pressing another long piece of the mirror to Rhena's throat.

Saiden grew stiff next to him.

"Sacrifice yourself," the individual said, "and we will return the Blessed one. We do not wish to spill divine blood, but we will do so if it rids this world of your death-bringer's corruption."

"I will come to you," Saiden said, her voice unusually devoid of emotion. She was stern when in the barracks, and respectful to Nakti, but Mozare had not heard her voice like this. She was hiding something, but he wasn't entirely sure what. Blood soaked the sleeve of his gear, and he could feel fuzziness creep into his thoughts. Saiden moved to step closer.

The Enlightened only pushed the shard tighter against Rhena, drawing a small trickle of blood.

Mozare watched Saiden freeze, and he could feel the panic she must have been feeling watching the young girl be hurt because of her.

"Drop your blades."

Saiden lowered her hands, still gripping her kindjal. She did not disrespect her weapons by carelessly dropping them but handed them to Mozare and then moved another step towards the Enlightened. When the Enlightened didn't press the glass harder against Rhena, Saiden took another step. And then another.

When she was an arm's reach away, the Enlightened released Rhena, who ran behind Saiden. Saiden half-turned to her, urging her to go to Mozare.

He held the girl tight, doing his best to keep his blood from dripping on her. He didn't know what Saiden was planning, but if it got violent, she would need to be able to concentrate without Rhena getting in the middle of it. He watched as his partner raised her hands as if in prayer and then, with one single movement, unsheathed one of her stiletto blades and pushed it up through the Enlightened's neck and out the top of their head.

He pulled Rhena further into his chest, turning her away from the bloodshed. She was shaking in his hold. Life in the Legion was a violent one, but she had had a hard enough day without the shock of watching someone's soul leave their body.

Saiden looked at him, her appearance now sullied with blood splattered across her face and her hair almost completely loose of its careful braids and four matching buns. She bent down to retrieve her weapon from the body, wiping it clean of blood on the Enlightened's garments before concealing it again in her jacket sleeve. When she was closer, he gave her back her kindjal blades, which were also quickly put away.

He wished he could tell her that there was nothing she could have done to avoid that death. That Saiden had been right in trying to protect Rhena. But he could see that his words would mean nothing right now, so he did not insult Saiden by sharing them.

Now that the fight was over and his adrenaline was fading, Mozare could feel dizziness settling in. He was losing too much blood.

Saiden ripped a piece off the bottom of her shirt and used it as a tourniquet around his upper arm.

He was glad she was there to worry about him because he could barely focus anymore as his vision started to get fuzzy.

11
SAIDEN

The sound of blood rushed through Saiden ears as it dripped down her fingertips and mixed with the red already spilled before her. She had collected her blades from Mozare on autopilot. The simple action helped to focus her slightly, but panic still clouded her mind.

She forced herself to notice what was most important, ignoring the stickiness already drying on her skin. Her partner was bleeding, the blood thoroughly soaking both him and Rhena where they were pressed together in a comforting hug. She knew he was trying to be strong for the young recruit, the same way she knew he would likely already be passed out on the ground if he weren't holding onto someone.

So she did what she did best—swallowed her revulsion and guilt—so she could help them get back to the barracks where they would be safe.

She pulled Mozare into her arms, wrapping his uninjured arm around her shoulder. He had lost too much blood. He was limp, barely hanging onto the edge of consciousness. It was times like this when she wished for the powers that made her Blood-Cursed. She'd be able to heal him immediately instead of needing to travel and depend on another person.

Saiden held Rhena's hand in her free one, keeping the terrified girl close. They made their way slowly through the city. The blood coating their skin caused people to move out of their way upon seeing them.

She sent Rhena into the inn to fetch their horses, offering a large tip if the horses came out fast. Once the animals were returned, she lifted Rhena into Sirius' saddle, tightening the stirrups so the girl's feet sat comfortably. Saiden doubted the girl was without experience, but she was clearly in shock.

It took more effort for her to get Mozare onto the back of the black horse, especially without anything to put his foot in. She eventually managed and climbed up after him. She sat behind him, keeping him steady in her arms and wishing she had saddled the horse. Even though Mozare preferred bareback, it would be much harder to get him home like this.

She pressed a heel into the horse's side, and Rhena followed.

They took the roads this time since speed was more important than cover, pushing their horses to go faster than they had on their way in. She would have to ask Rhena how she had managed to follow them on foot, but that question could wait until Mozare had seen a healer.

When they were near the compound, she turned to Rhena. "If someone asks you, tell them you saw us coming in on one horse, and you rushed over to help bring the horses in."

Rhena nodded and dismounted, grabbing hold of the reins from both horses and moving towards the stables.

Saiden would check on her once Mozare was healed, and she had debriefed Nakti. That promised to be a fun conversation.

She was supporting most of Mozare's weight now, since he had lost too much blood to sit up straight on his own. She went to pick him up and sent out a small prayer that he would forgive her whatever damage this did to his reputation. She ran with Mozare in her arms, using one of her shoulders to push the door open with a bang.

Healers rushed into the room. They took Mozare from her, two girls following after the man who held him. The fourth healer stayed behind to check after her, running hands over her and allowing the God of life's Gift to search for injuries.

Saiden was covered in blood, but none of it was hers. The healer was quick to see that she hadn't been harmed and rushed to where the others surrounded Mozare.

"I need to see Nakti. Take care of him," Saiden said. She walked out of the infirmary before the healer even had a chance to answer her.

Her nerves were rattled, and knowing that she was going to be yelled at for killing the Enlightened and letting her partner get injured didn't help. She wanted to take back the day more than anything. To stop Moze from getting hurt and Rhena from seeing her kill like the monster everyone feared she was. She kept reviewing over the fight, trying to picture a different ending. But all she could see was Rhena's blood on her hands instead. Saving the girl's life was worth letting death wield her like the weapon she was.

Nakti was waiting in her room, though she couldn't imagine how someone had gotten to the General fast enough for her to be already waiting, anger tainting her expression.

Maybe she *hadn't* known what a disaster her patrol was until this moment.

"What happened?" the General asked, her calm tone doing nothing to hide the disappointment Saiden sensed lurking under the surface.

"There was a fight," she started, her voice hoarse. "Outside of the temple." She wanted to scrub the blood from her hands, from under the broken edges of her fingernails.

"And what happened?"

"A piece of my hair slipped free in front of the Enlightened. They attacked us."

"And you killed them." It wasn't a question.

Pain lanced through her. "We did our best not to kill anyone."

"And yet, I can see it in your eyes that you have killed today."

Saiden thought of Rhena. Even if the excuse might free her of punishment, she knew she wouldn't make the day any worse for the young recruit. "We had no choice. The Enlightened had us cornered. *I* had no choice." She repeated that one sentence in her head, trying to force herself to believe it.

Nakti slammed a hand against the wall, the full of her rage on display. "You always have a choice, Saiden. You are the greatest soldier this Legion has ever trained. Death is not your choice."

The following silence was worse than her thundering reprimand.

Hidden in the harsh words was a compliment, but Saiden couldn't bear to acknowledge it. When she didn't answer or fight back against the unspoken allegation, Nakti left.

Finally alone, Saiden stripped away her blood-soaked jacket to be cleaned. She didn't bother changing the rest of her clothes, despite how soaked they were. She still had one last person to check on before she could give in to her own feelings. Then she could burn away the feeling of blood on her skin in a scalding shower.

She found Rhena hiding behind the stables, curled up and staring at the blood drying on the sleeves of her shirt.

"Mozare will be okay," she said in greeting, her voice deceptively calm. "The healers are already helping him."

She expected Rhena to look up and flinch away. When she finally did, Saiden saw relief through the tears in the girl's eyes.

She walked over and sat down, leaning back against the stables, making sure to leave space between the two of them in case Rhena didn't want her close. And waited for the right words to find her. Something to make this better.

Rhena moved over, dirt dusting her pants, and leaned into her.

Saiden felt the recruit's tears soak through the sleeve of her shirt, dripping onto the tattoos underneath. Unsure of what she could do to comfort her, she gently placed her arms around the girl. She had expected Rhena to finally see her how everyone else did.

Her actual response stunned Saiden.

She lifted her head from Saiden's shoulder and wiped her tears with the clean sleeve of her shirt. "You saved my life today," she whispered. "Is death always like that?"

"No, little one. Death is not always so violent. But things like that tend to follow me."

"You are good," Rhena said, her voice strong. "They attacked us, and you saved me."

She squeezed the young girl to her. "You need to clean up, and then we'll go have dinner, okay? And you'll see Mozare will be just fine." She helped Rhena off the ground and brought her to the showers, leaving when she was sure the girl was feeling more herself.

Then she slipped away, heading into the base.

12

MOZARE

Mozare woke in the healing tent and knew that Saiden had been the one to deliver him. She would have made it the first thing she did, despite already personally having helped to take care of his injury with the tourniquet.

He felt his arm finish knitting together. The new, healed skin was tight over the injury. He left the eye, where he had been cut, was still closed, but he opened the other one to see healers' hands over his face and his arms, likely trying to replenish the blood he lost.

"Well, you're a sight for sore eyes," he said. He would have laughed harder if he hadn't expected that would interrupt the healing.

"Shh," one of the healers said near his head. "You need your rest."

"You could come rest with me," he said softly.

"You senseless flirt," she answered, her hand pressing softly against his forehead. "You've lost a lot of blood. You need to sleep."

"I'd sleep much better with you, beautiful."

She laughed but didn't answer him.

His strength was coming back to him, the fogginess in his head clearing. He pushed against the thin mattress and, despite protests, moved so he was sitting up. "How's my face look?"

If Saiden were there, she would probably joke about it being as ugly as ever. But the healers liked him, so he wanted their opinion.

"Ruggedly handsome," one of them whispered, giggling into the sleeve of her robe.

The healer he had been flirting with stopped to look at him. "You're lucky you didn't lose an eye. The slice skipped right over it." She ran a gentle finger over the raised skin where their healing had closed up the wound. "You'll have this as a nice reminder of the day, but there's no other damage to your face."

He smiled at her, at the gentle way her hand had yet to leave his face.

"Did Saiden come in for healing?"

A different healer answered him. "I looked her over when she brought you to us, but she was in a rush to report. You know how she can be about letting us help her."

He knew entirely too well how stubborn Saiden could be about healing. She was one of the only people he knew who preferred healing the natural way. She only went to a healer when there was serious damage, like what he imagined she had done to her own knuckles, or when she needed to be fit for another mission.

"Any other visitors today?" he asked. He wanted to ask them straight out about Rhena, but he knew they would report her to Nakti and get the young recruit in trouble. If it had been any other recruit, he might not have been so hesitant, but Rhena showed kindness to Saiden. He didn't want that kindness whipped out of her.

The elder healer walked in at that question. "We were having a very peaceful day until you showed up. It would be nice if you considered our time before getting yourself injured constantly."

"But if I weren't injured so much," he said, laughing, "then you wouldn't get to see as much of this handsome face. And we both know that's the absolute highlight of your day."

13

LORALEI

Loralei was sitting in the throne room, still rattled from her visit to the prison. She hoped to find some semblance of stability from the grand seat and surrounding heavy stone pillars. Though it wasn't exactly a hiding place, as her advisors always found her. She just wanted to breathe before she was once again bombarded by questions about the decor.

In the end, Avestan was the one to locate the queen, long after her tears had finally dried. She was lucky that her skin didn't stay red when she cried, unlike Cara, whose tears stayed far longer than it took to cry them.

His bow was quick and shallow. "Your Majesty, there's been news of a brawl in town."

"Any casualties?" She cringed at the idea of another human being sent into the dark pit she had just visited, but brawls could not go unpunished. "Any prisoners?"

"We have one fallen, and a few others are injured. They claim to have been attacked by members of the Legion."

She tried to keep her voice steady. "I am sure there was a reason. Members of the Legion do not act out of turn without provocation." There had been too much anger and too much violence in her kingdom as of late.

"Your Majesty," her advisor prompted, "there are still those who wish to bring their grievances to you."

"Were there any additional witnesses?"

"Yes, Your Majesty. We brought two merchants from town who saw the fight happen."

"Bring them in first," she ordered, rearranging her skirts, hiding her shaking hands carefully behind the layers of cool silk, and sitting tall on her throne. She wanted to hear an unbiased report of what happened before she talked to anyone personally involved. Otherwise, she worried her view of what happened would be unfairly skewed.

"Of course, Your Majesty." Avestan left and quickly returned with two men, a father and son pair, from the looks of it.

Both men bowed deeply at the foot of her dais.

"Please tell me what you saw when you were in town today. Your honest recount of the day's events will help me with my final judgment."

The older man spoke, but she watched his son as he stood slightly behind and kept a watchful eye on his father. "We were traveling through town to the market. We've just been given permission to trade again after an issue with the head merchant. There were three legionnaires, though one of them seemed awfully young to be on patrol. Maybe a year or two younger than my boy. They were passing the temple when the Enlightened drew them into an altercation. I am not sure what specifically happened, but they attacked the girl. The Blood-Cursed girl," he clarified.

Loralei's mind conjured the picture of her she had seen earlier and tried to imagine her hurting anyone.

"She did her best to only disarm them, despite what people say of her. Then the leader took the younger girl captive. I was going to step in, try and reason with the Enlightened against taking a young girl's life, but the Blood-Cursed girl tried to stop them herself."

The son spoke up. "She gave up her blades, and the Enlightened gave up the girl. Then the Blood-Cursed one killed the younger girl's captor."

"Her partner was injured," the father continued, "so they left very quickly after that. But I do believe they did nothing that was not provoked and intended their actions only as a means of protection."

Loralei watched the men for a moment after he was done speaking, the sincerity of their words settling over her. "Thank you for your time," she answered and let her advisor come forward to lead the two men out of the room.

The door had not even closed before someone else had entered her throne room. In front of her were two of the Enlightened, bruises blooming on both of their faces.

"She killed our friend!" one of them screamed. "Murdered them right in front of us. There is nothing of the gods in her. She is only her curse."

Avestan stepped forward before Loralei had a chance to respond. "You will bow before Her Majesty and speak with reverence in her presence."

The other Enlightened practically spat her response. "We bow before none but the gods. We owe no reverence to a Giftless queen."

She spoke before Avestan could remove them from the room. "Then this queen owes you no help. I would appreciate your consideration while you are requesting my aid."

"In time, the gods will right every wrong," the first Enlightened said. "They will see how we suffer for them and reward us."

Loralei tried to keep her shudder from being too visible. She wondered how they would approach her if they knew she had been blessed by the gods they hold so dear.

"That Blood-Cursed world-ender—she spilled our blood without care!" the enraged Enlightened shouted. "We are pure, untainted by the world's desire or its greed, and she tainted the temple by taking life in front of it. Her existence offends the gods, and the kingdom would do well to rid itself of the pestilence she spreads within its borders."

Loralei again tried to match this image of the Blood-Cursed legionnaire to the girl who saved a child from an untimely death. She was glad the witnesses had come in first to speak to her. If she had heard this account first, fear might have pushed her to be irrational.

"I assure you justice will be served where it is due." She stood and left the room before the Enlightened had another chance to squeal their complaints.

14
SAIDEN

aiden returned to her room and gently closed the door behind her, trying to shut out the overwhelming feelings trying to drown her. She hadn't taken the time to wash the blood from her skin, and now it was crusted and itchy. Underneath the clean gear jacket she had thrown on, blood flaked off of her skin. She threw the outer layer on her bed and pulled the bloodied long sleeve shirt off, throwing it in the pile of dirty laundry. Next, she vigorously scrubbed her skin, doing her best to cleanse her mind of the screams echoing through it. When her skin was red and blotchy from her efforts, she finally stopped and pulled the gear jacket back on over her tank top.

She walked through the halls before going out into the open air. There were some shops in the compound for mercenaries. Saiden was a regular at the tattoo parlor and had set up an appointment after their last mission. The fight with the Enlightened meant she needed four leaves now instead of just three.

Her arms and a large section of her torso were already wrapped in vines, each leaf the marker for a single life she had taken. It was her way of remembering and honoring the dead. The tattoos kept her mind on the cycle of birth, death, and rebirth. Death paved the way for more life, just as life gave way to more death. There was balance in all things.

The size and spread of the design was the reason she always wore long sleeves. She hadn't needed to for the first few tattoos, but as her body count grew, the vines twisted down her arms. She could've lied about them, but that would go against their purpose, and so she resigned herself to the extra coverage.

The tattooist, Niran, was the only person besides Mozare ever to see the tattoos or know what they meant.

Saiden knocked on the door as she crossed over the threshold. Niran was prone to daydreaming, something she could not do as a soldier, and she didn't want to startle the woman.

"My best customer," the tattooist said, nodding at her.

Saiden had been surprised the first time she visited the parlor to see no hate in Niran's eyes. She was pure-hearted, though she explained the benevolence away as a ploy to get more customers. Saiden saw the truth, and it had made her like the woman, even if she didn't openly admit it.

She locked the door. Niran always respected her privacy, and Saiden felt better knowing no one would be able to come in without advance notice. She shrugged off her jacket and offered her right arm to the artist, where the vines only twisted down to her elbow. More were sure to come. She had space on her other arm as well, but considerably less than on her right.

"How many today?"

Saiden had never seen judgment in Niran's eyes. Only remorse.

"Four."

"I'll have to bring the vine down, then." She readied supplies at the counter and started sharpening the metal instrument. She was as careful with her tools as Saiden was with her blades, which had fascinated the legionnaire since her first tattoo. Next to it was green ink, the same hue used for all the other leaves. The label even read *Saiden's shade*, which made her smile.

When Niran started, Saiden ground her teeth together. The tattoos were slow, and the first few dips of the metal into her skin always hurt the worst. But the pain numbed with time, and it served as good penance for the lives she had taken.

Niran curled the vine down until it was a few inches under her elbow—she wouldn't have to bring it down for a few visits after that.

"You wear these like scars," the artist said, tracing a light finger over some of the earlier leaves.

There were real scars mixed in among them, though none were prominent enough for her to remember where they came from. Most of them were probably from training. It was a rare opponent that actually made contact in a fight.

Niran started inking the new leaves, commemorating the latest deaths. "You remember the dead like no one else. You are not the monster they think you are."

Saiden looked at her, tilting her head to the side. She could've guessed that Niran thought as much. The woman was always kind, but Saiden had never expected her to voice the words. Besides, there were so few people who truly believed in her that she couldn't believe they had it right and everyone else was wrong. But she would continue to fight to defend her place in their world. The gods did not put her there by accident, and she would show those who doubted and feared her that they were wrong in doing so.

When Niran was done, Saiden paid her, making sure to tip well to keep Niran in a good mood. It would be hard for her if she had to find another tattooist, and she doubted anyone else would keep ink mixed in her perfect color on hand.

She pulled her jacket back on before unlocking the door and heading out. Someone was sitting outside the door. She was surprised to see it was Mozare. She had been planning on picking him up from the infirmary for dinner, not on finding him waiting for her at the tattoo parlor.

"You shouldn't keep getting those. The weight is not yours to carry."

"Their deaths came from my hand. They are very much my weight to carry."

They had this discussion a lot, where Mozare tried to convince her to turn away from her feelings. He saw everything in the world so easily. The line for him was so clear. But she had been born on the line, one foot on either side of it, and she knew that things weren't as easy as they seemed to her partner.

15

MOZARE

"Nakti wants us," Mozare said.

Saiden was still busy looking him over for injuries, even though the healers wouldn't have let him out of their sights if he had still been injured.

The healers had done their best, but even their Gifts wouldn't stop him from having a scar. It started at one corner of his forehead, crossed over his nose, and ended in the middle of his cheek. It was an honorable mark, though he couldn't help vainly thinking about how it divided his face.

When she was done with her assessment, she briefly hugged him. Saiden wasn't really one for physical affection, especially if there was a possibility of a crowd. But he knew she was happy that he was okay.

They met a few other legionnaires outside of Nakti's office and fell into line against the wall in order of rank. The act often made him feel more like a schoolboy than a trained soldier, but he imagined that was part of the reason Nakti preferred they presented themselves like that. He believed the only other reason was to put the others in their place without actively reminding them that Saiden outranked them. It was clever on her part to maintain control of the situation the way she did.

The General came out of her office a few minutes after the last of their group had arrived. There were six of them in total, and the last to arrive was lucky he hadn't been late enough to incur Nakti's ire. The woman valued punctuality, even more so when her presence was required.

"You have been selected," she said, her back straight as she walked up and down the short line of gathered soldiers, "to guard the queen."

Two of the younger legionnaires, a boy and a girl, gasped at the end of the line. Clearly, they had not expected an assignment of this importance.

Nakti turned to look at them, and they straightened against the wall. She didn't even have to speak to correct them.

"The anniversary of her Choosing Day is coming, and they have ordered extra security for the event," the General continued.

Mozare and Saiden were aware of the threats against the crown, especially the young queen-to-be. It was why he and Saiden had been sent on so many missions lately to protect the queen's interests. In truth, they were to remove threats to her authority, which Mozare found ironic. If he were ever caught, he would be executed for being just that.

Saiden stepped away from the wall and dropped to one knee. It was a show of respect towards Nakti and an understanding of their mission. He copied her, and the rest followed. For them, it was an honor to be selected. For him, it was an opportunity.

When they were dismissed, he told Saiden he was tired and would be in his room before their shared training exercises. Between the lack of sleep the night before and the blood loss, it wasn't exactly a lie.

It was dangerous to head to the rebellion compound during the day, but his news couldn't wait. The rebellion would need time to organize a strike at the parade. They would need all the advance warning possible.

Unfortunately, shadows didn't help him during the day. It would be much too obvious that he was up to something suspicious. Instead, he utilized his rank. If he walked as if he belonged, there were very few people who would question him. He only had to worry about Saiden or Nakti seeing him, but the two of them were currently holed up in the General's office going over the security detail.

He walked until he was hidden by the trees, then sprinted through the underbrush. He still had gear on. The protective barrier easily pushed branches and thorn bushes out of the way as he ran past them. The material was tough enough that it would not rip, and it would protect his skin from scratches he couldn't explain.

He had been granted this opportunity to serve the gods, and that higher purpose had made sure everything had been set into place. It was what had always guided him, what gave him his understanding of right and wrong. It was why he wanted to see the queen dethroned, why he couldn't stand to serve a government that shunned the Gifted. Those in power were turning away from Ilona and Keir, and it was the greatest treason one could commit. To him, it was an unforgivable act.

He knocked at the door again, not paying enough attention to whether he had knocked three or four times. They would see him, the energy running through him, and know that any mistake had been caused by his urgency to share information.

The door was opened for him, though very hesitantly considering it was still daylight. They couldn't afford for anyone to realize the underground compound was a stronghold for the rebellion.

The thought sobered him. He couldn't get carried away with sharing information to the point that he revealed their location and got a lot of good people killed. It would go against the gods' will.

"Boy, you rush in here without care for our position," Revon started, not bothering to ask him for the code sentence created at the end of his last visit. The commander's face was bright red, and Mozare imagined if he got much angrier, smoke would most likely start pouring from his ears. The thought made him want to laugh, but he managed to contain it, if only barely.

"I am sorry to have come so hastily." He wasn't good at apologizing or being formal, so he did his best to speak as Saiden did. "But I have urgent news that could not wait." Mozare proceeded to tell him about the parade. That he had been picked as one of the Queen's Guard.

Revon listened, running a thick-knuckled hand over his face.

"This is what we've been waiting for. The public venue, the crowds, it would be almost too easy."

Mozare smiled, listening to Revon talking it over to himself. He wasn't a man that often asked for outside input, so Mozare just waited until he was brought back into the conversation.

"It's important you go back right now. We'll have a messenger come to give you instructions. For now, just maintain normal operations."

Mozare was used to this, reining in his nerves and hiding his intentions in plain sight. As always, he would have to watch out for Saiden. His partner could read him like an open book, which could get them all killed.

16
SAIDEN

S aiden sat with Nakti in her office, still reeling from the news of her next assignment. They were going to be in the Queen's Guard, one of the highest honors in the queendom. She couldn't help feeling that it shouldn't be given to someone like her. Someone impure and hated. And the timing of being given the task was so at odds with the past few days' constant reprimands.

The General had various maps and layouts of the parade route spread across her desk and littered on the surrounding floor. There was so much to consider when it came to guarding a queen. Especially in a public space with so many people coming out to see Her Majesty. Nakti pointed a finger at one of the maps. "This is the safest path for an escape route. I want you stationed near the queen. You're our best fighter, and she'll need you close if the situation becomes violent."

"We can have a small patrol of guards keep the path clear," Saiden suggested. "Dress them like civilians, so it's not an obvious route to dissenters."

"Smart thinking," Nakti commented.

It was the highest praise coming from the General, but she was careful not to let it go to her head. Nakti had very high standards, and she'd been recently reminded how quickly she could disappoint her. "Any other guards close to the queen need to know the routes as well, in case I get stuck in a fight," she added.

"Your priority is the queen. Stay at her side at all times. No staying back to fight, and no jumping to anyone else's rescue. Do you understand?" The General turned her full attention to Saiden and waited for her answer.

She couldn't speak under the woman's harsh stare. She just nodded and looked back at the map, memorizing each way to get the queen to safety.

"I'm proud of you, Saiden."

The words made her snap her head up, shock coursing through her. She knew that Nakti saw her accomplishments and was pleased with her performance. But the General had never voiced it aloud.

"Being selected for the Queen's Guard is a high honor, my daughter. I'm sure you will do me proud."

Saiden looked down again before Nakti could see her lips turn up into a smile. She wouldn't give her reason to regret this decision.

Saiden needed a clear head, and while she usually turned to training for that, she knew she needed a visit to the temple today. She had to plead forgiveness for killing the Enlightened and ask for guidance for the days to come. Those things were not going to be found in a training room.

There was a grand temple in the compound. It would be sacrilegious not to have one with so many Gifted gathered, doing their best to honor and fulfill the wishes of those above. The temple was decorated the same as the one in town, and Mozare had said they were decorated very similarly around the country. The ceilings were made up of collections of grand arches, and the walls were painted in black and white sections.

She had found it slightly unsettling at first. With her blood-red hair, she had hardly fit in with the coloring. But after visiting enough times, she had grown to find peace there. Saiden and Mozare had often attended prayer services when he had first arrived. It had helped his transition since he had been practically raised in one. She'd known the temple would still feel like home to him in a foreign city.

There were no statues or images of Keir or Ilona because the temple believed that no one would ever lay eyes on them in their true form. Saiden would never tell them that when she called upon them, they came to her in mortal flesh. She was sure the temple would have her lashed for such a bold claim.

Instead, there were pictures of terrain where it met the sky, koi fish, and statues of scales, all in black and white. Everything in balance, as the gods were meant to bring the world, and the Gifted were meant to protect.

She lit a candle and headed into one of the individual prayer rooms. Group prayer was good on some occasions. But she was in dire need of a conversation with the higher powers, and they would never come to her in front of a crowd.

Saiden placed her candle on the small pedestal, knelt down in front of it, and bowed her head. She put her right hand palm up on her leg to thank Keir for giving her this life. If she were normal like Mozare, she would have stopped there. But she flipped her left in the same manner and rested it against her other leg to thank Ilona for the peace she knew would come after death.

She could feel the room shift slightly, her body entering the trance-like state it often did when she visited them. But there was a part of her that belonged solely to the human world, and so she could not completely slip into the place between life and the everlasting. When she opened her eyes, she was no longer in the small room but on a vast plain. Rich, soft grass surrounded her, and she could hear the running water of streams nearby. The sky was a swirl of color. It was a peaceful place they brought her to this time, though they were not always so gracious.

She remembered when they had brought her to a live volcano, and the lava had burned her where she knelt. The burns had been gone by the time she returned fully to herself, but the memory of the pain had stayed with her.

Balance was needed even in their meeting location.

Keir, the father of life, stood to her right. He had skin like ivory, his features highlighted by silver streaks. He wore a loose tunic, and she knew if she touched the fabric of it, it would be like nothing she had ever felt before. His pants were loose, the cuffs tattered and hanging above his bare feet. The only part of him that had a different color was the crisp black of his hair.

She wondered if he had been the one to choose their location this time.

Next to him was Ilona, the mother of death. She had a kind face, and that had meant so much to Saiden after her parents died. Her skin was obsidian in color, a clear contrast to Keir. But where the sunlight hit it, there were sparks of other hues. She wore a long black dress that hugged her tightly in the chest with a skirt that flowed as she walked. Unlike Keir, the goddess had hair that dragged behind her for longer than Saiden could see, a river of pure white in the plush green grass.

Ilona placed a hand against Saiden's cheek. Without thinking, the legionnaire leaned into the touch. The goddess' skin was cold like ice but still comforting despite this fact.

Keir spoke first, his voice carrying like music on the wind. "You should already know that you are forgiven."

She had expected him to say that. He was always quick to forgive her.

She looked at Ilona and felt a small bit of her weight lift when the goddess nodded her head in agreement.

"You cannot expect to save everyone, my love. Death will come for every life." Her voice was clear, and Saiden often found herself entranced listening to it, even if it lacked the musical quality of Keir's.

The god of life knelt behind Saiden, pulling at her buns and letting her hair down. He said he preferred to see her that way. The deities thought there was no reason Saiden should hide her hair. She was Gifted not once but twice. She was their Gift to the world. But they did not understand what the people saw of their supposed favor. Still, she could not disobey a god, certainly not to his face.

"You have come to ask something of us?" Ilona asked when Keir was done with the task. They were standing together again, an ethereal pair. Especially in such a mundane landscape.

"There is clearly something that weighs heavily on your mind," Keir added.

"I have been appointed to the Queen's Guard. I worry that I am not the right choice for such an honorable position." She looked away from them, not wanting them to see the shame on her face. "I fear that my being there will cause more damage to the queen than any other threat could."

"You are our greatest warrior," Ilona said, ice cooling her tone.

"Perhaps," Keir started. He was given more to logic than emotion, so while Ilona was quick to offer her outrage, he was faster to offer advice. "Perhaps it is your reluctance and deep understanding of your shortcomings that make you the most suitable for such a position."

Ilona looked at her while Keir spoke, listening until she was calm.

Saiden looked at both of them and waited for someone to add more, but they remained silent, clearly satisfied with what had been said.

"Until we see you again, love," Ilona said, concluding their meeting.

Then they faded from view. The landscape started to blur.

Saiden closed her eyes, and when she opened them again, she was back in the temple. She understood what they wanted her to do, and she would do so to the best of her ability.

17
LORALEI

Loralei waited in her courtyard, pacing back and forth. Her parade was set for two days from now, so she was inspecting her new guard today. Truthfully, she would have very little choice in the matter. She wondered how much influence the advisors had or if they had left the choice to the General. Either way, it hadn't been hers. But it was tradition to stand and thank the soldiers for honoring her with their protection.

Cara stood at her side, a small comfort during this political farce.

General Nakti walked in after her advisors, followed by six soldiers. Loralei's eyes widened at the first legionnaire in line. The girl had her hair covered, but Loralei could see a few pieces of it coming loose, and the red was unmistakable. It was the Blood-Cursed girl, the one the Enlightened witness had told her about. Her advisors had honored her choice, even after the events in town.

She couldn't help but stare at her before realizing that her advisors would be watching. They would find it wrong that she was so entranced by a single guard. Loralei looked at the General and bowed her head, giving permission to continue with the ceremony.

The woman stepped forward—her gear decorated to represent her rank—and knelt down to present her arms. The others stood at attention behind her, waiting for their turn to prove their loyalty to their monarch.

"Stand, General," she said, her voice commanding the respect a queen deserved. She didn't need it, but it was what was expected. And she was so used to doing what was expected of her. In a few days, she would be in charge, and she could work towards changing things, but not today. "I am honored to have you here and to have your arms."

The General rejoined her line, now standing as an equal with her soldiers. Loralei found herself admiring her. There was much honor in that simple action, in being willing to stand with one's men.

The Blood-Cursed girl was second. Surely, she wouldn't be next when there was so much stigma around people like her—and yet, she was. It was fascinating that the legionnaire's rank was right below the General. Loralei hoped she managed to keep her expression neutral this time.

"I am Saiden," the young woman spoke. "Let my arms serve to protect you, and my life serve to shield you." She laid two blades at the queen's feet, joining the General's spear, and kept her head bowed.

"Stand, soldier," Loralei replied, watching Saiden smoothly re-sheathe her blades behind her back. "I am honored to have you here and to have your arms."

The other soldiers approached and introduced themselves the same way, but Loralei couldn't stop thinking about the Blood-Cursed girl—Saiden. To be honest, she hadn't stopped thinking about her since the testimonies in the throne room. She hadn't expected to see her so soon after, if ever.

When the last of the selected guards had finished introducing themselves, she would be free to go, though she admittedly no longer wanted to be finished with them. She spoke before her mind could catch up to her mouth. "Please, join me for refreshments before you return home. A token of my appreciation." She turned away without looking at her advisors. She already knew that their faces would only show surprise and disappointment at her breach of protocol.

Without hesitation or concern for the politicians, the soldiers followed her. She was in charge of them regardless of what her advisors thought. She sent Cara to the kitchen for drinks and charcuterie, and she sat among the pillows at the table.

The others remained standing, looking to the General to see what they should be doing.

Loralei saw the Blood-Cursed girl look at her and patted the pillow beside her. Saiden was clearly confused at being singled out but sat nonetheless, the ever-obedient soldier.

The rest quickly seated themselves afterward.

Cara was quick to return from the kitchen, followed by other servants with trays piled high with fresh fruits, cheeses, and dried meats. They set the trays down with practiced ease and started distributing glasses. There was wine, but Saiden refused, asking quietly for a glass of water instead.

Loralei was absolutely fascinated by this girl that never should have survived infancy. She didn't understand why the girl had been left alive, but she knew there was nothing in this world that happened without reason. She would just have to wait to figure it out.

"I would like to know more about you," she said, turning to the rest of the table. It would be too obvious if she asked only Saiden, but this way, she could pass it off as harmless curiosity. No one would think twice about it.

She listened to the two youngest speak, excitement clear in their voices. They had a few more years before life showed them its dark side, and she found herself somewhat jealous. She could've been sitting with them as equals, as another Gift-ed soldier, had she not been Chosen to become queen. Had she not been forced to keep such a big part of herself a secret. The emotion surprised her. She had never before felt such remorse toward what her position had made her give up.

In her peripheral vision, she watched Saiden pick an orange off the tray, peel it slowly and savor each slice of the fruit. She made a mental note to inves-tigate the rations in the legionnaire barracks. If they didn't have fruit, she saw no reason why she couldn't send some of hers to her soldiers, to Saiden.

When Saiden's partner spoke, she tuned back in. She had watched how the two of them kept an eye out for each other and knew that he must mean a lot to her. Perhaps he would be interesting to pay attention to as well.

"I was born to loving parents in Erast." He paused to take another piece of meat. "We ran a merchant stand, and my parents would travel and sell wares from different lands. They were very devout, and we were in temples often, praying even more than that. They showed me what was right in the world. When I was Gifted, they figured it was a reward for their devotion and sent me here. Pretty good, since I doubt Sai would have survived without me." He bumped his partner's shoulder.

She watched him go back to eating and wondered what it was about him that seemed so opposed to her presence. Something about the look on his face when he talked about the morals his parents had given him, the way he had stared at her while he said it, set Loralei's teeth on edge.

"Your Majesty, if you would be so pleased," the General said, bowing her head towards Loralei, "we should return for training. Saiden and Mozare are responsible for the recruits this week."

Had Loralei not met the General before, she would have misunderstood the woman's tone for rudeness. But she knew the woman was very organized with her troops.

"Of course. As soon as Saiden has told me about herself. It is only fair that they each share my attention before returning home." Loralei turned to Saiden without waiting for a response.

"I am an orphan." Saiden closed her eyes briefly before continuing. "General Nakti took me in when my parents were killed. The Legion is all I remember of my life, Your Majesty. I am afraid there is nothing interesting for me to share with you."

Loralei knew the legionnaire was trying to maintain a calm appearance, but she could see the emotions fighting toward the surface.

Before Saiden could continue, Lorelei's youngest advisor came over to whisper in her ear about the other meetings she had scheduled for the day. She bid her new guards farewell and left to attend to her royal duties.

18

SAIDEN

Saiden stood in the shadows outside the training room and watched Rhena tighten the laces on her boots for the seventeenth time. She was later than she had intended to be. No one had expected Loralei to invite them into the castle, and she took advantage of the fact that Rhena hadn't noticed her to watch the girl.

She stepped silently into the training room. "Is everything okay, Maus?"

Her brain took a second to process what it was she had said, and when she realized, she could feel the blood drain from her face.

"Maus? What's that?" Rhena asked.

Saiden felt sick. "It's something my mother used to call me," she answered. She ran a hand across her face and then pulled off her gear jacket.

"I was worried about you," Rhena said. "I thought someone might have tried to hurt you again."

"I'm okay. People attack me all the time." She had long ago resigned herself to that life. Trying to bring the attention away from herself, and she asked Rhena a question. "Why did you come to the Legion?"

"Because I'm Gifted. Isn't that why everyone is here?"

Saiden ignored the fact that she had never presented her own Gifts. She was an exception to the rule. "Not every Gifted individual comes to the Legion. There are other posts you could have taken."

She watched Rhena think.

"I come from a small village. The people there have mostly turned away from the religion of the gods. There hasn't been someone Gifted in our village in over fifty years. Until me, and I'm older than he was." She paused, breathing in. "My parents were ecstatic when I manifested. They knew that sending me here would mean they lost my help on our farm, but they would have a Gifted in the family. That still means a lot, even with people who've lost their way."

Saiden watched the emotions that crossed her face as she spoke about her family. There was a mixture of nostalgia and love that made Saiden feel a twinge of jealousy.

She had only a few small memories of her parents, and she suddenly wanted what Rhena had, even if the girl's parents had ultimately sent her away.

She had another question, one she was afraid to ask because she wasn't sure if she could handle the answer. "Why aren't you afraid of me?" Her voice was barely above a whisper. She'd never even asked Mozare that question.

Rhena just shrugged. "I know you're good. Whatever Gifts I have, from the Goddess or otherwise, they tell me that you are good."

Saiden could see plainly on the young recruit's face that, to her, it really was that simple. She smiled timidly and turned to grab two bo staffs.

"When can I use a real weapon?" Rhena asked. "You gave me a knife in town."

"I gave you a knife so that you would be able to protect yourself if you were in mortal danger. And it didn't help, anyway. You can have a blade when you wipe the floor with me."

"That's not fair," Rhena complained.

"A fight will not be fair. You asked me to train you. These are my rules."

"I don't think anyone has ever wiped you off your feet," the recruit said, but she wasn't arguing. She moved into one of the stances they had been practicing yesterday in their group training and spread her hands on the bo staff, ready to begin.

Saiden started off easy, going over the different blocks and strike points again. "You're small," she started.

Rhena scoffed.

"You might not always be small," Saiden continued. "But for now, people won't expect much from you. Use it to your benefit. Get in first and hit them where it counts."

Saiden moved them over to the practice dummies and showed Rhena the strikes. She let the girl practice, adjusting her and giving her pointers every time she made a mistake.

Rhena had good instincts. And despite her slight stature, there was power behind her hits. Whatever work she had done on her family's farm had definitely helped build some muscle.

"Put the bo down."

Rhena listened and watched Saiden as she went to the wall again.

She picked up the wraps she used to protect Mozare's knuckles when they sparred. She never worried about herself as much as she did about him. "I'm going to show you how to use this. Keep your knuckles covered if you're in here for practice. It will help you condition them without causing excess damage."

She reached out and waited for Rhena to cross the distance. She was quick to wrap the recruit's hands and step back to put space between them again.

Saiden settled into a good stance and put her hands up. "I want you to hit me."

"What?"

"You're going to hit me. It will help me to gauge what you need to work on with your punch. Don't worry. I've taken plenty before."

Rhena stepped into a punch.

Saiden adjusted her swing.

They went on like that, with the young girl punching and Saiden fixing things about her throw, her fist, and her stance.

"You want to punch through whatever you're hitting," she said. "If you stop when you hit the target, your force dissipates too soon."

She let Rhena get in a few more blows before she called it a day.

It was about time for dinner anyway, and she wanted to talk to Mozare. Something about sitting with the queen this morning had felt weird to her, and she needed to see what he thought about it.

19
LORALEI

Loralei knew her advisors wanted to talk after her unorthodox choice of entertaining her new queen's Guard with food, but they would have to wait. She now realized the identity of the mysterious prisoner and was desperate to talk to her. She took the stone steps two at a time, hiking her dress up so she didn't trip on its hem. The floor was cold against her bare feet.

"Guards, leave," she ordered. When they tried to argue, she just glared at them until they left. It was not queenly behavior, but they could just add it to the list of things she'd done today.

The room still smelled. She hated that the criminals were left in such conditions. No matter what horrible things they were accused of, they were still human and deserved the dignity of hygiene. She would be discussing the prison conditions with her advisors, even without a crown. This was unacceptable.

"Prisoner," she said as she slid to a stop in front of the cell. "What's your name?"

"You should know my name already, Your Majesty." The old woman stood, her hair tangled and her arms thin to the bone.

Loralei felt tears prick the back of her eyes. She called for the guards. This woman was no threat. She would have her cleaned and properly fed.

The guards ran back into the prison with their weapons drawn, obviously thinking her screams to be a cry for help.

"Release this prisoner, have Cara tend to her bath, and bring her to my chambers for dinner."

"But, Your Majesty…" the biggest started to say.

"That is an order."

"Yes, Your Majesty." They each put their swords back in their sheaths and clasped their hands against their chests, looking at her for further instructions.

Loralei pulled the smaller of the guards back while the other released the prisoner. "Be gentle with her. Any marks on her and you will be relieved of your positions. Do you understand?"

He nodded, and she let go of his arm. She hated this place, and when she could no longer tolerate being there, she walked to the exit.

Two of her advisors were waiting at the top of the stairs, anger stamped on their faces.

"What do you think you are doing?" one of them asked, stepping beside her as she continued walking.

"Your Majesty," she corrected. "You may be my council, but I am still Queen Chosen. You think your position grants you authority and the right to speak with me like an equal, but it does not. You would do well to remember that from now on." She hated hearing the words come from her mouth, but she couldn't stand the constant questioning at every turn. The gods had picked her. They would have to let her prove that she had been the right choice.

The man didn't reply.

"I am going to have dinner with that prisoner," she continued. "Alone in my chambers. I will position guards outside the door. After so many years of neglect under our own roof, I suspect she will be of no threat to me." Her voice was cold, her back straight as she stared at her advisors. "As far as my soldiers, if I want to sit and have fruit with them, I will do so at my leisure."

The two went back and forth between staring at her and looking at each other.

She was sure they had expected a docile queen, but she felt like her blood was on fire. Her mind was still racing after meeting Saiden. There was so much for her to think about. So many things she still did not know.

They did not offer more censure but silently escorted her on her path through the castle, ultimately leaving her at her door.

She sent one of the men guarding her room down to the kitchen to inform the chef to prepare her two plates to be served in her chambers. A light meal with lots of vegetables and chicken to provide protein without sitting too heavily in a malnourished stomach. Another person she would have to make amends with tomorrow for all the changes in the schedule today. But the chef was easy, quick to forgive, and had a special spot in his heart for Loralei.

It had already been a hectic day, and she imagined she would be faced with the repercussions tomorrow. Tonight, at least, she could allow herself to let her curiosity roam free. Tonight, she could be the little girl she had had to leave behind so many years ago.

When she was alone in her room, Loralei took what felt like the first full breath since that morning. She sat in front of her vanity, pulling the few pins free from her hair. She'd wanted to keep it down completely for the day, but loose hair was for children, not for queens. In that aspect, at least, she had maintained the appropriate, queenly custom. She ran her fingers through it, getting out the rest of the pins before she started brushing it. She had long black hair with soft waves, and it often accumulated quite a few tangles.

Cara was helping the prisoner with her bath, so she changed her outfit alone. She chose a less formal gown than before, then tied her hair back loosely behind her head. She wanted to appear more sympathetic to the captive. As a young woman instead of a queen.

There was a knock at each of her doors, the one coming up from the kitchen and the one leading to the castle proper. She called for them to bring in the food and went to the other door to let her guest in.

The prisoner looked clean now, but in the better light, Loralei could see the hollows in her face and the way her collarbones stuck out sharply. She looked like she had not eaten a full meal in all the time she had been there.

Loralei felt the overwhelming urge to cry rise in her again, and she carefully let some of the sadness and pity show through on her face. "Your name, please," she asked, her voice soft.

The woman sat across from the young queen but did not touch her food. "I am called Magdalena, though very few have bothered to call me that in years."

"I was wondering," Loralei began and paused, wondering if she could trust the prisoner with her greatest secret. But if Magdalena was who she truly expected she was, then she had held on to bigger secrets for much longer. She started over. "I was wondering if you might allow me to try healing you. I'm not sure how much I could help, but I should be able to do some good for you." Loralei was risking a lot in admitting her Gifts to a stranger.

Magdalena, understandably, looked shocked. She knew what it meant that Loralei was asking to personally heal her and not just offer to bring in a healer. She didn't answer at first, but picked up her fork and took a hesitant bite of her food with a long sip of water.

When the glass was empty, Loralei moved to fill it again.

Still, she did not answer the question. Instead, she posed one of her own. "Why is it that you have brought me here? While I am sure you have a kind heart, it is not typical for queens to share meals with their prisoners."

"I am starting to wonder if you have been unjustly imprisoned," Loralei confessed. She supposed if she were going to get the woman to open up to her, then she would have to be completely transparent. "And I believe I have had the honor of meeting your daughter."

At that, Magdalena's eyes widened, and her face paled.

Loralei doubted she could have shocked her more if she had said the sky was purple and made of peacocks.

"My. Daughter." The words were whispered haltingly, as if she needed to taste them anew. As if speaking them aloud brought her back to the years when they had lived together as a family.

"I was hoping you could tell me more about your child. The one you were trying to protect when you were sent to prison."

20
MOZARE

The air in the compound was buzzing with energy.

Mozare had to sneak out of the barracks tonight despite no messenger coming to get him. If he didn't go tonight, he wouldn't know what part he was meant to play in the upcoming attack, and that was dangerous for all of them.

He ducked through the hallways, watching his fellow revolutionaries run back and forth, sharing information and forming plans. He knew they had spent the past few days constantly planning, and now people were ready to act. They were getting restless, waiting for the time to be right.

Revon was at the front of the hall, standing tall at a makeshift podium. He liked to be the highest in the room so that everyone would be subconsciously drawn to look at him. Revon made eye contact with him and subtly lifted his hands.

Mozare let his shadows spread around the room, releasing some of the tension of his Gifts. People would attribute the show of power to Revon, which is what the older man wanted. He couldn't lead the Gifted if they didn't see him also representing the gods' favor. And what Revon lacked in his own, lackluster gods-given talent, he made up for by appropriating Mozare's skill for shadow bending.

When the room had quieted down, and everyone was looking only at their leader, their other tasks momentarily forgotten, the man let his hand fall back to his leg.

Mozare called the shadows back, letting Revon stand in the spotlight of their absence.

"Fellow revolutionaries, we stand tonight on the cusp of greatness. No longer must the Gifted—favored children of the gods—stand in service of those who turn away from the righteous path." His voice grew louder with rising fervor. "No longer will we serve an unholy ruler who shuns divine favor. Our oppression ends tomorrow, and a new reign of glorious prosperity will begin for all people." He placed his hands on the podium and leaned forward. "I know you grow restless now, with our victory so close at hand, but you must stay cautious. There are many who do not understand the gods' teachings as we do, who will strive to maintain brutal order. We must not let them succeed." He paused before continuing. "We are the new light of tomorrow, the hope for a new day. We must keep that hope wrapped around us as we fight to free our beautiful country from the grip of anarchy that has plagued us for far too long."

People cheered, forgetting themselves in the lines of Revon's speech. Forgetting that they were hidden underground, not far from the kingdom's best-trained killers.

Mozare waited, letting Revon bask in the glory he created, before pushing through the room to speak with him.

"What's my part in this tomorrow, Revon, sir?" he asked, adding the honorific as an afterthought. There wasn't a strict hierarchy in the rebellion, but Revon was their founder and the one who would lead them to a new life. So, he had earned at least that much respect.

"You should remain inconspicuous. If plans go well, you can step forward at the end. If not, you must do whatever it takes to keep your true alliances hidden. Your current position is too valuable to lose."

"I can do more than that," Mozare objected. "I can fight. We'll win the day tomorrow, and I want to be a part of that victory, not just someone standing on the sidelines."

"You've given us the opening we need. I am forever grateful for that. And you are loyal to our rebellion. I know that whole-heartedly. But you are also loyal to your partner, and I can't be assured that if she were to come to danger, you would still fall on our side."

"I have given you no reason to doubt me. I have sacrificed both honor and time to do this for you."

Revon clapped Mozare on the shoulder. "And those sacrifices will not go unrewarded in the age we will bring in together."

"And Saiden—you promised you wouldn't hurt her. That she wouldn't get swept up in all of this."

"I have given you my word that I will do nothing to intentionally put her in harm's way. I have passed those orders on to those who will be in the square tomorrow. But if she attacks them, you cannot expect them not to defend themselves. It is war. There will likely be casualties on both sides."

Mozare bristled at the calm tone of his voice. He had nothing left to say to Revon, and when it seemed Revon had nothing left to say to him, he turned away, stalking the other way down the hall and back into the woods. Despite being Gifted by the goddess of death, or perhaps because of it, Mozare had a distaste for the spilling of innocent blood. He didn't want just anyone to die for their cause, whether they were on his side or not.

21
LORALEI

Loralei stood in front of her mirror, admiring her dress, another rendition of the same one she had worn for her annual parade since her Choosing Day. It was a simple white garment decorated with vibrant purple flowers sewn into the hem among thick green vines. They had added longer sleeves and a tighter corset as she had grown. It was elegant, but wearing it still made her feel like a child. Perhaps that was the point.

Cara had pulled her long hair into a pile of elegant braids and twists, exposing the pale skin of her neck where she wore a beautiful opal necklace, the gem matching the three gems in her crown. The jewelry helped age up her ensemble.

She also donned a green velvet cloak. The winds of winter still clung to their streets, and she couldn't have anyone see that the cold wasn't bothering her. She ran her fingers up and down the soft fabric in a useless attempt to calm some of her nerves.

She had forced her feet into slippers. Her advisors had wanted her to wear heels, and she refused, though they didn't know. So, the hem of the dress was a little longer than it should have been. She didn't mind since it gave her more space to stretch her legs.

Since Loralei had allowed Alastair to lead the parade, she was forced to walk out with him. She had tried to insist that she didn't need an escort, that she was old enough to walk outside without a guide. They had refused her, of course, believing it indecent for her to be unescorted. There would be prospective princes and lords at the parade today now that she was old enough to court.

The thought made her want to vomit.

There was a parapet set up for them a few feet above the rest of the crowd. She had always hated the separation. When she was a small child, she had hated it because it kept her from the other children playing in the streets and eating pastries. She had been able to smell them, could smell them now, but she had never been given one to eat herself.

As she had grown older, she had hated seeing how dirty the people looked. She didn't understand why they were forced to endure a parade when it didn't seem like they had even eaten. She once tried to speak to someone, but they had considered her a foolish young girl and ignored her.

Now, she looked out from her parapet and saw the people she would need to care for. All the things she had tried to change but had been "too young to understand." When the crown was handed to her, she could make true changes. Her brain started to wander to all the ideas she had—all the ways to better her kingdom and improve the lives of her people—when trumpets sounded around them. She pasted a smile onto her face and waved, hoping they couldn't see that her heart wasn't in it today. Her people cheered anyway.

Alastair began to address the crowd, and the noises of celebration quieted down around them.

She could see her guards positioned around the parapet, each standing in gear and at the ready. She didn't know if they were already expecting an attack, but she felt sure that if something were to happen, at least one of her guards would be able to help her.

"On behalf of the Queen Chosen," Alastair began in a nasal voice, "I would like to welcome you to the palace on this anniversary of her choosing. We are here to remember the tradition of Choosing Day and to remember our queen's humble beginnings. No single person here is worth more than another, and each is vital to maintaining the balance of our country."

Loralei rolled her eyes. She couldn't stand listening to him speak about the people like he actually cared about them. She watched the people instead, watched how they hung onto his words. It was the only thing that kept her from interrupting Alastair and calling him out on his lies.

There were a few people in the assembled crowd that didn't seem to have as much faith in his words, and she had to keep herself from staring too long. Their faces were dirty, and even from her place above them, she could see the hard press of their lips. There were no cheers or smiles on their faces, sending a chill down Loralei's spine that had nothing to do with the weather.

At the edge of the crowd, she watched as a few large men inch their way closer to her guards. While her legionnaire guards stood closer to her, the uniforms of the soldiers in the crowd marked them as ordinary military. She watched them, unsure what would bring so many men to their sides while her advisors were still giving their speech.

She took her time turning to watch her other advisors, trying to gather if they were seeing the same thing she was. But they were just watching Alastair, nodding and beaming up at him. They had likely written the speech together and were just happy to hear their own contributions spoken aloud. Arrogant fools, all of them, though she currently had little control to change that.

The rest of her audience stood equally captivated by Alastair's words.

From the makeshift throne they set up for her each year, she couldn't see Saiden. But she knew the Blood-Cursed legionnaire guard was positioned where she could quickly get to her if something were to go wrong. Despite Saiden's subordinate status, the respect the General had for her soldier had been palpable.

In front of so many people, Loralei felt small in the big chair. And weak, in her dress-up gown, with her advisors speaking in her place.

She turned her attention back to the crowd and watched with horrified stillness as one of the large men quickly pulled a blade from under the vest he wore and used it to cut the throat of the guard next to him. She almost screamed, but no sound came from her throat. Her heart raced, and her powers swirled inside her, begging to help, wanting to heal him. She pushed against the feeling. She couldn't imagine how many more of her people would get hurt if that secret got out.

In the crowd, her people screamed as her guards tumbled to the ground, their blood spilling in rivulets onto the cobblestones. She stood from her throne, hand clutching at her own throat as the square broke into chaos. Her people ran, pushing into the others beside them, trampling over anyone who might have fallen in their path. She felt the tears streaming down her cheeks before she even realized she was crying.

Someone touched her shoulder, and she flinched away from the contact. Loralei hadn't even noticed the way her advisors stood around her, putting their bodies between hers and danger. But the hand belonged to Saiden, reaching for her hand and trying to take her away from them, away from the chaos.

She hiked up her skirts, grabbed the hand of her Blood-Cursed savior, and ran from the crowd where her people were dying.

22
SAIDEN

Saiden ran with the queen, pulling her through the tumultuous crowd. People were screaming everywhere, and she couldn't exactly tell what was going on. She kept the others in the corner of her peripheral vision, keeping her focus largely on the queen. She could see some of the people who had attacked the guards pushing through the crowd, trying to reach them. Panic crept into her mind, waiting for a moment to overpower her completely. She needed her mind sharp, now more than ever. Despite all the plans she had made with Nakti and the different routes they had discussed, Saiden was still trapped, the square seemingly surrounded on all sides by combatants.

At least running with her hair clearly visible made the parade goers quick to step out of her way. For the queen's part, she did seem a pretty competent runner despite the layers of her skirt and years of being pampered in a castle.

Someone jumped out at them, and Saiden pushed the queen between her and the brick wall of a leaning store next to them. Next, she drew one of her stiletto blades from in her sleeve and stabbed the assailant in the chest. She didn't wait to see if they died. They were safe so long as they couldn't pursue.

Her mind raced, and she finally figured out where to take the queen, though she was sure she would be reprimanded for it. "I am sorry, Your Highness," Saiden said as she pulled out the shorter of her kindjal from its sheath.

Loralei's expression went from scared to confused. Before she could say anything, Saiden bent down in front of the queen and used the blade to cut two deep slits in the now dirty fabric of the fancy dress. She pulled the pieces of the fabric together and tied them, freeing the queen's legs. Loralei was going to need to be free of tripping hazards where Saiden was taking her.

She re-sheathed her blade and moved to check around them again. Two men were searching the alleys around them, likely looking for the queen. She pulled two short daggers from her thighs, holding one in each of her hands. Taking a deep breath, she ducked around the corner, throwing one blade and then the other at each opponent, listening for the sound of their bodies hitting the cobblestones. When Saiden was sure there weren't other nearby pursuers, she walked a few steps from the queen and pulled a sewer cap loose, resting it next to the manhole it uncovered.

"I'm sorry, Your Majesty," she repeated, but Loralei—much to Saiden's surprise—was already preparing herself to climb underground. Saiden handed her one of the stiletto blades to protect herself while she shut the manhole up again. She didn't want to leave any signs as to where she had taken the queen.

Saiden was going to reach her hand out and take her blade back from the queen, but Loralei was holding onto it tightly. She let the queen take it, unsheathing her kindjal instead and walking slowly through the sewers back in the general direction of the castle. She took a few steps, keeping her hand behind her to keep track of the distance between her and her charge. Then she paused, her breathing hitching as she heard the small splash of someone behind them.

The sewers were too small to defend the queen safely. She cursed herself for not realizing that the sewers might be a good place to hide, but they were a terrible place to fight if you were also trying to protect someone with no experience. She pulled another dagger free, keeping Loralei behind her as she waited, listening between each of her own deep breaths for the sound of whoever was following them. She heard a footstep to the left and threw the dagger, simultaneously reaching to pull her other kindjal out with her free hand. The blade clanged against the metal wall of the tunnel, splashing into the water. Whoever was following them must have dodged it, though she wasn't sure how they had even managed to see it in the darkness.

As the fighter raced towards them, Saiden just made out the glint of metal through the small shaft of light coming through the hole of the sewer cover. She raised one of her own weapons, striking it across the soaring blade and knocking it to the ground. Before she even had a chance to shift her stance, a man was in front of her, two thin blades in his hands.

With him crowding towards her, she barely had room to raise one blade to block the strike he aimed at her collarbone. She stepped to the side and then immediately regretted it, realizing how it left Loralei vulnerable. Her attacker kicked, a small blade shining at the toe of his boot. Saiden stepped wide, plunging her blade through the leather of his shoe and stabbing the man through the ankle. She pulled her blade back before he could pull her off balance, the metallic smell of his blood tinging the grimy air around her. He dropped, rocking in the filthy water around them as he pressed his now empty hands to the wound at his foot. He cursed, and Saiden paused for only a second to run her blade through his heart, the only thing she could do to make absolutely certain he didn't follow.

She could hear drips of condensation echoing around her, but as far as she could tell, there weren't any more footsteps, which was what really mattered. The queen was only a step behind her. Loralei was shaking, fear so thick around her that Saiden could almost taste it. Her stiletto blade was still held tightly in her hands, now slightly in front of her body in protection.

She felt pity for the queen, having so much power and yet being so powerless. To Saiden, she seemed young to be responsible for so much, though she imagined they were around the same age. And now, to be dealing with rebels attacking her, she couldn't imagine the stress on the woman's shoulders. Saiden glanced at her again and saw blood on her hand—the way she was holding the blade had cut into her palm slightly—and she knew that the queen hadn't received any kind of training. She didn't understand why the kingdom's obsession with modest rulers meant they couldn't also be strong.

She sheathed the shorter of her kindjal, keeping the longer one in her dominant, right hand for easy and swift access. She removed the glove of her other with her teeth and ran it against the wall. It was slimy and wet and surprisingly cold, which made for a disgusting sensation on her fingers. But since she couldn't see the line maps, she needed to feel for them. The path to the castle would be marked with a crown—not very creative, but good for clarity. She followed the path she felt with her hand on the slimy wall until they came to another set of stairs.

"Ah!"

Saiden pulled the queen behind her when she heard the woman scream. She was looking for someone who might have grabbed the queen from behind, but no one was there. She looked at Queen Loralei, and the royal's cheeks were red. "Your Majesty?" she asked.

"There was a mouse," Loralei said, looking down at her soaked slippers.

They made Saiden wish she had another pair of boots. Instead, she took off hers and gave them to the queen, whose feet were more important than hers. Saiden had plenty of calluses on her feet already, anyway. Besides her feet being cold and wet, the sewer wouldn't do anything to her.

"No mice in the sewers, Your Majesty," Saiden said, watching the relief on the queen's face. "Only rats." The queen paled again.

She felt bad for joking with her, but that was often how she reacted to tough situations. The queen, on the other hand, looked like she was only a few seconds away from succumbing to shock. While Saiden didn't imagine she would be hard to carry, she didn't need to explain why she was carrying a passed-out queen through the sewers.

Loralei shook her head, trying to give them back, but eventually accepted the offer and slipped the boots on graciously.

Saiden was a bit surprised to see her reluctance after the way she had confidently ordered the palace staff around a few days ago, but the circumstances were obviously very different.

Without any underground danger present, she motioned for Loralei to sit behind the ladder, moving the queen's hand on the blade so she would be able to actually use it if the need arose. Then she climbed the ladder first, carefully pushing open the hatched door, and peeked her head out, looking around for signs that the chaos of the parade had moved toward the castle. She couldn't see anyone, and the sounds of the parade still seemed far away. She climbed back down and offered a hand for the queen to pull herself up.

When Loralei almost fell, Saiden rested a hand against her side to steady her. It was improper, but it had been a quick and necessary reaction. She helped the queen up the last rungs of the ladder, watching the adrenaline quickly leave the woman and exhaustion setting in just as fast.

"Where are your maids?" Saiden asked Loralei. She hoped no reprimand for the informality would come, but they needed to get her somewhere she could sit and a warm towel for her head. Otherwise, Saiden was quite sure the queen would faint right there in the hall.

Loralei pointed weakly, and Saiden grabbed her weapon back before the queen could accidentally impale herself. She kept an arm out in case the queen suddenly fell, but despite her clear exhaustion, Loralei made it to what Saiden assumed were her chambers before she sat down. Saiden looked around for a way to call for someone, but their footsteps had been enough warning.

Two young girls came quickly into the room, unable to hide their shock at the mess that Saiden and Loralei presented. They left just as quickly as they'd come and returned with towels and water for the girls.

Saiden refused.

They were in the castle, but that did not mean they were in the clear. Until Loralei's soldiers returned to the palace, Saiden would have to be on guard.

Loralei called one of the girls over and handed her Saiden's boots. "Have these cleaned and dried for my guard."

Saiden didn't mind them being cleaned, though she would have been capable of doing so herself once she'd gotten back to the barracks. But the queen hadn't asked, and she had been informal enough already without contradicting royal orders.

"Please sit," Loralei said, rubbing at her legs with the towel.

"With all due respect, Your Majesty, it would be better if I stayed standing." Saiden had more to say, but they were interrupted as four guards burst into the room.

She jumped to put herself between the queen and the men, pulling both her kindjal free.

"Stand down, Saiden."

It was the General, coming in behind the men. Her face was a weird mix of anger and pride that Saiden couldn't quite understand, but she sheathed her weapons nonetheless.

"Your Majesty," Nakti began. "We have two of the rebels in chains and have sent others after the rest. You can rest assured that no man will be free of punishment." She knelt in front of the young queen and presented her arms.

Loralei smiled and placed a still-slightly-smudged hand on Nakti's shoulder. "Thank you, General. As you all can see, I am quite well. Nothing a bath won't fix." Loralei had clearly been trying to joke, but no one laughed. "You are dismissed."

23
MOZARE

Mozare scanned the crowd, watching the rebel fighters get into place. He could see them clearly, despite being left out of the planning. He worried at his nails, hoping no one else could, otherwise their chance at the Queen Chosen would be over before it had even begun. Revon wouldn't tell him how many soldiers he had sent, and now Mozare found himself trying to count them all.

He could hear speeches going on but was so focused on counting the fighters—at understanding how big Revon had thought this fight was going to be—that he couldn't make out the individual words. When the speech was finally over, he heard the call to attack and braced himself.

Revon had planned for him to disappear during the chaos. Mozare wasn't one to run from a fight, but in the end, he had to listen to Revon. He had sworn allegiance to him and the rebellion, and he never went back on an oath.

He looked for Saiden, worried that some of the more superstitious fighters would target her even if it was the queen they were there for. They wouldn't be able to help themselves. He got a single glimpse of her hair in the middle of the fight, making her way toward her charge.

The royal advisors stood in a tentative circle around their yet-uncrowned ruler. They were clearly not familiar with the brutality of battle, which was wrong considering they sent others to fight. Mozare hated them. Hated that they sentenced others to death when they were too cowardly to do it themselves.

He tried to make his way to Saiden, but when he looked back, he couldn't find her. Panic rushed through him. Revon had promised him that he would give the others instructions not to harm her, despite his own dislike of her, but in the heat of battle, there was no controlling what others did.

When Mozare noticed that the queen herself was also missing, he wondered if they had succeeded, but only for a few seconds before he realized Saiden must've gotten to her and helped her escape the melee. He ran into the twisting alleyways between the cramped together buildings, listening for footsteps, for any sign of which way Saiden had taken the target. When he found his partner, the two women were sneaking into the sewers, where he knew he couldn't follow.

The rebellion had failed. Mozare couldn't blow his cover now. Besides, in a one-on-one fight, he knew he stood no chance against Saiden and no part of him wanted to hurt her. They were partners, and though they stood on opposite sides of a revolution, he would not raise a weapon against her.

His feelings tangled together in a chaotic knot. The rightness of what he was doing and all his beliefs fought against the creeping feeling of these deaths. He understood in that moment more than any other why Saiden got her tattoos. Why she honored the dead with her skin and memory.

He ran back into the crowd and grabbed a rebel. It was an older man, one who often raised trouble with the new recruits, and one he knew harbored a pure and deep hatred that wasn't altruistic like Revon's desire to help the people.

"Traitors to the crown!" Mozare yelled, the words bringing bile to the back of his throat. "You have failed in your mission and will pay for the crimes committed here!"

He knew this man would be executed for raising a hand against the Queen Chosen, but he would die with honor. His death would further their cause. Even the man saw what had to happen and had become resigned to it, dropping his weapons on the ground, but not before looking at Mozare, that pure hatred gleaming in his eyes.

Around him, he saw others fleeing, running away with their wounded. He watched a young girl get captured, a guard grabbing her by the tail end of her braid. His heart went out to her. He didn't think she was even part of the rebellion, but he doubted she would walk away from this.

He brought the prisoner to Nakti, where she was standing with her broad sword dripping blood on the cobblestone streets. He could smell the blood. The sharp, metallic scent that sat in the back of his nose didn't help his nausea.

The man he had grabbed was thrown into a circle of other prisoners, heavily guarded. He was sure that they would die today, and while he had been blessed by Ilona—Death, herself—it still made him feel uneasy. To kill in battle was different, but what he had just done was cold-blooded murder, and he wasn't entirely sure he would ever be able to repent for that.

Mozare stood with the other guards and watched the square thin out. Palace soldiers searched every parade goer for weapons or evidence of rebellion, but they found no other fighters in the people remaining in the square.

Nakti ordered the soldiers to bring the prisoners to the dungeon, announcing she would take four of them with her to find the queen. And although they were palace guards, and not technically under her command, every man and woman there immediately listened to her and started escorting the group of prisoners to the cells.

Mozare stayed behind. He hadn't been included in either of the groups to whom Nakti had assigned tasks, and so he went around the square offering blessings to the deceased. Someone would come soon enough to bring the bodies away to be burned, but he wanted all of them to have the gods' eye, not just the palace soldiers.

24

LORALEI

L oralei held tight to Cara's hand as they snuck around the corner, doing her best to avoid where she remembered there would be guards posted. She wished she had paid more attention at those boring meetings where her advisors had droned on about security, but she couldn't change that now. And after the parade, her guards had changed rotations, so the information was likely irrelevant now, anyway. Besides, she was the queen-to-be. If she wanted to be out and about in the palace, no one could really stop her. Especially since all of her advisors had retired to their city homes for the night.

Behind her, Cara giggled, leaning over to kiss Loralei's shoulder. "What are we doing, my love?"

Her voice was louder than it should have been, and Loralei froze, hoping the guards hadn't heard. Still, she couldn't bring herself to quiet Cara, and the feeling of her whispering—however loud it was—sent shivers down Loralei's spine. It was so pleasant a feeling that she almost decided to forgo her original mission in favor of locking them in one of the unused bedrooms for the evening. She knew it was risky bringing Cara. She couldn't really afford the distraction, but she needed the time with her just as badly as she needed answers. Nighttime was the only opportunity they had together without her advisors breathing down her neck about the impropriety of it all. She sighed, then moved around the corner, pulling Cara to follow her.

Focus, she reprimanded herself. She had too many close calls in recent weeks, and something told her answers were waiting if she only knew where to look.

She almost hated how easy it was for her to sneak past the guards. It made her protectors seem incompetent, but she was also grateful to avoid their questions. And the reprimands of her advisors once they learned she had visited the Archives on her own. Technically, they belonged to her, but until she was officially crowned, her access to them was limited. They never let her forget that.

She opened the door carefully, pushing it open only far enough for them to slip through to avoid the rusted hinges' creak whenever pushed too far. Her bare feet didn't make a sound on the stone steps, though she paused and gently pulled Cara's shoes off to stop the echo from giving away their location.

Unlike Loralei, Cara was frequently cold, so she never went without her sturdy shoes, the soles worn from use.

Loralei made a mental note to order her lover a new pair.

She had no true idea where to start in her current search for information. Just a hunch that something down here would explain why her people had been so inclined to rebel. And why her kingdom had imprisoned Magdalena for all these years when her daughter wasn't a threat. There were too many mysteries recently, and she knew that if the answers couldn't be found here, no one would ever give them to her.

"A dusty old library. How romantic," Cara said from behind her, kissing the sensitive stretch of skin behind her ear.

Loralei leaned into her, forgetting for the briefest of moments that there was a kingdom resting on her shoulders. That she needed answers. That she needed anything other than to bring Cara closer to her. She smiled and turned around, ignoring the part of her mind that was pressuring her to stay on task. She took Cara's face in her hands, and her smile widened before she pressed a searing kiss to her lover's lips, holding her there for a second too long before she pushed her away, running a finger down her nose. "I knew you would find a dusty library romantic, Cara." She smirked. "But you also know that I need to read and not just kiss you." No matter how much she wanted to do just that.

Cara pressed a kiss to the corner of Loralei's mouth. "Where should I start?"

The tone of her lover's voice sent warmth shooting through the queen's body.

"Look for anything about the Blood-Cursed." Her gut told her this still had something to do with the turmoil, that the gods' hands moved in all the questions she had.

Loralei could tell that Cara added an extra swish to her hips as she walked away. "Does this place have any kind of organization?" she asked, picking up a dusty file by its corner.

"None that I've ever been able to understand."

"Good, so this should be easy." Even with the sarcasm, Loralei appreciated that Cara was able to take the time to dig through dusty old documents with her when there were plenty more enjoyable things she could be doing with her very limited time off.

They hadn't been down there long enough for either of them to find anything worthwhile when Loralei heard loud footsteps, the metal clang of armor echoing down the stairs. She was quick to shove her files back into their places, grabbing Cara and pulling them behind one of the more hidden shelves and praying they wouldn't get caught. She had never used her Gift around Cara, and she hoped that the small power she used to bend the light around them wouldn't reveal that secret.

They hid only long enough for the guard to leave the Archives before following him themselves, too shaken to risk discovery again.

25
SAIDEN

Saiden walked to Nakti's office once she had finished washing up and getting dressed in clean clothing. She had been summoned immediately, but knew that going there dirty and smelling of the sewer would only add to the General's frustration. Unfortunately, a faint odor still seemed to cling to her. She didn't bother knocking on the door. Judging by how angry Nakti had seemed earlier, she couldn't imagine her superior would have anyone with her until she had gotten the chance to speak to her. When Saiden opened the door, she was pacing, a glass of Taezahli whisky clutched in her hand.

The General saw her and put it down.

Saiden stood straight and looked Nakti directly in the eye. She had prevented the queen's death. And though her methods may have been unusual, no one else had managed to even get close enough to protect Loralei. Her advisors wouldn't have stood a chance against even the lightest trained warriors.

"Gods, Saiden," she said, anger clear on her face. There was nothing else mixed with it this time. "You took the queen into the sewer system! What were you thinking?"

"I was thinking the fighting was happening above ground, and taking the queen underground would keep her protected."

"And filthy. They don't think they will ever be able to fix her dress."

"They're worried about her dress? She's alive because of me."

Nakti glared at her. "The sewers might be fit for you, but not for a queen."

The room fell silent. Each of the words hit Saiden like a poisoned arrow, the pain coming from the injury and the way it seemed to settle in her bones.

Nakti's face was still marred with anger, but her eyes went wide.

Saiden couldn't wrap her mind around it. She tried to speak, opening her mouth several times and closing it without any words coming out.

The General had been the one to convince her own general that killing a six-year-old girl, despite being Blood-Cursed, would go against the gods' wishes. She was the one who had brought Saiden to the Legion and trained her when she was little. Given Saiden a home when she had lost her parents. And now she was telling her that the sewers were a fine place for her.

She had no way to defend herself, especially when Nakti was so mad. She hadn't expected anything said during this meeting—any conversation with the General—to hurt her so much. Finally, she managed a response. "Because I'm Blood-Cursed? Tainted?"

Nakti looked at her, as if just realizing what she had said.

But it was too late. Saiden was already out of her office and—though the thought crossed her mind—she did not slam the office door. The General wouldn't follow after her, anyway. In the heat of the moment, she had wanted to hurt Saiden, and both of them knew that, so there was really no point in her trying to apologize. Saiden ran to the stable.

She wasn't sure where Mozare was. She hadn't seen him since they had been in the square, but the thought was distant in her mind. At the moment, all she could think about was distancing herself from the barracks and from the pain of Nakti's words.

Saiden took Sirius from his stall without even taking the time to saddle him. The stable hands didn't look up at her as she rode him away, the doors banging shut behind them.

Sirius was an excellent horse, and he was good at finding paths in forests even when there wasn't a clear way through. It was partly why he had become her horse. She pushed him to go faster, riding away from the barracks and away from the city. Away from all the pain she had faced today.

She took Sirius to a secret place in the depths of the woods. When she was little and they had first taken her away from her home and her parents, she had tried to run away almost every day. It took her a few weeks to find this place. A small oasis in the middle of the woods where she could find peace. Saiden broke through the tree line and quickly dismounted her horse, trusting that he wouldn't stray far from the fresh grass that grew there. She went and sat at the edge of the river, pulling off her boots so she could put her feet in the cool water. She heard branches ruffle behind her, but she didn't turn and waited for Mozare to come sit next to her on the sun-warmed rocks.

"You saved the queen."

"I didn't take the paths Nakti had set before the parade."

"I saw the fighting. You couldn't have taken that way, and you know it."

"The sewers are not a fit place for a queen," she said, repeating the words that continued to spiral through her head.

Mozare leaned against her. They both knew when she was in these kinds of moods that there was nothing he could say to bring her out of it. But she was glad for his presence, so at least she didn't have to be alone.

"I'm thinking of going for a swim. The current doesn't look too strong today," he said, standing up from the rock and stripping off his shirt.

She shook her head at him, at the lengths he was going to drag her out of her slump.

"Listen, even if you don't want to, maybe you could do it as a favor to me. You reek so bad I've been holding back tears since I stepped through the trees."

She laughed, only lightly, before taking his offered hand. She punched him in the arm, payback for his comment about her stinking, but she really was glad for his company. Otherwise, she might have wound up with bloody knuckles again.

She pulled off her pants, washing the sewer muck from them before wading into the river next to Mozare. She left her shirt on. Despite Mozare having seen the tattoos before, she didn't want them out in the open. She didn't need a reminder of the deaths she had caused.

They stayed there—swimming some of the time and relaxing in the grass—until her head quieted again, and the sun began to set in the sky.

26
MOZARE

"**Y**our plan failed."

Mozare listened to Revon speak, a false blanket of calm still settled over the conversation. He doubted it would last long. Revon wasn't one to keep his anger at bay. He expected people to know he was angry and grovel for his forgiveness. But Mozare would not give him the satisfaction. He had given Revon advanced notice of the parade, and then he had been left out of the planning. He could not be blamed for this failure.

The rebellion's leader tapped his fingers against the table in a steady rhythm. It irritated Mozare, who always preferred a silent room to one filled with useless ambient sounds. Eventually, the man slammed his hand against the table. "Do you have nothing to say for yourself?" he asked, his voice growing louder with every word.

He pushed against his own anger. Mozare had lots to say about it not being his plan, about him having no part in it but to maintain his cover, but he said nothing. There was no consoling or confronting Revon when he was in this state, and if Mozare were to embarrass him in front of the others, he wasn't sure how the leader would respond.

Revon got up and started pacing back and forth across the room. "This was our chance," he said, though it sounded more like he was speaking to himself than trying to address his small audience. Mozare wondered if perhaps he wouldn't be so flustered if he tried doing anything without witnesses, but

Revon wanted to be seen. "Twice now, we've failed to kill a teenager. For gods' sake! She's a coddled girl with nothing to protect her."

A girl speaks up from the wall. "There will be other chances. Our fighters didn't provide any useful information before their execution." She goes quiet. "Loralei would have told me about it. She doesn't see me as a threat at all."

Mozare knew he had seen her around before, but he had never really cared to introduce himself to anyone beyond the people Revon saw fit he knew. He was completely at the older man's mercy in all of this, something that really only hit him now.

Revon's footsteps became lighter as he listened to the girl, a sign of his anger subsiding—if only slightly.

Mozare spoke for the first time since returning to the bunker under the shade of nightfall. "We should allow the fighters to rest tonight. There will be plenty of them who are in mourning, and they will be discouraged after our failed mission." He was careful to avoid admitting any guilt because Revon would latch onto someone else to blame. "Then, tomorrow, we remind them why we fight."

27
LORALEI

Loralei sat in her bedroom while Cara brushed her hair. She hadn't slept well, but she had an early meeting with her advisors and needed to look as if she had. They had already wanted to excuse her from her duties today after the ordeal at the parade, but Loralei had known that sitting around the palace with nothing useful to do would only bring her misery. She needed her brain to be doing something besides thinking about the blood currently running through her streets.

Her advisors were sitting around the table when she walked in, each of them trying to talk loud enough to be heard over the others. They didn't notice her entrance immediately, giving her the rare opportunity to watch them without their knowledge. They were more energetic when she was not around, hands flying and wildly gesturing.

One of them eventually noticed her and tapped the advisor next to him, leading to the room quickly going quiet.

"We are sorry, Your Majesty," said Umbrian. "We did not notice your arrival."

"Please, there is no need to apologize." She had not minded watching the way they engaged with each other, even if they did so because they believed her absent. "I understand we have a few important matters to discuss." She sat down at the head of her table.

Her advisors followed suit, each sitting down in their respective seats and pulling their chairs into the table.

Alastair pulled out some papers and tapped them against the table, pretending to straighten the already even pile.

"We have been considering the ball, Your Majesty," began Oscan. "We think it might be unwise to host such a large event in the wake of such tragedy."

Umbrian interjected. "We do not all agree on this matter."

"The ball is tradition," said Loralei, carefully picking her words. "We cannot forgo centuries of tradition in favor of fear. We must show the people that we are still able to rule and protect them. That a small attack will not stop us." She waited for pushback, but it seemed that her word settled whatever dispute had arisen among the men.

"I have sent Cara to the dressmaker with some alterations for my gown in mourning for those lives lost," she continued. She had thought of it last night and had written out basic instructions for what she had in mind. She was sure the tailor would do an excellent job of bringing it to life. Again, she waited for dissent, but none came. She had to admit to herself that she was a little curious at how non-argumentative her advisors were being. They did not usually allow her much decision in such matters.

"I will also be appointing Saiden as my new personal guard."

At this, the room burst into sound, a symphony of outraged rebuttals ringing through the open hall.

"She's Blood-Cursed, Your Majesty. Surely that is not how we should represent the crown," she heard one of them say.

"She's a mercenary! A trained killer, not a guard," another joined in before his voice was lost to the cacophony of the others.

"Filthy trash—"

"Tainted!"

"Spoiled—"

"Unfit—"

"Should have been killed—"

She slammed a hand against the table, bringing the room back to silence.

101

"She is the best, and that is what I need. We cannot doubt that they will try to attack again. They are getting bolder and putting more people than just me at risk. Saiden was the only one of the Legion who was able to secure my safety. Therefore, she is the one I choose as my protector. Her blood does not define her, as your blood does not define you. Speak another ill word against her, and you will be punished severely."

She wasn't sure exactly what had taken over her, but she felt herself wane at the end of her speech. She was troubled by the pure hatred she had seen her advisors exhibit at the mention of a name. The fear of grown men based on superstition. Superstition that would have also seen her removed from the court if they knew the truth.

She took a deep breath, then continued. "You will send word to the Legion that she is to be moved to the palace. Her partner may come as well if he wishes." She added the last bit on as an afterthought and looked around for any objections.

Her advisors could barely look at her, but she wasn't entirely sure if the look on their faces were shame or anger.

"Let us adjourn for the day." She had barely been in the meeting for more than a few minutes, but couldn't continue dealing with her advisors. She stood from the table and left before waiting for another word.

28
SAIDEN

When Saiden returned to the barracks late the next day, after sleeping in her forest paradise, she was surprised that Nakti was summoning her again. She did not expect her to apologize—the General never did—but she also was not expecting a repeat of the day before. She shook out her muscles and straightened her back, passing Sirius off to be groomed and fed by one of the new recruits. She paused again to shake the tension from her muscles before knocking on Nakti's door and waiting to be called inside.

The General was standing at her window, the glass from yesterday absent from Saiden's sight. That, at least, was a good thing. Drink was a sure sign that Nakti was pissed off, and so its absence meant that even if she were to be reprimanded again, it would be a gentler reprimand.

"You have been summoned by the queen," Nakti said, slowly turning to face Saiden. "She wishes you to be moved into the castle and ready for duty tomorrow by midday."

"'Ready for duty,' General?"

"She means for you to be her personal guard, Saiden." Nakti pulled a page of paper from her desk and held it out. "She was apparently rather impressed by your quick action at the parade."

Saiden didn't look down at the paper but watched the General. She could see the hesitation in her face and wondered if it had to do with the reprimand she had given her when their queen thought that Saiden's actions were deserving of promotion.

"I'll send recruits to bring your cases to the palace."

Nakti was dismissing her, so Saiden slipped the now-folded letter into her sleeve and left. She could swear she heard Nakti mutter something that sounded like a prayer as she stepped out of the office, but the words had been unclear.

Standing outside the General's closed door, she looked at the paper in her hands. The edges were wrinkled where someone had held on to the letter too tight. Saiden couldn't believe that she was leaving the Legion. She had grown up within these halls. And now she was to live in the palace. It was such a wild notion that her mind couldn't wrap itself around it.

Mozare was waiting for her in her room and was quick to pull her into his arms. It was strange how many people had touched her in the past few days when there were so many people who avoided her completely.

He let go and stepped back. "I was worried last night when you didn't come back," he said, watching her. "Why'd you stay away so long?"

"I needed the peace." She folded her clothes and placed them into an empty chest. "You really shouldn't be worried, Moze. I'm the scariest thing out there."

He laughed, and she tried to join him, but the sound was wrong.

"What is it?" he asked, seating himself on her bed. "And why are you packing?"

She handed him the letter and waited for him to read it. When enough time had gone by that he could've read the letter three times over, she looked up at him.

He had gone pale, his new scar startlingly pink against his face.

"Moze?"

"You're going to be the queen's new personal guard," he said, staring at the letter.

"It's an honor."

"It'll put you in danger."

"Because I'm cursed? I'll be in no more danger in the palace than I am here. Or anywhere else, for that matter."

"You're making your existence very public. There are many who will step forward as your enemy."

"What is it that you think is going to happen? A tournament to the death?"

He looked at her wide-eyed—like that was exactly what he was worried about.

She put a hand on his shoulder, the edge of a leaf sticking out below the cuff of her shirt. "I will be in the shadows," she reassured him. "No harm will come to me."

He still seemed hesitant. "Then I'm coming with you."

"Normally, I would say yes, but I need to ask that you stay here and keep an eye out for Rhena. Befriending me, however briefly, will have made her a target as well, and not just of the other recruits. I need to know she's safe here."

He stood in front of her and reached out his arm. She grabbed it at the elbow. It was a Legion oath.

He would do whatever he could to protect the young girl, and she would do whatever she could to protect the young queen.

Walking into the castle, knowing it was her new housing, was a very strange experience. Saiden couldn't really remember what her home had been like before she had been taken into the Legion, though she would catch a smell every once in a while that pulled her back to her childhood. Going from the barracks to a life in the palace was going to be an adjustment for her, to say the least.

The first thing she noticed was there was so much light. The walls, if they could even really be called that, were filled with large panels of glass everywhere. It was beautiful, but Saiden couldn't help feeling vulnerable under the sunlight.

Loralei met her at the door, stopping Saiden before she could kneel and present arms. "If you kneel every time you see me, you will spend far too much time on the floor." She put her arm through Saiden's and started walking down the hallways, two of the palace guards trailing some distance behind her. Loralei leaned in to whisper, "Don't mind the brutes. My advisors have little faith in my ability to make decisions, so they've sent them to babysit."

Saiden kept her face blank, but inside, her mind was reeling. She didn't understand why the Queen Chosen was confiding in her, and shame swept through her at the idea that *she* was likely the reason for Loralei's current supervision.

The royal watched her face for a moment. "Don't worry about it."

Saiden wasn't sure what Loralei had seen to make her concerned and didn't respond.

"They'll find something else to occupy their time shortly. They have a worse attention span than small children."

She was surprised the queen personally escorted her to her new chambers. She had expected to be passed off to a servant and given a chance to put on better gear before presenting herself, but that didn't seem to be the way Loralei intended this new position to play out.

"Someone will bring you dinner, though I will expect you to join me for breakfast in the gardens tomorrow." She reached over and opened the curtains to let in the light from the setting sun. "One of my lady's maids will be in to set the bed, and someone will be coming by to get your measurements for new gear. I can't have my personal guard dressed like an ordinary legionnaire grunt."

Saiden's mind swam with the influx of new information.

Loralei must have understood because she bid Saiden goodnight and quietly slipped back through the door.

With the queen gone, Saiden pulled her boots off and lay on the bed, watching people come in and out to light candles or bring in her cases.

A set of petite women came in and took her measurements, turning her around and directing her to lift her arms or stand straight. She did what they said and, when they were gone, she crawled into her bed and slept.

29
LORALEI

Loralei slept much better, knowing that Saiden was in the castle with her. She knew it was ridiculous. If something had happened last night, Saiden wouldn't have known or been able to do anything from her separate room. But the knowledge had comforted the queen nonetheless.

Before going to bed, she had let the kitchen know that she would take breakfast in the garden for three, so they would be prepared in the morning.

Loralei woke with the sun, as she often did, and stretched. Cara was next to her in the bed. She loved having her there, tucked in close to her. She leaned over her lover and started planting small kisses against her shoulders, moving towards her neck, kissing under her ear. She felt Cara start to stir underneath her. She was a heavier sleeper than Loralei, but not heavy enough to stay asleep under such loving ministrations.

Cara rolled over underneath her, smiling up at Loralei. She looked almost magical in the morning, in those first moments between sleep and wakefulness. Her copper hair spread on the pillowcase, and the sunlight made her cheeks blush.

That might have been Loralei's favorite thing about having her spend the night. Besides the kisses, of course. She leaned down and kissed Cara fully, bringing her completely into the day.

Cara wrapped her arms around Loralei, turning so they were lying side by side, still connected.

They lay in bed that way, kissing and pulling each other closer for a while, until both of their stomachs began to protest. She knew Cara would have to leave soon before anyone else came in to wake Loralei or help her dress for the day, but she wanted to live in the moment as long as she could.

When her lover finally left, Loralei stayed in bed, soaking in the warmth of Cara's vacated spot, until another lady's maid came in and told her she was going to be late for breakfast. She had forgotten breakfast with Saiden amidst the all-consuming kisses. She was quick to pick out a dress for the day, a simple, unadorned dress made of purple silk. It was a color she knew Cara liked, and since she would be joining for breakfast, Loralei wanted to look desirable.

She rushed down the stairs, not even giving the stones a chance to cool her feet. She hadn't worn shoes. Her dress was long enough to forgo them, and she loved the feeling of the grass under her feet. Despite the various protests of her advisors, she tended to her own garden, and the grass there was some of the softest in the entire kingdom. Not that Loralei had been very far from the castle. But she still imagined there was nowhere as nice as her garden.

She paused at the outside door, taking a deep breath and composing herself. Different voices circled through her head, reminding her that a Queen Chosen should not be excited to meet a mere guard. Shouldn't walk around shoeless. Shouldn't take a female lover. Shouldn't have Gifts. All the things a queen shouldn't be, and nothing that she should.

She tried to change the thoughts in her mind. A queen should care for all her people. Should find comfort in her kingdom. Should love freely. A queen should be impartial regarding the Gifted and the Giftless. She repeated the new statements in her head as she took her first steps outside.

Saiden was sitting at the table they kept in the garden for Loralei, and the legionnaire stood when she saw the queen come out. She wasn't in gear today, but her clothes were still unusually warm for the weather. Long pants and a long sleeve shirt with something else clearly worn underneath. It was a weird choice of clothing, but Loralei did not mind. It was an outfit that fit what she understood about Saiden.

"Please, Saiden. You mustn't display so much decorum when we are alone."

"We are not alone, Your Majesty," she replied, bowing slightly and gesturing towards Cara.

It might take some time to break Saiden of her formality.

"Cara is my lover," Loralei said, shocking even herself. She had never said the words out loud, but saying them to Saiden felt right. She knew her guard would not betray her trust by sharing her secret. "You are free to speak and act however you like when she is with us."

Saiden looked at the queen curiously.

"You are also free to ask whatever question you wish. I can clearly see there is something you desire to know."

Saiden waited—Loralei wasn't sure what for—before speaking. "Should the queen not take a male lover? Someone with whom to produce an heir?"

"I have had male lovers," Loralei said, though more hesitantly than her announcement of her relationship with Cara. She had not spoken openly with her lover about her other affair and now was not an appropriate time to do so. "I will have to take a husband eventually, but he will have to be okay with my arrangement if it still exists at that point. But I also do not have to worry about an heir since the divine will choose my successor."

She watched her guard's face. She could see nothing of disgust or anger. She wondered if there was anyone Saiden would show revulsion toward. She made a mental note to watch how the legionnaire interacted with other people in the future.

Cara came to join them, having finished pruning the dead flower heads from the rosebush. Loralei had had the roses planted specifically for Cara after learning they were her favorite flower and was happy that Cara had liked them so much.

The queen placed a hand against her leg, and the three of them waited in content silence for breakfast to be brought out. When it was, they were served fresh plates of eggs and crisped meats, as well as plenty of fresh fruit after she had seen how much Saiden seemed to like them.

She asked the legionnaire all kinds of questions, to which her answers varied greatly in depth. When she asked about the mercenary's childhood, her answers were short and terse. But if she asked about the Legion or weapons, she could see Saiden relax in her seat. Those were the questions to which her answers were most descriptive, and it was interesting seeing the expressions on her face, hearing the passion in her voice.

She stayed close to Cara, liking that they could be close—that they could be together in public—even if it was just in front of Saiden. It made their relationship more real, which she enjoyed even if she hadn't realized she had craved that kind of validation before. She hadn't needed to be so careful with her last lover. Her advisors hadn't liked the situation, but he had at least been male, so they tolerated it. They would likely have Cara exiled, or worse. She was quick to push the thoughts from her mind.

"Perhaps," Loralei said, interrupting a small period of quiet, "it would be best if you trained me as well." She had been thinking about it. Training had been one of the pivotal reasons why she thought Saiden was the best choice as her guard, and she had been struggling to keep it to herself. Her advisors would definitely not approve.

"If that is Your Majesty's wish," Saiden answered, eating another piece of the crisp white fruit she had picked from the plate.

She had expected an argument. If she had brought the wish up in front of anyone else, they would have argued that a queen should not be trained or armed. She changed that sentence in her head as well.

A queen should be able to protect her people.

Loralei was excited Saiden was willing to start her training on the very same day. Cara had the day off, and while she had joined them for breakfast, she always went to visit her family when she could. Loralei couldn't begrudge her. If she could visit her family, she would've taken every opportunity to do so.

She wasn't even sure if her aunt was still alive. Even so, she was glad for the distraction to keep her mind busy until Cara returned.

There were no meetings today as her council was likely still reeling from her putting her foot down yesterday. They hadn't even bothered to come into the palace proper all morning. It made it easy for her and Saiden to prepare a makeshift training room, and for her new personal guard to send for training weapons from the Legion.

She had tried to assure Saiden that she could hand her a real blade, but that would be impossible without disclosing her powers. And while she doubted Saiden would hate her for being blessed by the gods, she knew Saiden was religious, so there was always a possibility that she would find a Gifted queen a horrendous abomination.

Saiden hadn't bothered changing into gear.

Loralei didn't know if it was normal to train dressed like that, but she had always imagined them training in full gear. She had changed out of the nice silk dress, opting for something with higher slits. She was not allowed to wear trousers as other women might. She didn't mind dresses. And she would need to fight in one anyway if she were attacked again, so training in one probably wasn't a bad idea.

Saiden was waiting for her, holding two long wooden poles in one hand, resting her other against her hip.

"This is a bo. It's the first weapon we give recruits to train with." Saiden handed one to Loralei. "It helps to understand the way your body moves and how you fight. Then you can pick another weapon."

"Like your blades?" She had wanted to ask about them since she saw them at the parade.

With her now free hand, Saiden pulled out the two blades that had been sheathed at the hollow of her back. "These are kindjal, good for fighting multiple attackers and in close proximity. They were given to me because I exhibit great balance, and," she paused, "because I have often been attacked simultaneously by different people."

She said the words with shame, and Loralei hated that they lived in a place that had treated her with such disdain for something that was a natural result of her birth. She could not imagine Saiden had done anything to deserve such scorn.

"And your others?" Saiden had given her one of the thin blades when they had been in the sewer.

"Stiletto blades. I get all my gear jackets altered to have a spot for them in my sleeves. Good for piercing armor or internal organs."

Loralei felt dizzy thinking about Saiden trying to stab someone so viciously. She knew that life outside the palace was very different, so she tried to wrap her head around a life where that kind of knowledge was necessary.

"We'll find something suitable for a queen once we figure out your fighting style," Saiden said simply, ending their discussion.

Next, the legionnaire held the staff out in front of her, showing Loralei where to place her hands. Saiden moved then to stand beside her, and they began going through the motions. It was clear Loralei wasn't the first person Saiden had trained. She was good at showing others what to do and manipulating a lesson to fit the student.

Loralei was quite impressed by it all, but something inside her wanted to get to the action. "When do I get to actually fight?" she asked, trying to hide some of her eagerness.

"You still need more foundation before you can take on an opponent."

Loralei called for one of the guards she knew was waiting outside. Her advisors did not trust the Blood-Cursed mercenary, and the queen had quickly noticed the extra palace guards following them.

Saiden looked at her, confusion clear on her face.

"If I cannot fight," she said, motioning for the guard to come into the middle of the room, "then I hope you will at least indulge me in a first-hand look at how our strongest soldier fights."

Saiden nodded, pulling her sleeves down over the backs of her hands before readjusting her grip on the bo.

Her guard did not take the other staff, but pulled his own sword from its sheath. She realized too late that it was possible the guard would mean to do Saiden harm, but when she tried to speak to stop it, she saw Saiden shake her head ever so slightly. She wasn't sure why Saiden wouldn't want her to break up the fight, but she trusted the legionnaire had a good reason.

The guard struck first, swinging his sword toward Saiden with speed and fury.

Fear and panic mixed in Loralei, dancing through her chest. Each footstep matched the beats of her heart.

The bo cracked and split in two, leaving Saiden with a piece in each hand. She blocked with one half of it and struck out with the other, flipping it in her hand so it landed against the guard's side with a loud thud.

He flinched and shifted to the right, but quickly recovered.

When both pieces of the bo were reduced to only what Saiden had in her palms, she dropped them to the floor and pulled her kindjal from her waist. The guard swung at her again, but she blocked it, rolling on the ground and standing up behind him. She was fast, and his bulk kept him from being quick enough to strike her before she moved again. Saiden crawled up his back, cuffing his ears with the palms of her hands.

He dropped his sword with a clatter.

Then, in some move Loralei could not understand, Saiden had the guard pressed against the floor, a blade pointed above his sternum while the other rested against his throat. Saiden was quick to release him.

Even from where she was sitting, Loralei could see the pure fury in the guard's eyes. She was relieved that he picked up his sword and left them, retaking his earlier post. There was honor in losing—if one lost honorably.

"Why did you let that go on?" Loralei asked. "When you knew it would be more than sparring."

"Because he would not have had it any other way." Saiden sheathed her blade as a messenger walked into their room and bowed in front of Loralei.

"The Legion requires your seal on their mission, Your Majesty," the messenger said.

"Their mission?" Saiden interrupted.

"They are requesting to be sent to the northern mountains."

Saiden moved to stand behind the queen, reading the letter over her shoulder.

Loralei just watched her, unsure why she was reacting this way to news of a mission. The General was frequently requesting her signature for different businesses of state. This wasn't any different.

"Your Majesty, could I be allowed to deliver the letter back to the General?"

Loralei paused a moment before answering, trying to imagine what the motive was behind Saiden's request. In the end, she simply said, "Yes."

Saiden nodded her head, and though Loralei could feel the soreness radiating out from the woman, she still picked up the broken pieces of her bo and removed them from the training area before motioning for Loralei to take her spot at the center of the floor.

Loralei dismissed her other guards, taking an extra second to memorize the angry guard's face, filing it away so she could punish him later.

Saiden stood across from her and demonstrated the first of the training exercises again, which Loralei took to easily. She had never had the opportunity to test her Gifts out in a combat situation, but she could feel the way she was attuned to Saiden's life and the lives of the guards lingering outside.

Felt how easy it would be to *take* those lives.

Loralei shook her head, trying to clear that thought from her mind.

Saiden noticed and put her weapon on the floor before saying, "I think we should take a break for today."

Loralei wanted to keep training, but now that she wasn't moving, she could feel her muscles smarting.

And Saiden was still clearly put off, her mood soured by the General's letter.

"Good," the queen replied. "I have something to show you."

30

SAIDEN

Saiden wasn't entirely sure what the queen had in mind as she led her through the halls of the palace and back to her own royal quarters.

Despite their training, Loralei seemed giddy, but Saiden's mind was too preoccupied with thoughts about Nakti's missive to puzzle out the change in the woman's attitude.

"Your Majesty, what are we doing?" She didn't have it in her to be patient, to wait and see.

"This castle was built at a time when war frequented our borders. So, in order to protect the reigning monarchs, all the old sections of the palace were lined with secret passageways." Loralei pushed aside one of the tapestries hanging in her room and revealed a small opening behind it. When the queen pressed one thin finger into the hole, Saiden heard the wall hiss. Instinct had her reaching for her weapons.

When nothing came out from the panel, Saiden let her hands relax slightly, though she never let them stray too far from the blades. Whatever doubts were swirling through her head about her own abilities after seeing Nakti pass her up for a mission were secondary to her duty to protect the queen.

Loralei watched her for a second, and Saiden couldn't quite tell what thoughts were swirling in her head, couldn't read the quick flash of emotion on her face. The woman turned and entered the passage, giving Saiden no choice but to follow her.

The hallways behind the hidden entrance were surprisingly dry, and there was a small, unlit lantern resting on the stone floor beside the revealed doorway. Loralei was so quick to light it, Saiden wasn't sure how she managed it, but she barely had time to question it before the queen launched into a story.

"When I was a child, these hallways were some of the only things that brought me joy. It is an honor being Chosen, but it is lonely too," she admitted.

Saiden's heart went out to her. If anyone could understand the loneliness of being set apart by destinies, it would be her—the Blood-Cursed girl meant to die.

"My advisors hated that I knew about them and wanted to punish whoever it was that had given me this hiding space. I never told them who it was. Eventually, they just got used to it. They never really wanted to raise a child, so when I would hide away, they would pretend to look for me for a short while before going on with their day."

Loralei motioned for Saiden to follow her down the left side of the tunnel. "I had an aunt. She was all the family I had left before I was Chosen, and I was hers. They never let me go see her, but I found a way out once. I was so happy to see her, but I knew if I ever went up to her, they would punish her. It's hard being separated from loved ones like that, though I'm sure you know that already." Saiden watched Loralei gently wipe her cheeks, erasing the tears that had spilled from her eyes. "I'm not saying I had a bad childhood. I mean, what kid doesn't want to live in a palace? But I understand what it is to be left out."

Suddenly Saiden understood why Loralei had brought her here, why she had shared this part of herself. "Your Majesty, you have shown me a great kindness by sharing this story with me." She placed a hand over her chest, but Loralei stopped her before she could bow.

"I would like to ask you a question."

"You may ask me anything you wish, Your Majesty."

"What about that letter upset you?"

Saiden couldn't tell if it was curiosity or pain that flickered across Loralei's face as she asked her question.

She took a second to find the right words to explain how she was feeling. "Fighting is one of the only things I am good at. I never thought I would have that taken away from me, as well." As soon as the words were out of her mouth, she wished she had picked something different to say.

"There is no reason why you couldn't go on this mission," Loralei spoke, making sure to keep eye contact even as Saiden wanted to bow her head. "Your life here is not meant to limit you in any way. When you return to the barracks, petition the General. If you have her permission, then I see no reason for you not to go."

Saiden didn't want to question her generosity, so she pushed down the montage of questions bubbling up and bowed. She led them both back out of the tunnels the way they came and took her leave as soon as she had secured another guard to watch the queen.

31
MOZARE

With Saiden gone and Rhena in training with someone else today, Mozare had time to slip off to the rebel hideout. With their failure at the parade, things were still tumultuous there, and he imagined Revon could use his help.

He knocked on the door and was helped down into the entrance hall by one of their older guards. "I'm looking for Revon. Do you know where I can find him?"

"He's meeting with his palace informant. They're in one of the interrogation rooms, I think. Unless he decided to meet with her elsewhere."

Not exactly a helpful answer, but he could check the interrogation rooms before looking for Revon in the other places the man tended to haunt.

Mozare was lucky, though, as he knocked on the first of the interrogation rooms and heard Revon answer from the inside. He let himself in, dragging a chair from the hallway in with him. He watched the informant pass an old leather-bound book across the table but couldn't tell if there was anything on the cover before Revon tucked it into his jacket.

He nodded to the hooded girl across the table and sat next to his leader. Whatever intel she had, he was sure their leader would share with him anyway, so it wouldn't hurt for him to sit in on the meeting.

Revon continued his conversation. "You've come with news. What is so important you came weeks before we next expected to see you?"

"The Blood-Cursed girl, the one he," she nodded her head towards Mozare, "protects. The queen has selected her as her personal protection."

"Mozare has already informed us of that fact," Revon stated plainly. "If that is all the news you bring, then I am afraid you have wasted a trip."

"Loralei knows something about her condition, she went back to the Archives without me and she read something about it that left her shaken. She hasn't told me what it is, but I think it would be worth it to read into the Blood-Cursed and see if there's any information that could benefit us."

"I will send scholars out to research it in the morning."

"And Saiden—the queen is fascinated by her. I've never seen her take to a stranger as fast as she has to the girl. She could be the opening we need to get to Loralei."

Mozare slammed his hands against the table, ready to jump across it if needed. Revon grabbed his wrist and kept him from moving any further.

"You will not endanger her," Mozare said through gritted teeth. "If we really need an in, you should be it."

"You know she cannot just kill the queen, Mozare. I must be present at the death of the monarch, or the rebellion will not be able to lay claim to the throne. We are not going through all of this just so her board of advisors can rule until there is another Giftless monarch."

Mozare sat back down. They'd had this discussion multiple times, and every time it ended the same way. But he worried that his mentor's protection of Saiden wouldn't stretch far enough.

If Revon could use Saiden to get to the queen, he would. And he wouldn't care if she got hurt in the process.

"Thank you for the information," the rebel leader said. "You are free to go."

Their informant left, sneaking out the back room, leaving them alone.

"Saiden is innocent," Mozare said without turning to look at him.

"And I have always done everything to shed as little innocent blood as possible."

"Then you can't use her. She'll be branded a traitor, no matter what side wins. She has had enough hatred to last her multiple lifetimes."

"I will not give anyone a reason to hurt your partner, my boy. I have always given you my word, and that has not changed." He took a breath. "Now, it's time for you to leave as well. It was reckless of you to come during the day."

Mozare nodded, letting his anger simmer away, soothed by Revon's reassurances.

32

SAIDEN

Saiden had been planning to take a horse, but the stable boy at the palace had taken so long that she simply decided to run. She hoped the exercise would burn off some of the excess energy, both from the fight and from her anger at learning she'd been excluded from such an important mission. It, unfortunately, didn't have the desired effect, and she arrived at the barracks just as bitter. And completely out of breath.

She hadn't bothered knocking on Nakti's door. The General hadn't been respecting her lately, so Saiden had no reason to offer the General special treatment. She knew it was childish, but behind it, there was genuine pain. She was a perfect soldier, and she deserved this mission.

Nakti was talking to two of last year's recruits, perched on the edge of her desk. She stood up as her door banged against the wall, hand reaching for a weapon. The other two did as well, stopping when they realized it was Saiden, and looked to Nakti for directions on how to continue. She waved them away, dismissing them from their conversation.

"Shouldn't you be with the queen?" Nakti asked.

"My responsibility to the crown does not supersede my ability to complete missions. Her Majesty even said so in her letter." She handed Nakti Loralei's response. "So, why are Moze and I not assigned to this mission?" Saiden was angry, and even she could hear how it laced through every word.

"Because I did not assign you."

"You know we're the best choice for a mission this important. Whatever selfish reason you have for being a coward," she saw the General's fist clench, "you need to get over it."

"The mission has been assigned. If you wish to take it over, you will need to do so by duel. Those are the rules."

Saiden knew this, but had never personally dealt with it. She was used to Nakti giving her the missions that she was best at, and no one had ever tried to challenge her.

"Who do I need to find?"

"Oliver and Melana are in charge."

Internally, Saiden sighed. Oliver was one of the biggest mercenaries in the order. Saiden wasn't altogether surprised that he had been picked for this mission, but she wished it had been someone who would have been easier to fight. She could already feel exhaustion setting into her muscles from fighting Loralei's guard and then running to the barracks. This fight was going to be hard.

She left Nakti's office, careful this time not to slam the door. They might have been at odds for the past few days, but she didn't want it to last any longer than it needed to.

Saiden went to find Moze first. If she was going to be challenging Oliver to a duel, her partner should be there as well, even if she knew Melana would not fight. The girl was a timid, life-Gifted individual and had been partnered with Oliver in an attempt to balance his brutality. It had not worked well, but Melana had stayed by his side regardless, probably too afraid to request a new partner.

Moze was in his room, lying on his bed and throwing a ball up and then catching it. The act looked so mundane it stopped her for a second until she realized he was staring at her, waiting for her to say something.

"I'm going to challenge Oliver to a duel."

Mozare didn't even flinch, as if he had already expected her. He sat up on the bed and reached over to pull on his boots.

"Tired of the palace already?" he asked, teasing her. He must have known she would do this. He was usually pretty adept at figuring her out, and he knew she would want to be on this mission.

In the corridor, she saw Rhena sharpening a small dagger. "You gave her a blade?"

"You were handling blades when you were much younger than she is. And she's pretty good at it," Mozare said. It was one of the things she liked about him most—that he had so much faith in people. But she still worried about Rhena.

When the recruit saw Saiden, she slipped the dagger into a holster at her hip and stood up to hug her.

Saiden smiled and then let go, hoping Rhena would get back to sharpening her dagger. Unfortunately, she decided to follow them. Saiden just hoped that it wouldn't further cement Rhena's position on the periphery.

She found Oliver and Melana in the mess hall. He had a plate piled high with meats and cheeses while his partner sat nibbling on fruit.

"Oliver, I challenge you to a duel for lead on the mission."

"You dumb, Blood-Cursed bitch," Oliver said, slamming his hands against the table. The room went silent, everyone turning to watch them. "Thinking you're so special because they ain't killed you yet. This is my mission. Get lost."

Mozare stepped in. "She has the right to challenge you, Oliver. You have the choice to accept the duel or to hand over control to Saiden now."

Oliver growled at him, and Saiden reached for her blade. She would not let him threaten her friends when she was the one he was angry with. Rhena had also reached for her dagger, but Saiden stepped in front of the girl before Oliver had a chance to turn his wrath toward the young recruit.

"I've issued the duel, so you pick the weapons." He wouldn't turn it over to her without a fight. "We'll meet in an hour in the training hall."

She pulled both Rhena and Mozare out with her, hoping that neither of them would be stupid or impulsive enough to push Oliver any further. She had expected pretty much the exact response she had gotten. Oliver had never liked her and had made that clear from the beginning. She pushed it from her head and started pulling her thoughts together for a fight. At least she had already been training today and, though her muscles protested another fight, she would be ready.

33
LORALEI

Loralei took another look at the letter. She hadn't been raised the same way as Saiden, so she still found it hard to understand why she was upset, but her instincts told her it was the right thing to let her go back to the Legion.

Your Majesty,

We've received word that there is a group of rebels at the border between Kaizia and the northern kingdom who have developed a weapon of mass destruction.

From what our spies say, this weapon would have the ability to harvest a Gifted person's power and strip it from them, turning it into volatile energy that can be turned against their enemies.

Given the number of Gifted in our kingdom, and the tenuous agreement between us and the northern kingdom, we believe it best to send a team to stop them now before they have finished developing their weapon.

Your obedient servant,

General Nakti

She read the letter twice more before adding it to the pile of papers to be filed. Request for leave for Saiden had not been a part of the letter, and she wondered if that would get the legionnaire in trouble when she returned to the barracks.

As she let the knowledge of the mission fade to the back of her mind, anger filled her. She couldn't believe that one of her guards had attacked Saiden with such rigor. She had him summoned back into the makeshift training room and she called the lady's maid waiting in the hallway, and told her to bring three more guards, strong in the arms. All her guards were well-trained, but she was going to need muscles for this punishment.

The girl returned a few minutes later with three bulky guards behind her.

Loralei pointed to the fighter. "Two of you grab him, relieve him of his breastplate and shirt."

The guard she had called into training earlier looked at her in question but did not move as he was stripped of his armor and the sweat-soaked shirt underneath.

"I hope one of you wields a whip," she said and addressed the three guards standing and watching. "Two of you will hold him, and the third will deliver seventeen lashes."

She looked the guard directly in the eyes. "You will get the violence you sought earlier. Hopefully, you will remember that pain has a way of coming back to people."

She waited for the guards to move, to overcome the hesitance written across their faces. Guards were as loyal to each other as they were to the kingdom, and this punishment would affect all four of them.

"You may begin."

She stood watch as the guards delivered each blow, mentally counting the strikes. The guard's back arched with each lash, blood splashing across the floor. The other guards cringed as well, trying to hide the hate and fear crossing their faces. The disgust at having the blood of their comrade splattered across their uniforms.

As the seventeenth hit struck his back, he collapsed, and the other guards let go, not watching as he hit the floor.

"Bring him somewhere where he can heal. He is not allowed to see a healer," Loralei said, getting ready to leave. "And send someone in to clean up the blood."

THE LEGIONNAIRE

She walked out of their training room, not turning to look back at the blood soaking into the stone floor. Her hands at her side were shaking, anger warming her chest but leaving the rest of her cold.

She tried taking deep breaths, moving through the castle, ignoring the way her heart pounded in her chest as she walked up the steps and knocked gently on the door to the room where Magdalena was staying. She was still trying to figure out how to reintroduce her to her daughter without shocking either of them too much. With Saiden gone, at least she could check in with her and make sure she was being taken care of.

The former prisoner answered on the third knock, peeking hesitantly around the edge of the heavy wooden door. There was color in her cheeks now, but she was still frail, her years in prison having sapped her of her strength.

"I was wondering," Loralei started, breathing carefully through the anger that still threatened to consume her. "If you would like to go for a walk with me. I thought the sun might do you some good and I could show you my gardens." She smiled, and she hoped Magdalena couldn't see through it. She didn't want to show Magdalena the side of her that had a guard whipped by his peers.

The older woman offered Loralei a small smile of her own, slipping on a pair of slippers before joining her in the hallway.

She offered Magdalena her arm, slowing her steps so she didn't rush her down the stairs.

She felt her body relax as they crossed over the threshold, the smell of her flowers perfuming the air and bringing her a sense of peace. When they reached the grass, it was soft under her bare feet and she paused to curl her toes in it.

"You grew these flowers, didn't you," Magdalena said, a statement more than it was a question.

"How could you tell?"

"The look on your face. The pure joy of having created something good. That's how I feel about my Saiden."

"You should be proud of her. She's survived insurmountable odds, and she's still a good person." Loralei wondered if the same could be said about her with the satisfaction the guard's cries had brought her.

"I would like to see her."

"I want that more than anything, Magdalena. When Saiden returns, I will do whatever I can to see you reunited."

"Where has she gone?"

"To the mountains." She was sure that Saiden would end up being sent on that mission, despite not knowing how that would happen. She was the General's best soldier, and they would want her on a mission like this. It was why Loralei wanted her at the palace to begin with.

She and Magdalena walked together in silence. Loralei enjoyed her company. She wondered if having a mother, knowing her own, would bring Saiden the same peace that being with Magdalena did for her.

It didn't help Loralei's anger to think about what the woman had lost, what she had to give up before she even understood the consequences. She squeezed her hand into a fist, nails piercing the inside of her palm, and pushed the anger and sadness to the side. Then she smiled at Magdalena and wished for nothing more than a return to the happiness she used to know.

34
MOZARE

Oliver had unsurprisingly picked maces. He was big, and his arms were as thick around as trees, so he would want a weapon he could really swing with. Oliver was big, and while Mozare had no doubt Saiden was the better fighter, he could still do a lot of damage. They weren't supposed to purposely hurt their opponent in a duel, but Oliver was filled with rage, and Mozare knew that line was very easy to cross. Still, he knew that picking such a weapon meant he had underestimated Saiden, who was especially fast in a fight. She was crafty, too, having spent hours training with each of the weapons in the training hall. He wasn't worried about her in the slightest.

Rhena, on the other hand, was standing next to him and shaking her leg so hard he thought she might split the floor.

He put a hand on her shoulder. "Saiden will be fine. She's a better fighter than everyone here. It's why Oliver hates it so much that she challenged him."

But the recruit kept fidgeting, passing a small statue from one hand to the other. Mozare wasn't sure what it was, but he figured now was not the right time to ask.

He had offered to help Saiden warm up, but his partner had declined. Most likely because she knew the young girl would need someone to calm her down. Saiden was always looking out for the people around her, but he worried she wasn't looking out for herself. He wondered how the two came to care for each other so quickly, but maybe the gods had just put them in the right place at the right time.

He stood next to Rhena, leaning down so she was the only one who could hear him. "Who do you think has the advantage?"

The young girl paused, eyes going back and forth between the two opponents. "It's hard to tell," she admitted. "Oliver picked the weapons, so it's likely one he feels confident with. And he's strong. But Saiden is fast, and she's been training longer."

"So, is strength or skill more important?"

"It likely depends on who's wielding it."

Mozare was surprised by her answer. Even though she hadn't quite picked a side, she had done a good job differentiating their positions.

Together, they watched Saiden stretch in the middle of the room.

Others had started to join the crowd. This fight wouldn't be one people would want to miss.

Mozare thought it was stupid. They all fought all the time. He didn't understand why they needed to see more violence. Still, he was there, even if it was just for Saiden, so he couldn't necessarily argue with any of them.

When Oliver walked in, the talking stopped. His partner was behind him, but Melana moved to sit toward the side of the room once they got through the crowd.

Saiden stood up as Oliver joined her in the middle of the training room. Her hair was neatly tied in its four buns, with all its loose ends tucked away. It was how she preferred to fight. One less thing to be grabbed by.

Saiden's opponent walked to the weapons wall, taking his time to look over the maces before picking two. Some might have given their opponent a shittier weapon, but not Oliver. He handed her a mace.

Mozare imagined he didn't want anyone to say he cheated and only won because she had an inferior weapon. Even if he wasn't going to beat her.

Someone from the side of the room started a countdown. When the count reached one, the fight began. He swung straight away, aiming for Saiden's side.

She waited until he was dangerously close before dodging, bringing her own weapon up to parry his.

Rhena was holding tight to the handle of her dagger next to Mozare, the statue clenched in her other fist.

Oliver moved again, trying to bring the mace down from above. Saiden rolled, moving under his open legs, and standing up again behind him. He tried to turn around, but Saiden used the handle of her mace and jabbed it into his ribs. He slid sideways, changing weapon hands and swinging at Saiden again. She took the hit to her arm, and her mace made a loud clanging noise as it hit the training room floor.

Rhena gasped.

Mozare just watched. No matter the odds, his partner wouldn't lose the fight, and those who thought it was over were sorely underestimating her.

Oliver pulled his mace back and aimed for Saiden's head. It would have been a killing blow, no doubt, with Oliver's strength behind it. When it hit the floor, it left a hole.

Saiden had moved seconds before the mace would've hit her, twisting on the floor and grabbing Oliver's leg to knock him off balance.

He started to sway, and she used the momentum to pull herself up, swinging around and propelling Oliver's body to the floor with his own strength. He slammed into the stone, his mace flying into the air.

She caught it before it had a chance to land on him, though Mozare would have liked to see Oliver knocked out by his own weapon.

She held the spiked end of it to Oliver's throat. "Kill shot," she said. It was the quickest way to end a duel. She removed the weapon and offered a hand to her defeated opponent.

He spat at her, pushing himself into a sitting position. Melana rushed over, and though she, too, tried to help him up, he pushed her away. Clearly, he couldn't stand another stab at his pride in front of a room of mercenaries who just saw him toppled by an unarmed girl.

Mozare ran up to Saiden and clapped her on the back. "I had no doubt you could do it."

"Really?" She bent over, taking in a few deep breaths. "Because even I was starting to doubt it towards the end there."

Rhena joined them, checking herself to see that Saiden was okay. She pulled back a sleeve to reveal an already darkening bruise.

His partner must've been really out of it to let the younger girl push her sleeve back at all, though it didn't pass the boundary of un-tattooed skin.

"Do you think it's broken?" Rhena asked.

Saiden moved her arm and shook her head. "Banged up pretty good, but not broken. You shouldn't have come to watch that, Rhena." She turned towards Mozare. "Why did you let her come? What if something had happened?"

Mozare shrugged. He had let Rhena come because he doubted he would have been able to stop her. The girl was just as stubborn as Saiden, not that he would mention it to either of them.

"When's the mission start?" he asked, redirecting everyone's attention.

"We'll go tomorrow. Plan to leave here just before nightfall."

He nodded. He had assumed as much, but since Saiden had fought for the right to this mission, she deserved to give out the plans.

"And our team?"

"I can't imagine anyone will want to come with us besides Rhena, and she isn't coming."

Next to him, the recruit pouted, but she didn't argue. He wondered if she was remembering the last time she had tried to go on a mission with them without being ready for it.

"Besides, we work best alone," Saiden continued. "It'll be an easy job, in and out."

35
SAIDEN

When Saiden returned to the castle, this time on horseback, she was surprised to find the queen waiting up for her in her chambers. It wasn't that it was late that shocked her, but that the royal seemed to be worried about her. She was pacing in front of the large window, and Saiden watched her as the last of the sunlight bled from the sky.

Loralei turned around as Saiden closed the door, the soft click sounding through the room. There was something in her eyes that Saiden couldn't read. A secret she was keeping.

"Oh, Saiden, you're back. I'm sorry to be in your quarters without an invitation. It's just that—"

"It's all right, Your Majesty." She unstrapped her weapons' belt and sat down to start unlacing her boots. "Has something happened?"

"No, everything is fine. I just wished to apologize. I had not realized my guard would react that way, or I would never have suggested such a thing."

Saiden thought she could see something else in Loralei's eyes, but she was sure it wasn't the right time to be curious. "Your Majesty, there is truly nothing for you to apologize for."

"But that hatred," Loralei paused. "The hatred they feel for you is unlike any I have ever seen before."

Saiden didn't try to argue with Loralei. They would both know it was a lie, and she would not discredit either of them by doing so. "Hatred is a very powerful emotion." She was used to being hated just for being born, for living to be nineteen. For living at all. It was her burden to bear. "Please do not fret on my behalf, Your Majesty."

Loralei looked at her arm, where her sleeve must have ridden up, and the bruise Oliver had given her was peeking out. The barest tip of one of her leaves began to peek out as well, so Saiden was quick to pull down her sleeve.

"Did he do that to you?"

"No, Your Majesty. There was a fight at the Legion. I challenged another mercenary to a duel for the right to run the mission. I trust you will be alright with my absence for the next few nights?"

Loralei didn't answer, which made Saiden nervous. Perhaps she had misunderstood the queen's letter, and she was not free to run missions as she had thought. She couldn't imagine how embarrassing it would be to tell Oliver the mission was his after all.

"Of course, you are not my prisoner," Loralei said finally. "But you shouldn't go while injured."

"There are not, to my knowledge, healers kept on palace grounds. Are there?"

The queen studied her in silence, and she couldn't help but feel like her soul was being judged, and she wasn't entirely sure she wanted to know what the woman was thinking.

"Not officially, no," Loralei eventually said. "But there is another secret you should know if you are going to be working with me in close proximity."

Saiden watched, dumbfounded, as the queen approached her and knelt at her feet. So shocked that she did not resist when Loralei grabbed her arm and pushed the sleeve of her shirt back, letting her other hand hover over the large bruise. A tingling sensation of magic spread on her skin, and she stared as the bruise got lighter, the black fading to greens and yellows to brown before disappearing entirely. Saiden wasn't entirely sure what she was least comfortable with, the fact that her tattoos were on display or the knowledge that the queen—*her* queen—was Gifted. It was against public decree, and yet she had seen the proof with her own eyes.

Loralei had been blessed by Keir, Gifted with healing and life magic.

They were two people who weren't supposed to be what they were.

Loralei watched her from where she was crouched in front of Saiden, then she stood and moved the chair from in front of the vanity so they could face each other.

Twice today, the queen had trusted her with personal secrets, and the legionnaire wasn't sure what to make of it.

Saiden pulled the sleeve down. "You're Gifted." It wasn't a question, and it didn't really need to be said, but she could think of nothing else to say.

"They found out when I was fourteen when I started growing flowers from my balconies," Loralei started. "I thought it was the most wonderful thing ever, but everyone around me was so angry. The advisors hope that whenever someone is Chosen, she will be malleable and timid, but then I had more power than any of them. They've done their best to keep me suppressed, and I haven't done anything to stop them." Her voice became quieter as she spoke. "The last person to find out who wasn't one of my advisors disappeared."

She doubted they had just disappeared, and she knew Loralei was too cunning to have believed that lie, either.

"I will keep your secret, my queen. But there must be no others between us. I will not be able to protect you without complete understanding." She watched Loralei and made sure she understood. If there were going to be any more revelations, they needed to come out now.

Loralei did not speak, but she looked troubled.

Saiden wondered what it was like to be hiding such a big secret. Her blood-red hair made it impossible for her to hide hers, but Loralei seemed normal. She wondered if that was harder somehow.

"If there is something you wish to say, Your Majesty, then you should say it."

"I am trying to figure you out. Twice you have learned that I am not a typical ruler, but you are unshaken by both secrets."

She wondered if the queen was trying to shake her in the first place.

"You are unlike anyone I have ever met."

"I am unlike anyone you have ever met," Saiden repeated in agreement. "I shouldn't be here at all. They should've killed me. How could I ever judge someone else for standing outside of society's standards?"

"People would so quickly judge you for being born." Loralei looked like she regretted her words as soon as they came out of her mouth, but they did not bother Saiden. The queen spoke the truth, and there was no point in hiding from it.

Saiden shrugged her shoulders. "You should rest, Your Majesty." She moved to pull back the covers of her own bed, expecting Loralei to let herself out.

"May you rest with the gods tonight, Saiden," she said.

When Saiden heard the door click closed, she couldn't help but wonder if she ever had.

36
MOZARE

Mozare was only back at the barracks for a few hours before he had another reason to return to the hideout. He was slightly worried about how Revon would react to his news, especially since he hadn't been civil at their last meeting. But this was important information, something that threatened the entirety of their rebellion.

He knocked and used the newest password to gain entrance to the stronghold. The guard was shocked to see him, and it made him wonder what information Revon shared about him after his last meeting. He didn't have time for gossip, but the thought of Revon spreading rumors about him didn't sit well. He pushed the feeling away. His reason for coming was more important.

"He doesn't want any visitors tonight."

"I only have tonight. And he's going to want to hear what I have to say."

"He's in his temple."

That was another thing Mozare didn't agree with. No one had any more claim to the gods than someone else. Revon keeping a private temple bordered on blasphemy. Mozare was one of only a few people who even knew where it was. He had voiced his worry shortly after joining, but the leader had explained that his piety, the way he was raised, had no place in the stronghold. Revon needed to know what the gods wanted of him, and so he thought it was important for him to have private, unencumbered access to them.

He turned down one of the collapsed tunnels, carefully ducking under broken pieces of the ceiling and pushing through crisscrossed lumber. Hidden behind the rubble was a small, carved-out room where Revon knelt, his left palm facing up as he called on Ilona for guidance.

As he stepped into the rudimentary space, Mozare could feel the goddess' energy calling to him. As much as he hated ignoring her call, he needed to speak to Revon as soon as possible in case Saiden went looking for him. It was a huge risk, coming on the night before a mission, but he was placing his bets that she would stay at the castle for the night to prepare guards to take over in her absence.

From behind him, Mozare could see Revon slump as he left the trance he was in.

"The Goddess sent me away because she felt you here," he said, anger lacing his voice. He did not turn to look at Mozare. "Her favored child refusing to speak with her. And you believe me to be the blasphemer."

"We need to speak. I will offer recompense to Ilona later. She will understand."

He knew her wrath could span centuries, but she would understand. She wouldn't want unjust harm to come to her children because of the actions of bigoted people.

"Saiden and I are being sent on a mission."

"I thought the world-ender had been charged with the queen's personal protection."

Mozare bristled at the old nickname for Saiden.

"She fought for the right to run this mission, signed and sealed by Her Majesty herself. She will be given leave for the time it takes."

Revon finally stood up from where he was kneeling, turning around to look Mozare straight in the eye. "And what mission would permit the queen's personal guard to leave her majesty's side?"

"There are rumors of a group of people in the northern mountains who strive to rid the Gifted of their power. They want to strip the gods' favor and turn it into weapons for their own cause."

Anger bloomed across Revon's face. There was nothing their leader believed in more than the gods' favored children and the Gifts they possessed.

"The scientist responsible…" He paused. "What are you meant to do with the one who created such a weapon?"

"Orders are to have her returned to Legion for questioning. In case there's something else they're planning or someone else who can build the weapon."

He could see a tirade of thoughts swirl through Revon's head.

"You could question this creator. Figure out what it is that the Legion thinks is so important to know, and then kill them. Someone with that ability can't be allowed to live in anyone's hands."

Mozare had already realized that would be Revon's response long before he had spoken the words aloud. It was why he came to the stronghold in the first place. Because he needed Revon to sanction the part of the mission, obviously to be kept secret from Saiden. The ruthlessness he would need to commit in order to protect the people he cared about.

"I expect a full report upon your return." Revon's dismissal was clear enough, and he let his mind settle into his task as he climbed back through the debris of the collapsed hallway.

The sun was shining when he got back to the barracks. Saiden was waiting for him beside the stables. He added a bit of a stumble to his step and hoped that she would overlook the lack of alcohol on his breath. He knew it was a risk. She noticed most things about everyone. He just hoped she would trust in him enough to not question it.

"I've saddled the horses and prepared packs. We should be able to ride the first days if we go through the forest, and then we can send the horses back. Sirius will know the way."

"Sounds like you really thought this through. But I thought we were leaving at nightfall?"

Saiden shrugged. "It took me less time to get soldiers in line at the palace than I had anticipated." She seemed to bounce with energy, and he knew she needed this time away from everything more than she was letting on.

She bumped his shoulder as they went in to grab breakfast. A tradition of sorts since a warm meal would last a lot longer in their stomachs than the bread and hard cheese they'd be eating on the road.

Rhena was waiting for them at their table, sitting with a tray full of food in front of her. The recruit turned to look at them and smiled, an orange slice covering her teeth. He laughed, and he could feel Saiden beside him laughing too. They waited in the short line to get their own breakfast and then joined the girl at the secluded table in the back.

Other recruits walked by, and he was slightly surprised that they didn't look at Rhena with the same hatred in their eyes as he knew Saiden feared they would. There was clear respect on their faces, even if they weren't going to make the same decision she did. He assumed she was excelling in her training and felt pride at that.

"You should take me with you," the girl said before they had even pulled their seats in. Apparently, all her apprehension from yesterday had disappeared.

"You know we can't, Maus."

Mozare knew what that name meant to Saiden, and he was happy that she had that connection with Rhena. That they had each other.

"You've gotten much better, but you still need training before you can take another mission," his partner finished.

"One day, Rhena, we will be happy to take you with us," he added.

Satisfied, the young girl went back to her plate, and the three of them ate in companionable silence. The meal was over as quickly as any other at the Legion, and they were saying goodbyes before he knew it.

They rode fast and hard, weaving through the trees and pockets of sunlight in the forest. He could see the sun streak across the sky as the hours went on. They slowed as darkness began to fall, looking for a good place to camp for the night.

37
SAIDEN

Saiden busied herself with setting a fire as Mozare hunted for game in the forest surrounding their chosen site. She doubted he would find anything, but knew the routine calmed him, so she didn't argue. And if he did manage to find something, then at least they wouldn't have to immediately rely on the rations she had packed.

As the fire burned and crackled in front of her, she listened to nature. Forest sounds always soothed her, and she wanted to enjoy that peace as much as she could before she needed to be brutal again.

Near-silent footsteps sounded behind her on the forest floor, and she stilled.

"You really do have a death wish, Moze, don't you?"

"You always know it's me. And I trust that you would never hurt me. So, I can't see why I should worry about death."

"One day, I could slip up and gut you before I even have a chance to look at you."

"Doubtful."

She sighed, turning to see if her partner had brought anything with him to eat. Surprisingly, across his shoulders was a good-sized creature native to the woodland they were traveling through. She made space for him to prepare and cook the food. He knew that much blood made her uneasy, so he never made her do it.

They sat in silence as the meat dripped and sizzled, cooking over the fire. Whatever they didn't eat tonight, they could pack for the rest of the trip. She hadn't been stingy in packing, but fighting could certainly make them hungry. And they needed to keep their strength up in case anything went wrong.

She leaned back on her bedroll and looked at whatever stars she could see through the blanket of trees. "Tell me another of your stories, Moze."

"You've heard almost every one of them, Saiden. I'm not full of infinite stories, you know."

"But you're the best storyteller I know."

"That is true." He laughed. "Fine, I guess I can think of another one for your enjoyment. Once upon a time, in a land far away lived people not Gifted by any magic. They lived ordinary lives, with ordinary dreams, and they died ordinary deaths."

"That's your story?"

"Only the beginning," he said. Then he dove in. Mozare had a way with words and made them feel real.

Saiden listened to him speak until sleep pulled her into its peaceful kingdom.

When morning broke, they rode another day and a half before moving their things into packs and sending the horses back to the Legion. There was a nearby town where they could buy new steeds on their way back. The path through the mountains was far too steep and unpredictable for them to bring animals, anyway.

Her and Mozare's hours of training made it easy for them to make it through the mountains to the small basin, where their targets were rumored to be hidden. They made easy work of the hill until it was in sight. She grabbed Mozare, pulling him behind a tall rock before they could be spotted by any guards that might be on duty.

"It's late. We should take watch and learn what we can tonight. It will be better for us to attack in the early light, where I can still have daylight on my side. Not all of us can wield shadows."

"Sound reasoning, as always."

They moved around each other, each picking a different vantage point, and settled in to wait for darkness to finish cloaking the mountains in darkness.

Saiden let Mozare sleep in the last few hours before dawn. She had no idea how he managed to find enough calm to do so while crammed into a mountain crevice.

Nervous energy pulsed through Saiden, and she wished for more room in their hideout to pace. She always felt like this before a mission. There was always too much to plan, too many things that could go wrong. But they had a job to do, and so she waited for the feeling to settle down. For the battle calm to slip over her.

Her partner woke up with a gentle sigh and wiggled out of his hiding place to join her in her spot. They were given orders to do everything they could to avoid casualties, but as she watched the people walk back and forth, her faith in their ability to get through without killing anyone dwindled.

"Where did they all come from?" Mozare asked from beside her.

"They've been gathering here all morning, coming in from all over the mountain. Most of them were bringing baskets, so maybe supplies? But I can't be sure."

"I should've gone down last night. Used the darkness to search the campsite."

"They came today. Going down last night wouldn't have even made a difference."

"We might have had better luck understanding a way in if I had looked last night," Moze insisted. "We could've at least guessed what weapons they have. What powers they could use against us. I feel like we're going in blind."

"We already know they hunt the Gifted. They might've been able to see through your shadows, and we couldn't risk that. Besides, I have a way in," she said, pointing at the small entrance the people had been using.

"Then when do we start?"

"As soon as you're ready. Our stuff must stay here since we'll be too slow with it. Hopefully, we can grab it on the way back out."

She went over her plan with Mozare, and when she was done, they set off scaling down the side of the mountain where other rocks hid them from view. She repeatedly checked her weapons before making her way down. There were plenty of ways she knew to incapacitate an opponent without causing fatal harm, and she mentally went over them as a way to keep her focus off the great distance between them and the ground.

She had only brought her weapons as a last resort. If something went really wrong, and they needed to truly fight their way out, she didn't want to have to rely solely on her wits and fists. She knew he felt the same way. She'd checked his ax harness' straps were secure before starting their descent.

She focused on her breathing, taking each step to prepare herself for the unknown they were about to face.

They reached flat ground faster than she hoped, although she was glad not to be climbing anymore.

Mozare stepped down next to her, grabbing her hand before calling a thin layer of shadows around them.

It wasn't enough to hide them. The shadows would be too obvious as the sun shone brighter in the sky. But it would be enough to keep anyone from noticing unless they were truly looking. She kept her hood tight on her head. Even here in the mountains, they would recognize its blood-red shade and know who she was.

They moved toward the door she had singled out. People were still going in and out, so it wouldn't be too suspicious if the barrier opened. They snuck through after a woman carrying a full barrel of grains, some of it trailing on the floor behind her.

They had no idea of what it would be like inside the building, which made Saiden even more hesitant as they moved forward.

Mozare let the shadows fall, and they crept into a hallway, careful hands hanging near their weapons.

She led the way, listening for any footsteps getting closer to them. She could blindly trust her partner would have her back.

"Where would a scientist hide in a building like this?" she asked, whispering the words so Mozare could add any input he might have.

"A basement? Some kind of evil lair?"

She slapped his arm.

But a basement wasn't a terrible place to start looking, so she set out trying to find a staircase or a ladder. She assumed these people thought the mountains were secure enough, since they didn't encounter any guards or even locks as they went through. They easily searched any room they passed and couldn't find any of the people they had seen coming in.

When they finally did find a ladder, they were careful while climbing down into the darkness beneath it. Mozare had the benefit of relying on his shadows to know what was around him, so she let him go in front this time. He moved quickly through the room until he found a torch and lit it.

Judging by the scattering of papers and tools, Mozare's idea about the basement had been right. Neither of them had much of a mind for science, but they had been told to bring back anything they could carry, any plans they could find that would let the Legion know what was going on.

Another door opened, and a tall woman walked through. She wore thick-rimmed glasses, pushed up and resting in the curls of her blonde hair.

She spoke first in the language of the northern kingdom, and when they didn't answer, she tried again in the common tongue. "Who are you?" She had a beautiful accent, rich with the sounds of the mountain people, but she was distraught, and Saiden didn't need her to raise an alarm.

"We're new. And we got lost," she said, rushing to say the first thing she could think of.

The scientist nodded and moved toward one of her tables. Saiden watched her, trying to keep an eye on anything that might call people to her aid.

"You think I don't know who you are?" the woman said as she reached for a tool on her table and threw it at Saiden's head.

She ducked, rolling out of the way, and then charged toward the scientist before she had the option to throw anything else. She struck her chest with the palm of her hand, knocking the frail woman onto the stone floor.

"Get whatever plans you can," she told Mozare. "We need to leave before anyone else knows that we were here."

"You Gifted wench! We will rid the world of tarnished people like you."

"You can try," Saiden whispered to the woman. "But I am not Gifted, and I can kill like any other man. Don't forget that."

She pulled the scientist up from the floor, binding the enemy's hands together behind with only enough slack to keep her shoulders from being pulled too tight. Mozare was beside them soon enough, his pack filled with whatever papers he could gather from the desk.

"We need to leave, Sai. Before anyone notices we were here. Or that their precious scientist is missing."

They crossed back to the ladder, pushing their captor to follow behind Mozare.

"If you take a step out of line, I can skewer you before you can even scream," Saiden warned. She didn't want to hurt this scientist, but she needed her to believe every rumor she had ever heard about her ruthlessness. Hopefully, that reputation would be enough to keep her from trying to run. She let the woman climb up in front of her, keeping a hand out to catch her if she were to fall.

They retraced their steps through the cobblestone hallways, keeping a heavy hand over their scientist's mouth. She didn't want to have to threaten her again, but she would if someone saw them.

By the time they reached the door, Saiden was having a hard time believing they were lucky enough to get out without being seen. Just as the thought crossed her mind, she heard an alarm call sound through the camp. She handed the scientist to Mozare, trusting him to get her out, and drew her blades. She didn't want to hurt these people, no matter what harm they might wish on her.

Two men approached, dropping their baskets and running toward them. She turned towards the faster one and ducked under his swing, striking the back of his knee with a rear kick, and knocking him out with a swift hit to the back of the head. The other assailant was harder to dislodge, but she had him passed out with only a couple of hits.

She pushed herself to run faster, even though Mozare was struggling with keeping their scientist away from the people trying to free her. Even from a distance, she could see blood on the blade of his ax. She cringed and ran harder, her footsteps pounding in her ears.

It would be hard for them to climb the mountain with the scientist's extra weight, but Mozare had a rope tied to his belt intended for just that. It would be slower and harder, especially if there were people pursuing them.

She stopped at the foot of the mountain, pain lancing through her head at the thought of what she had to do next. Saiden always did whatever she could to prevent needless death.

Now she had no choice.

38
MOZARE

Mozare waited with the scientist at the top of the mountain and watched Saiden climb. Her hands left red streaks for the first few feet until whatever blood was left on her fingers dried or was wiped off. He bundled their scientist into an alcove and wondered if he should just kill her before his partner even reached the top. But he couldn't bear to keep his eyes off his climbing companion, worried about the danger she was still in. Until they put more distance between them and the compound, he wouldn't feel safe getting rid of the scientist. And Saiden would need to feel like those deaths were for something, even if he was going to eventually take that away from her. Guilt tore through him, but he did his best to rest during this brief reprieve. If his partner knew what he was doing and why, he trusted she would understand.

As Saiden's hands reached over the cliff top, he extended his free one to pull her the rest of the way up. He was careful not to let go of their scientist, who would no doubt run back to the people desperate to protect her. He couldn't blame the woman's survival instincts when death's song played for her in the wind.

They pulled their gear on, hastily securing the straps on their shoulders and tightening the knots holding the scientist's arms behind her. He wondered if their captive had any skill at protecting herself. If she would be a hard target. He wasn't cruel. He wanted her death to be quick and painless. He wouldn't revel in her end but would in the relief that such a horrific weapon would no longer be a possibility. The bag full of her plans ruffled at his side as they ran down the steep rocky paths.

Saiden was behind them, carefully doing her best to hide their tracks and lead any would-be pursuer on a different path than theirs. They had this routine down. It was far from the first time they had been forced to fight themselves out of a situation and go on the run. They worked perfectly in sync, and he only stopped running when the trees were dense enough to cover them from sight.

Beside him, their scientist was bent over at the waist, her breath coming out in heavy puffs. He was honestly surprised she wasn't screaming, trying to alert her friends to where they were hiding. He watched her carefully, his head tilting curiously as he wondered what else she was protecting.

"We need to keep going," Saiden said. She was scrubbing furiously at her hands. "There's a stream not far from here. We can go there and interrupt any footsteps or trail I might have missed."

He knew she also needed to wash the blood from her hands. Looking at it would keep her mind trapped in the fight and the killing.

She took the lead, grabbing the scientist and forcing her to keep pace with them. At the back, Mozare wove a tapestry of shadows, moving with them and keeping them out of sight of any followers. It was harder to do with how fast they were moving, but he had lots of practice.

They reached the stream, crossing through the water until they were far enough away that it would be impossible to track them. Saiden had washed as they were running, something she was quite adept at, and let them rest at a small outcropping so she could go into town to get horses. He didn't like letting her go alone, but he knew that he needed the time alone with his target. This would probably be the only chance he got.

He watched Saiden leave and, when he was confident she was out of earshot, he turned to the scientist. "You've been awfully quiet." He pulled a small dagger from a sheath over his thigh and used the point to clean the blood out from under his fingernails.

"My fight is worth more than my life."

He felt a kindred spirit within her that matched the pieces of him that fought for a better system for his own kingdom. He recognized and acknowledged how, in different circumstances, they could have been on the same side.

"Why do you hate the Gifted?"

"They are cursed, and allowing the gods to have such a strong hold on our people will kill everything. Destruction follows where they go."

"I am sure they will forgive you when you meet them in the end for your misunderstanding of their graces." He truly believed that even those who hated the gods would still belong in the paradise that waited for all of them. Welcomed and embraced by those with more wisdom and love than any human could possess.

He went up to her and rammed his small dagger between the bones of her ribcage, striking fast and deep. It was soon over, his final mercy. He pulled her into his lap, doing what he could to make it look like he had been trying to save her. The sound of horses pulled him from his thoughts, and he watched Saiden enter the clearing and blanch at what she saw.

Her face was the only thing that made him regret killing. Even his victim's blood cooling on his skin didn't give him the same repulsion as seeing heartbreak and defeat take root in Saiden's expression.

"Wh—What happened?" Her voice was barely above a whisper.

"Someone must've followed us." He said, careful to hide any of his true emotions behind the wobble in his voice. "The blade came from nowhere, and there was nothing I could do about it."

Tears streaked down the dirt on Saiden's face as she kneeled next to them, praying over them both and blessing the dead scientist. Then she stood, clearing the ground a few feet deeper in the forest.

"We need to go," he said, not wanting to run the risk that his lie was true and someone had actually followed them.

"She deserves to be buried properly, Moze. We failed to protect her when we were the ones who put her in danger in the first place. I—I have to do this." She started digging.

They didn't have the right tools, meaning the digging would take hours, but he couldn't imagine taking this away from her. Even he was hesitant to leave the scientist's body to rot and be eaten by animals.

If there was honor in nothing else, there could at least be honor in death.

39

SAIDEN

They stayed in the woods longer than they had planned, but without the extra rush of bringing the scientist home, Saiden had needed the time to deal with her grief. And to plan how she would explain this failure to the General. Not only had she left the queen behind and fought for the right to this mission, but she had also insisted she was the best equipped to carry it out. And now, she had nothing to show for it.

Mozare was mostly quiet while they lived in the woods, slowly moving closer to the barracks with each passing day.

She couldn't tell what exactly was bothering him, and she was too stuck inside her own head to really push him to talk about it. They were so different in this matter. In how they handled grief. She knew he would eventually need to talk about it. And when he did, she would listen, even if she would never reciprocate and share what she was feeling.

The vibrant green of the trees and vines now seemed dull, death tainting everything around her. She couldn't pick out any color besides red. Like the blood that had stained the front of the scientist's smock. That *still* stained her hands, no matter how many times she washed them.

The horses she had bought weren't as strong as the ones bred for legionnaires, so they often found themselves walking beside them, the dirt smooth under her boots. It made her think of the shallow grave she had dug for the scientist. How each of them would someday return to the dirt they came from.

When the forest became especially familiar again, she started pushing herself through the motions of burying her grief and building up the mask of the perfect soldier over the pain she felt inside. Judging from the way Mozare was moving, she imagined he was doing the same. When they finally reached the barracks, they were themselves again, at least on the outside.

Since they had managed to clean themselves off that morning, they sought out their General immediately upon arriving. Their mission report would be a mess, and she wanted to get it out of the way. And to deal with whatever punishment Nakti was sure to dole out to them.

They found her outside, going over her own training regimen with some of the wooden dummies left out in the arena. Sweat dripped down her dark skin, soaking into the tank top she was wearing.

Mozare spoke first, getting their superior's attention, and requested a moment alone with her.

Nakti eyed them warily, grabbing a towel and some water before going to sit on the nearby bench.

Saiden couldn't sit, and standing felt awkward with what they had to say, so she kneeled. Mozare followed, waiting for permission to speak.

"You are four days late returning." It wasn't a question, so neither of them answered. "Our informants say their camp is in an uproar, and yet I see you've come back empty-handed."

She waited for a clear question, something she could latch onto that would prove their mission hadn't been a complete waste.

Mozare took matters into his own hands and pulled his bag in front of him, offering it to the General. He had guarded it so well on their journey home that seeing him give it up felt wrong.

Nakti didn't take the bag, leaving him kneeling with it in his hands like an offering. "What happened?"

"We had her, General. But she was killed by an assailant as we were fleeing," Saiden answered.

"Two of my greatest legionnaires—and some random rebel was able to get by you both?"

Saiden let her head hang in shame and waited for punishment to be given.

"Saiden, you are to return to the palace. Don't come back here."

Mozare spoke up. "You can't ban her from the compound!"

"I can do whatever I want with my soldiers. And I am not banning her, just sending her to do her duties to her kingdom before I make her incapable of doing so." General Nakti stood, anger striking through her muscles as she walked away.

Saiden felt hollow, waiting for relief or grief or any strong emotion to burst through her. But nothing came. She stood and left her partner kneeling there, heading to the stables for Sirius.

Rhena was waiting outside, talking to one of the other recruits from her group.

She didn't even say hello to the girl before riding off, leaving her and Mozare behind.

40
LORALEI

Loralei had waited in the observatory that overlooked the front gate of the palace every day since her personal guard's expected return, hoping to see the red-haired legionnaire ride through the gates. Her advisors were practically ignoring her at this point, far too happy that they didn't need to consider her opinion for her liking. But she hadn't bothered with them either. She had worried the first day that Saiden hadn't come back, and her worry had grown every day after.

The queen's heart leaped in her chest when she finally saw the woman approach. More than relief flooded through her, but she didn't give herself time to think about it. She hitched up the light blue fabric of her skirts and ran as fast as she could to the front door of the palace. She didn't care that it wasn't proper, or that she was sure to get an earful from her advisors as soon as she started going back to meetings.

She opened the front door before any of her guards had a chance to do so, or to step in to stop her. She only slowed at the top of the stairs. Otherwise, she likely would have tackled her, and she wasn't sure the legionnaire was up to that kind of contact. Even from a distance, she could see that something dark hung heavy over her personal guard's thoughts.

Saiden dismounted, turning towards the queen and bowing deep before making her way up the steps.

Loralei grabbed her hand, completely dismissing any kind of protocol in favor of showing her friend that she wasn't alone.

Saiden's room was ready for her, but Loralei didn't think she could bear to leave her alone in the big room. She brought her to the gardens instead, weaving through rows of different flowers until she reached her hidden spot.

She turned to her guard and placed a gentle hand on her cheek. The warmth from her fingers leached into the legionnaire's ice-cold face, and she watched the girl start to crumble. She grabbed her, pulled her to her chest, and sank into the rich ground with her. She didn't care about how the dirt might be staining her new dress. She held Saiden as tears wracked the fighter's body, and she stayed there, huddled around her long after all her tears had dried.

41
SAIDEN

Loralei came to wake Saiden early on her first official day back to service.

She heard the queen knock on her door and was surprised at how quickly she had learned to recognize the queen's knock. She pulled on a long sleeve shirt, sat up in bed, and called out, "Come in."

Her muscles were sore, and her skin itched where she had seven leaves added. She was lucky Niran preferred working at night since Loralei would need her around all day today. She didn't like to wait too long after the deaths to get the tattoos, even if the rule was hers alone.

Mozare was likely still sleeping in the barracks, and Saiden found herself envious. It surprised her. It wasn't something she felt often. It was probably because she was tired and sore, her mind and body still recovering from their mission.

The queen walked in, lilac pink skirts billowing behind her. She stopped when she saw Saiden still in bed. "I'm sorry, I figured you for an early riser. I thought you'd be up."

Her ruler blushed, which she thought was funny.

"It's alright, Loralei," Saiden said, and the queen's eyes widened. "What is it?"

"You called me Loralei."

Saiden didn't realize the change until the queen pointed it out. "I'm sorry, Your Majesty. I felt it would be appropriate since we've been working together."

And since Loralei had been there for her, making their relationship feel less like one of duty and more like a true friendship.

"No, please. It is much better than the formality. It's nice to have a friend."

Saiden pulled back her sheets. It was getting warmer in the kingdom now, so she had been sleeping in just her tank top and underwear. Loralei was quick to look away, but Saiden didn't care. She was used to changing in front of people. There were shared showers for the girls in the barracks.

Without turning around, Loralei handed Saiden a package wrapped in burlap and tied with twine. "I had something made for you."

Saiden took it and set it on the bed. As she untied the string slowly, the fabric fell to the side. She pulled the first piece of clothing from the pile and held it out. It was a gear jacket made of finer leather than what they usually used in the Legion. It was mostly black, as was expected of legionnaires, but the bottom was designed with flowers. She wondered if it had something to do with the queen's dress, which was always decorated with beautiful blooms.

Loralei had even had them add the spaces for her stiletto blades.

She set the gear jacket on the bed and pulled out the matching pants. The leatherwork was extraordinary. They had enough space for her weapons belt and pockets for the other small things she liked to carry with her, like basic first aid materials, a good luck charm, and small throwing knives. One could never have enough weapons.

A pair of new boots sat at the bottom of the container. Saiden picked one of them up. The cobbler had added more flowers, and she wondered why someone would put so much effort into a pair of shoes. It was one of the nicest gifts she had ever been given. She didn't know what to say and looked at the young queen, who was finally watching her, hands pressed together against her chest.

"If you don't like them, we can have them returned and have something new made," Loralei said.

"They're wonderful." She picked up the gear jacket again and slid one arm in. It felt light on her skin, but she instinctively knew the material that lined the sleeve would be strong enough to deflect a blade. She quickly strapped it up and grabbed the pants to pull them on. Everything fit incredibly, and she was glad they had spent that time on her first day to get her measurements. Next, she belted her kindjal sheath and buckled up her pants.

She stood in front of the mirror, something she had never desired to do before, and pulled the blades out, standing there before re-sheathing them. She was worried that the new gear would make her more noticeable, but Loralei had been thoughtful enough to have them add a hood. It wasn't standard in gear, but Saiden always wore one with hers, and she wondered if Loralei had personally noticed that.

"Thank you."

Two maids entered, carrying breakfast.

"I figured you'd be hungry," Loralei said, smiling.

Cara was the second of the maids, and she did not follow the first out of Saiden's quarters after the food had been arranged. Instead, Loralei and Cara sat down while Saiden braided her hair before quickly joining them.

There were plenty of fruits and dried meat. Loralei seemed to prefer that for their breakfast every morning, and Saiden appreciated the routine of it all.

"So, our plans for today, my queen?" she prompted.

Loralei frowned at her, but something inside Saiden felt weird being so intimate with her while they were in front of other people. Perhaps one day, she would get over it. But today was not that day.

"I like to go out once a week to see my people. To bring food and supplies for the needy. My advisors haven't let me out recently because of the attacks. But I figure with a guard as," she paused, choosing her next word carefully, "*well-known* as you, they wouldn't be able to argue. And with my coronation tomorrow, I want the reminder of what it means to be queen. I want to see the people I am meant to serve."

Saiden nodded in understanding.

When breakfast was finished and Cara left to do her chores for the day,

Saiden strapped on her new boots. She checked her weapons again and pulled out one to give to her charge.

"Only if you need it," she said, making sure Loralei understood that she should leave her protection to Saiden unless absolutely necessary. When Loralei nodded, she backed up, and they left.

She knew the queen wasn't meant to be armed, but she figured no one would be able to see a blade beneath all the chiffon layers of the skirt. Loralei, at least, seemed more comfortable having the weapon.

Two royal advisors joined them in the hallway, looking like they'd much rather be anywhere else.

"Your Majesty, we must advise against this once more," the first one said. "There are people out there who wish you harm."

"Any of the people you try to help today could turn against you," the other added.

The queen paused, pulling her spine straight and looking both of them in the eye before speaking. "These are my people. I will not hide from them like a scared little girl because of the threats from one group of outrageous rebels."

The two advisors looked at each other like they were both waiting for the other to come up with a better argument. When neither said anything, Loralei turned around, her skirts trailing after her.

Saiden was only a step behind her, feeling proud that the queen had stood up for the chance to see her people.

They took the front door of the palace, and Saiden was slightly shocked by the view of the town from where they stood. She had never taken the time to look at it from the steps, but the palace was built to be above everything. She could see all the way down to the barracks.

"Where do we start?" Saiden asked.

"At the beginning."

42

LORALEI

Loralei led the way. She had developed a circular path through the village where she could see each of the people she knew needed her most. She hated that she couldn't do more for them outside of food and fresh bandages, but if she used her Gift, she was sure to bring scorn and violence to the palace door.

Religion was such a big piece of the culture of her kingdom, and she couldn't deny them their beliefs. Even if that very thinking decreed neither she nor Saiden should exist.

It was strange to have found such solace in Saiden and the way the legion-naire lived in a world that would happily see her dead. The two of them really were an odd duo. She smiled at the thought.

The first stop was a little house neighboring the palace where a small family lived there. They'd had a limited harvest, half of which had been stolen by bandits.

She knocked at the door, and she and Saiden were let inside. The people knew when to expect her, and were always kind, but she hesitated walking in this time in case they wouldn't be the same to Saiden. She didn't want to choose between her people and her guard, but Loralei couldn't tolerate the unjust hatred toward Blood-Cursed individuals.

Eustace bowed. "Your Majesty." He was old to be a father of children as young as his. And yet, he had the same youthful look in his eyes as his children when he laughed. His wife and their children bowed as well, and then the smallest child, their daughter, Eloise, came up and hugged the queen. She swirled the young girl around and then carefully placed her feet back on the worn floor of their house.

"I've brought fresh bread and two weeks' worth of meat." Loralei pulled the food out of her bag and passed it to Eustace. She wanted to show he was still in charge. Her charity was in no way meant to remove the normal roles of the household. He smiled at her, making him seem younger.

Their house was as quick a stop as it usually was. Soon enough, Saiden and Loralei were back on the cobblestone streets. The legionnaire had her hood up, but Loralei could see by the way it was moving that the guard was still keeping an eye out for potential danger. Loralei liked her dedication, proving she had been right to choose her as her personal guard, regardless of her advisors' doubts.

They didn't visit every house like Loralei had tried to when she first started these charity days. However, there were many people close to the palace who did not actually need her help and would still take it while others were without. She had spent hours looking over maps, marking which people truly needed assistance and how often she should visit them to bring aid.

The next house was a few streets farther from the palace, and their troubles were more complicated. It was a young married couple without children. The husband had been hurt in a mining accident, and his leg was still healing. Loralei had wanted to heal him, wanted to help every time she went to visit, but had to keep reminding herself how they would look at her if they knew the truth.

She knocked at the door.

The wife, Alisa, opened it and quietly let them inside. Her husband was propped up in bed as usual, but there was finally color in his cheeks again.

Loralei smiled at him and found she was genuinely happy to see the small changes in his manner. She'd brought food and fresh bandages and was prepared to change his leg wrappings herself but didn't argue when Saiden put a hand out for the supplies. She imagined the legionnaire would be better at this than her since she had the gods-given Gift of healing and hadn't needed to rely on anything but her powers in a long time.

When Saiden pulled her hood back, Loralei saw Alisa's husband flinch slightly, but he still let her guard tend to his leg without argument.

She didn't know why having Saiden with her put her so on edge, ready to step into the middle of a conflict without hesitation. The Blood-Cursed fighter could clearly handle herself. Loralei had seen her do so multiple times. Still, her fascination grew whenever she got to see her guard do something new.

It was another quick visit, even shorter now that Saiden was the one tending to his wounds. She had deft and skilled fingers, and the creams and bandages were applied within seconds of the old ones being removed. Loralei wondered how many times Saiden had needed to apply bandages to others. How many times she had needed to apply them to herself?

They took a back pathway to the next home, sneaking underneath two double-level houses that leaned so close to each other that she was sure neither could be moved without collapsing the others. She liked seeing it. It reminded her of how dependent people were on their neighbors, for better or for worse, and how dependent they were on her.

Someone yelled, and people jostled against each other as they came out to a crowd on the other side of the alleyway. Saiden stepped in front of her, one hand reaching towards the blades sheathed on her back. There were more people on the road than Loralei had ever seen gathered there, and she could see no reason as to why.

"Your Majesty," Saiden spoke, her words hushed. "We need to turn around. This is not a place for you."

She moved to follow her guard's instructions. She had no desire to be trapped in another mob. Her people shouldn't see her fear so closely. It would start to topple their faith in her.

"You're right about this being a bad place to bring a queen," a voice spoke from the shadows. "Foolish of you to bring someone so valuable into the slums. And your poor hem is absolutely ruined."

Loralei heard the people laugh, and panic crept through her. She had no idea how many were hiding out in the alleyway. Couldn't see how many people wanted to kill or harm her.

In front of her, Saiden slid off the new gear jacket Loralei had commissioned for her, handing it back to her without turning to look.

"You don't want to do this," Saiden said, and she sounded every bit the formidable warrior her reputation made her out to be.

Loralei could see nothing of the girl she knew in the defender now standing in front of her.

"There are eight of us and two of you. Ain't much of a fight, is it?"

Saiden didn't answer, and Loralei saw her hands creep to her thighs. Faster than Loralei could track, two short blades sailed from Saiden's hands. She heard the dull thud as they connected with human flesh.

"Six," her guard said, pulling blades from her back and stepping towards the next assailant. She was a storm given life as she moved around the alley, never letting anyone get close to Loralei. She had already killed two of them, the shorter of her blades still stuck in the chest of a short hairy man.

She felled a third and a fourth before someone grabbed her, slicing a blade down her arm and successfully knocking the other kindjal blade loose. The clatter as it hit the cobblestones echoed in Loralei's head.

She waited for Saiden to pull her stiletto blades, then froze as she realized they were tucked in the jacket the legionnaire had given her. She didn't know if Saiden even had another weapon on her after throwing the small daggers.

The larger of the men, the leader if she had to guess, pressed a blade to Saiden's throat, pulling at her hair until it began to unravel around her shoulders.

"Stop." Loralei forced as much of a command into her voice as she could. "Let her go, and I will go with you."

"You'd give up your life for this cursed garbage? Maybe there is still honor left to the crown, after all." He let Saiden go.

The legionnaire sagged to her knees, eyes watching as the queen stepped forward silently on slippered feet.

Loralei had one chance to get this right. If the gang knew she was armed, they would kill them both. And she wasn't a good enough fighter to stop it from happening. She stepped forward until she was in between the two men, Saiden at her back.

When they went to grab her, she pulled Saiden's stiletto blades free and ran each of them through.

Shock passed over the leader's face before he fell to the ground.

Loralei felt nothing for a second, and then shame bloomed in her chest. She hadn't even thought about what she was doing. She just wanted to protect her friend.

Saiden was beside her in an instant, looking her over and checking for injuries.

Loralei's hands were shaking, but she had not been close enough to the attackers long enough for either of them to do her any harm.

Her guard, on the other hand, was still bleeding steadily from the deep cut on her arm.

She grabbed her, ignoring the resistance Saiden tried to provide. She knew the men were dead, but she still looked around before calling on her Gift, letting it knit the skin on Saiden's arm back closed. Through the rip in her shirt, Loralei could clearly see the tattoos that covered the other girl's skin for the first time.

"What are these for?" she asked, trying to flush the panic from her system by focusing on something else. She imagined both limbs were covered in leaf tattoos.

"Each of these is a life I have taken."

She pulled Saiden's arm closer and, through the fabric tear, kissed one of the leaves.

"Maybe you should consider how many lives you have saved."

Loralei was trying to take deep breaths, standing in front of the mirror. She would ascend the throne and officially take over responsibility for the kingdom today. That was more important than any dress she wore or braids in her hair. Still, she was happy with the alterations the dressmaker had made in such a short time, adding sheer black paneling to the back portions of her skirt. She felt it looked much more regal, and it recognized the death her people had faced in the past few days.

Saiden entered her room on silent feet, her presence filling the space with potent energy. Loralei had wanted Cara to be there as well, but there were too many preparations to be made for her to be able to get away.

"I had something made for you as well," she said without turning away from the mirror. She didn't intend to be vain. She just wondered if she would see herself differently with a crown on her brow.

"I thought I would be fine in my new gear. The flowers make it a bit more presentable."

Loralei turned to see Saiden looking down at her gear. "Leather is a good look for you, but it's not appropriate for a coronation." She went into her wardrobe and pulled a long bag down from the hanging rack.

"You had them make me a dress?" Saiden sounded incredulous. "I haven't worn one since I was a very small child."

The soon-to-be-crowned queen pulled the bag free, revealing a deep green dress. Flowers like the ones on Saiden's gear were embroidered on the hems and around the bodice. Loralei thought it was an absolute masterpiece, and the color reminded her of the tattoos she had seen her guard hiding.

She had asked for a last-minute adjustment for this dress, needing the seamstress to add sleeves. Knowing the truth about Saiden's tattoos, she couldn't imagine Saiden wanted them on display. The skirts were long, but she had left a slit in the side so the legionnaire would have full mobility if she needed to fight.

"Put it on."

"Is that a command, Your Majesty?" Saiden asked, humor lacing the words.

"It will if it has to be."

"I will wear your dress, but I'm keeping my boots."

"But they made you such beautiful slippers."

"Slippers don't do anyone much good. Ever."

Saiden had a good point, so she didn't push her any further about wearing them.

"There's one more thing. This one is more practical than the slippers." Loralei went to her desk and grabbed the two thigh harnesses. "Since there isn't much more space for you to keep a blade."

Saiden laughed slightly, pulling off her boots and then stripping the tight leather pants off her legs.

The queen turned to give her privacy, even though the legionnaire didn't care about that. Unless it came to her tattoos. Still, it felt right to look away.

"You know, I'm going to need help with this. There are way too many laces."

Loralei laughed, too, and took advantage of this one peaceful moment before the burden of being a crowned monarch fully became hers.

43

SAIDEN

Saiden kept an eye on where Loralei stood in front of the temple head, two different emblems in her hands, offerings to Keir and Ilona. She couldn't exactly recognize what they were from her post in the temple, but it had the best view of what was going on around the queen, so she couldn't regret it. She still hoped they wouldn't mar the coronation with bloodshed, but the people trying to hurt her ruler were getting bolder, and she doubted they would be above desecrating this holy place to get their hands on Loralei.

She scanned the temple and moved closer to the altar. People were gathered in the pews, waves of black and white dresses and elaborate suits. Her red hair was a beacon among the lack of color, yet people barely spared her a glance. She wondered what it was that made them temporarily set aside their hatred for her. Did they feel that such hate could not exist inside the temple walls? Or were they just so excited about the coming festivities that they didn't care enough to be angry?

She still couldn't believe the dress she'd forced her to wear. The way the fabric clung to her was completely unlike anything she could remember wearing before. Saiden pulled at it, though it had very little give. Her gear was tight, but not the way this laced corset was, where it pushed at her skin and shaped curves she was relatively sure hadn't existed that morning. She was lucky she had been able to convince Loralei to let her keep her boots, at least, and had tucked the stiletto blades into the sides of them. There were flowers on her dress—as if

Loralei had known she would fight her about wearing it—so the boots didn't look absolutely horrendous.

Saiden had gotten some weird stares because of them, but didn't mind. They could complain about her boots until the end of time if it meant they weren't looking at her hair. Loralei had forced her to leave her tresses out of the usual buns, so the curls rested against her back. It was an unusual weight, but the different hairstyle hid her pair of kindjals where they rested against her shoulder blades. Not an ideal place to store weapons, but the dress left her very few other options. The holsters Loralei had given her were heavy with her throwing knives.

Mozare had laughed hysterically when he saw her, and she had returned his amazed look with a glare. He got to wear formal gear. Even with him positioned further away, she could still see him trying to keep in his mirth. She desperately wanted to punch the look off his face, but that would have to wait.

Saiden turned her attention back to Loralei. There were two temple acolytes beside the presiding priest, each decked out completely in monochromatic outfits. The man standing in as the hand of Keir wore white, and the woman as the heart of Ilona wore black.

She wondered if the hate toward her would come back if she dared say neither of them looked even slightly like the gods they wanted to evoke. That she, alone, had born witness to their glory. But she would not tell them, just as she had told no one before. It would become a burden as people sought her out to invoke the gods' will directly or ask for their divine favor. Saiden would become nothing more than a hollow conduit, and that was not the path they had set for her.

She could see what Loralei was holding more clearly from her new position. In her right hand, in front of the man, the queen held a tall black candle, its glorious white flame melting the wax in rivulets down the side. In her other, she held a flower, dirt clutched in her cupped palm. Saiden recognized it as one of the roses from her private garden and wondered if Loralei had grown it herself. How ironic it would be for her to hold the reason why they would deem her not fit to be queen.

She watched the onlookers, but none of them moved in their seats. A few were perched on the edge of them with the excitement of the day. For many, this would be the greatest moment of their lives, the day they witnessed the crowning of a new monarch.

For Saiden, today was perhaps one of the most dangerous of her life. She had an awful feeling about Loralei's attackers. If they were so bold as to attack them in the street, surely they wouldn't pass up this opportunity.

They wouldn't succeed. There were at least seven of Loralei's newly named Guardians, so titled for preserving life instead of taking it as mercenaries, spread throughout the temple and even more standing vigil outside. All the guests had been checked for weapons, and while Gifted might be able to still do damage without steel, there were few who would dare stand against the Queen Chosen.

It was strange what the gods' Gifts did to you. Saiden could listen to hours of Mozare and Loralei talking about the power flowing through them, the way they automatically felt more connected to everything in this life because of it.

She couldn't exactly be jealous. If she had manifested true powers, they would have driven her mad. But she wished she could feel, even for the briefest of moments, what that power felt like.

The crowd grew silent, so Saiden turned towards the front to watch the blessing. Without actively thinking about it, she rested the backs of her hands against her thighs in prayer.

The high priest spoke, arm raised towards the stand-in Ilona. "Memento mori."

"Remember that I am to die, that I am given this death to humble me," Loralei replied.

"Memento vivere," he spoke again, raising the other hand.

"Remember that I must live," Loralei said. "And, in doing so, give my life to the service of my people."

"Acta deos numquam mortalia fallunt."

"Remember that in all my acts, I am guided by powers higher than mine. That whenever there is doubt in my heart or worry in my thoughts, they are with me. That I am never out of their sight."

The two temple workers stepped forward to take the candle and the flower from Loralei, and Saiden watched pieces of dirt fall to the floor. Loralei had been much more careful with the bloom than the life-Gifted temple worker now handling it, and Saiden now knew for sure that it had to be one she had grown herself. The queen had told her that she felt connected to them, and Saiden wondered what she felt when it was taken from her.

But Loralei did not glance toward the woman taking her flower and kept her eyes forward as she was handed a goblet. It was undeniably the most important part of the ceremony, as it had been forged by the gods and given to the first Chosen monarch before he had risen up against his predecessor. Each king and queen had shed their blood into the cup and drank the blood of those before them. It reminded everyone of the cycle of the crown. That power did not last forever and must therefore be shared. When she was done drinking and turned back around, Saiden could see blood seeping through a bandage on the queen's hand and knew Loralei had not healed herself, unable to risk anyone noticing she was not bleeding as expected.

Saiden moved even closer to the altar as people in the crowd jumped from their seats to cry out for their new queen. All around them were exaltations of, "Long live the queen, and may she forever be known for her kindness." In the back of the room, she could see some of the people Loralei had aided and knew their cries for longevity were genuine because they had seen what she was capable of. Because they already knew what kind of ruler she was going to be.

44
LORALEI

Loralei took a deep breath as she and Saiden walked through the palace halls, followed by a few newly-appointed Guardians. She only kept Saiden in the palace, but the others would always accompany her on formal occasions, as was befitting of a queen. It was the only way she managed to convince her advisors to let her keep Saiden after the villagers she had killed during the attack in town.

She was glad she had picked a dress that looked okay with Saiden's gear. The boots would have been completely out of place, otherwise. On anyone else, the combination would have been ridiculous, but Saiden had the right energy to pull off the look. Besides, anyone who looked at her twice would see that she wasn't someone to mess with.

Out of the corner of her eye, she saw Saiden habitually rubbing her wrists and had wanted to offer to heal them until she realized the itching was the healing of new tattoos. She looked at her guard and implicitly understood that this was her way of making peace with what she was so often forced to do. In the end, she had not offered her assistance.

Loralei met her advisors outside of the ballroom. Her guards would walk in first before the procession, dispersing among the crowd to keep a watchful eye. And then her council would lead the way for her eventual entrance. Each of them was dressed in formal regalia, white sashes lined in violet strapped across each of their chests. They had swords as well, fancy ones with elaborately jeweled handles, though she sincerely doubted any of them could truly wield the blades.

The doors opened, and she could hear the music and chatter in the ballroom cease as they waited for their newly-crowned queen. The ceremony in the temple had been a modest affair, meant for only the devout, and the ball was where she would find most of the courtiers she would have to deal with in the next months. She found the rich were never truly faithful. They could not see past what they possessed in this life. A shame for them, really, though she could not say that out loud.

Loralei made her entrance. The lavish setting was brilliant to look at, like walking through a still-life painting filled with bursts of color. The light from the high arching windows accentuated the jewels in women's dresses and reflected off their glasses.

A prolonged moment of silence reigned. Then the room around her sprung into motion with a sudden force that almost knocked her back as people cheered and the music started up again. Loralei kept her eyes forward, making sure to keep the crown she had chosen carefully balanced on her brow. People would see her today and judge her entire reign based on what they saw, despite having seen her countless times before. It was why today had to be perfect. So, she did her best to walk slowly, taking small steps to give everyone a chance to look at her.

They had raised a dais for her at the far end of the room, and she took the steps carefully one at a time, letting the long trail of her dress fan out on the steps. She turned to face the people—*her* people—and smiled. She was truly happy to see them there, even if the event was loud and boisterous. Most of them wished her the best. Seeing their faces reminded her of what there was to fight for.

She sat and gave her advisors their chance to address the crowd. It was another piece of tradition from the first Chosen King. She had heard it recited so many times that she did not listen now, opting to watch the crowds of people around her instead. From behind her, she heard speaking, and she forced herself to go against the instinct to jerk her head around to see who was behind her.

"You looked regal walking up the aisle, Your Majesty," Saiden said.

They had not agreed on her position behind the throne. Saiden, as usual, had desired a place among the shadows of the ballroom where she could have walked through the crowds unnoticed. She had eventually given in to the queen's request, as she had with the dress, and Loralei was glad for the company. If she had to stay up there all by herself, she may have been too worried to climb the dais in the first place. But with Saiden there, she felt more confident.

"Your advisors," the legionnaire spoke again, "not so much."

Loralei wanted to laugh and turned her head just enough to look at her guard.

A smile pulled at the corners of the girl's mouth, but she did not laugh, looking straight forward into the crowd as if she had not spoken at all.

When the advisors were done speaking, the ball took up again in earnest and the dancing began. It had been the one thing she had truly always loved about her new life since her Choosing Day. The way music moved through people and carried them some place new and magical. Many men came to ask for her hand, and she gladly danced with each of them, knowing that Saiden would be watching from her post above them.

When she was finally given a brief reprieve, she returned to her throne. Saiden sent a servant to bring her a cool glass of water. She was in desperate need of a drink and was glad her guard had thought of it. She watched one of her other Guardians, the dark-haired boy that was Saiden's partner, approach her dais.

He bowed low. When he offered a dance, though, it wasn't to the newly-crowned queen. But to Saiden.

Loralei smiled. She knew there was nothing romantic between the two of them. She could read it in their movements whenever they were near each other, but she knew Mozare was an important part of her personal guard's life that she had to leave behind when she came to the palace. She was free to see him whenever she wanted, but her visits to their barracks had been few and often only to report for missions.

She watched Saiden shake her head at the boy, clearly motioning to Loralei. Mozare pulled on the arm of a large legionnaire, the sleeves of his formal gear barely holding his muscles. "Oliver can take your place. It's just one dance."

Upon hearing his name, the man stepped forward with his arms crossed and a fierce expression aimed at the Blood-Cursed legionnaire.

Saiden tried to shake her head again, but Loralei grabbed her hand and placed it in Mozare's, practically pushing her off the dais. The woman could return to her post after a dance. Nothing would happen to the queen with the pile of muscles standing at the foot of her dais. She couldn't imagine anyone fighting him and winning.

She took the time to watch her favorite guard. Saiden was dancing with her partner, not in time with the music and completely separate from the formal dances taking place in her direct view. They were talking, and she was laughing and spinning around. Loralei had never seen the tension leave the Blood-Cursed girl's body before, never seen her move without constantly looking over her shoulder.

She realized then that Mozare was to Saiden what Saiden was to her. The legionnaire trusted him so intrinsically to protect her that she didn't have to worry herself. It was amazing to see the dynamic between the two of them and how truly carefree the girl was when the world wasn't sitting on her shoulders.

When the dance was finished, Saiden returned to her post on the dais, slightly winded and with red cheeks. Both Mozare and the beast Oliver bowed to her and set off across the dance floor in opposite directions, likely returning to their own posts. She passed her half-drunk glass of water to Saiden, who quickly emptied it with a big gulp, then handed it off to the same servant girl who had brought it to them.

Loralei wondered if Cara was in the crowd somewhere, and longed briefly to be dancing with her instead of the lines of suitors and various noblemen.

Still, dancing was the best part of balls, and she took great pleasure in being carried away by the music.

45

MOZARE

Mozare wondered if Saiden could tell what was going on in his mind. If she could tell that he had danced with her because he wanted one more moment where they were still partners. When he was still sure of his place in her life.

He wished he could warn her about what was going to happen, about what Revon had planned. But he didn't have the time to prove what he was doing was right for the kingdom. And Saiden wouldn't blindly follow him, no matter how much trust they shared. She would want to protect the queen from what was coming for her.

He worried about her safety as well, worried if she would make it out of this safe. Revon had promised, but the man couldn't control every soldier they had brought to the palace tonight. Mozare knew some of them would want to kill her just for the notoriety. Especially after she had thwarted their attempts at the Choosing Day parade. He had never felt this scared for her before, despite the many dangerous missions they had gone on together. But he wouldn't have been at fault before if something had happened to her during those. Now, however, her blood would be on his hands.

He turned a corner and waited for guards to pass. They wouldn't think anything of him patrolling, but he couldn't risk any of them getting suspicious or realizing he wasn't stationed as an interior guard.

The rebellion's cause had always seemed so clear to him, but doubt crept along the sides of his mind, eating away at his confidence. He believed with all his being that Ilona guided his movement. Surely she wouldn't guide him down the wrong path?

He checked an exit and deemed it too visible. There were too many guards there. No way to sneak in rebels that way. Or to abscond with the queen. He continued down a servant's stairway.

If only he could have scouted the castle earlier. But with all the new additions, the map Revon had from his childhood was long out of date. They needed an exit, and it was important for Mozare to find it before plans were set into motion.

He checked three more doors, each one straying from the ideal he had set for their escape path. Some were too small for soldiers to rush through, and others were too busy with servants bustling back and forth with trays of refreshments.

He finally found the best option down another dark hallway. Cobwebs filled the upper corners of the door, and he knew it had been out of use for a long time. He opened it gently, waiting to see if the hinges would creak. However, despite its lack of use, someone had still been around to oil them, a fact he gave thanks for.

He tied a small ribbon on the outside handle of the door. The red shade made him think of Saiden. Hopefully, reinforcements would see it. Otherwise, they wouldn't have much luck getting through the castle's extra guards. He needed to get back to the ballroom.

Saiden might excuse his absence for a short while, believing him lost in the chaos of the ballroom, but she would eventually come to look for him. She would stop them if she knew what they were doing, and he couldn't allow her to get in the way of their righteous path.

Eventually, when the dust settled, he would be able to show her why the rebels' cause was just. He just hoped when that time came, she would see and trust him.

46
SAIDEN

anging echoed through the ballroom, and Saiden stepped in front of the
queen before she had even figured out what was going on.

Loralei's hand rested against her back as if she had been going to stand
before the legionnaire had moved to shield the woman. On the edges of the
room, the perimeter guards were already drawing weapons against shielded
assailants. Watching the fighting, she realized the enemies were not powerless
but *Gifted*. There were Gifted fighting alongside the rebels.

Saiden looked briefly for Mozare, but she couldn't see him, which she
imagined was what he was going for. If they were going to fight in the shadows,
there was no doubt that her partner would be fighting the same way.

She grabbed the queen. "It's time to go, Your Majesty."

Loralei pulled against her. "My people—"

"Your people will be safer when their queen is safe. We need to get away
from here." She wasn't sure if she was lying or not. She couldn't tell if the in-
surgents cared about innocent loss of life or if they were so bent on getting to
Loralei that they would kill whoever they needed to.

Still, her job was to get the queen to safety.

She jumped off the back of the dais and turned to help Loralei down. In
her ceremonial shoes with the layers of her dress, the queen would've more
likely fallen on her face than made it to the floor successfully. Saiden had had a
small part in planning the event, as far as security went, and the dais had been

built with easy access to the crown room's secret passageway. She pulled Loralei through, making sure no one followed before slipping the door shut. Saiden grabbed her hand and ran, leading them through the tunnels she had spent hours studying. They weren't included in the official orders since they were strictly confidential, but after Loralei had shown them to her, Saiden had spent a long time mapping them out in her head. She hadn't known they would be useful so soon, but she was glad she hadn't waited.

Loralei followed, her skirt train clutched up in her hands. She was running quickly, though her heels were slowing her down. Saiden pulled her around a bend and bent down to pull them off. She had told Loralei to wear slippers underneath, and she was glad to see the stubborn royal had actually listened to her. At least she wouldn't risk stepping on something in the unswept tunnels.

When Saiden found the door to the queen's personal chambers, she pulled her inside. Next, she walked around the room, barricading the doors with furniture and brooms—anything close by that would buy her an extra second.

"Strip now," she said, pulling off her boots.

Loralei looked at her, but didn't move.

"You're putting on my dress, and you are getting out of here." Saiden did her best to be careful with the laces so they could be re-tied, but she could hear people in the hallways running towards her room. They were running low on time, and Loralei needed to be gone before anyone made it through the barricades.

When the queen finally understood, she started unlacing her own garment, undoubtedly more complicated than the other. But she was still able to remove it with ease. Loralei was more hesitant while unclothed, so the legionnaire immediately threw her own dress toward the royal, leaving her tattoos completely exposed. Saiden saw the woman visually trace them, seeing how many lives she had taken. She tried not to let it bother her.

"Put it on, now," she said, reminding the queen they were on a tight schedule.

Loralei did so. It wasn't the right fit, but it would have to be enough for now.

If Saiden managed to convince them that she was the queen, Loralei would be safe, and it wouldn't matter what dress she was wearing. She pulled on slippers and pulled the coronation dress on, letting Loralei properly lace her up. Her outfit would have to be more believable, even if years of exercise had made her hard in all the places where the real royal was soft.

She heard the footsteps steadily growing closer. "Listen to me very carefully. You are going to hide back in the tunnel. No one should know about them, so you'll be safe there. Do not come out—no matter what you hear. Someone from the Legion will come and find you, I promise."

She opened the hidden door again and pushed Loralei through, handing her both of her kindjals. The queen was meant to be unarmed, and she didn't want anything to happen to her favorite blades or for them to alert the rebels that she wasn't who they thought. If Saiden got lucky, they would think the queen's protector had left her in a barricaded room to go fight off invaders, and they wouldn't look for Loralei. If she didn't fool them, they might both die today.

The plan was already a huge *what-if* game. She looked around for one of Loralei's cloaks, specifically one with a hood. If they caught sight of her hair, it would never work. Saiden pulled the hood tight over her face, and though she wanted to stand and fight, she went and hid in the corner as she imagined an untrained and docile queen would do without her guard there to protect her.

The footsteps grew louder, and she felt the calm settle on her that always came when she was preparing for a fight. If her ruse didn't work, she would fight until her last breath to keep them from finding the queen. Hopefully, someone else would come to Loralei's aid when she fell.

She heard them pound against the door, bodies slamming into the thick wood, trying to push through her barricades. She smiled. At least she would have a few extra minutes. She hoped Loralei had the sense to run far away from the room. That way, even if the rebels found Saiden out, they would still have to give chase.

She started panting, despite knowing regulating her breathing was important. But she didn't know who her adversary was or if they were clever enough to notice such a small detail.

The door opened with a loud crash, the sound of wood cracking and splintering as the armoire slammed onto the floor. There was a bright flash of light. *Life-Gifted*, she thought.

And then they were pulling a hood over her head.

She smelled something slightly sweet, and then darkness consumed her.

Saiden woke up with a banging in her skull. Her arms were sore and heavy, and she lifted them to see shackles trailing from metal cuffs at her wrists to rings embedded in the floor. She pulled at the chains. The cuffs dug into her skin and drew blood. She had doubted they would budge, but without anything else to try, she still tugged at them.

Her cell was dank with a small bucket left in the corner. The metal gate of the cell was rusted, and the walls glistened with moisture. There was no bed, no blankets, nothing to keep the biting chill from sinking into her bones.

Loralei's dress was shredded where she imagined they must have dragged her, but her legs seemed free of scratches or bruises. She wondered if they had truly been careful with her or if they just had a talented healer on staff.

She yanked on her bindings again.

"You really are wasting your energy," a voice spoke to her.

She turned around, putting her back to the wall and stepping away from the stranger. The closer she got to the wall, the slacker the chain became, giving her more to use as a weapon.

There was another light suddenly in the cell, though not the same blinding one that came from the life-Gifted who had taken her from Loralei's chambers. This was pure candlelight. It filled the room with a soft, golden hue and gave her a small view of the man she imagined was in charge.

He carried himself like he thought he was important, and though he knew who she was, he didn't look afraid.

"What a trick that was. Disguising yourself as the young queen. My stupid fighters fell for it without a second glance. I've had them all removed from duty, in case you were curious. Can't let a mistake like that go unpunished."

She felt sick. She knew this man meant that he had killed them, and he wanted her to know those deaths had been her fault.

She tried to keep her face neutral, free of disgust. Men like this only grew more terrible when they saw how their actions affected others.

"You, of course, could be a very valuable asset to us. A Blood-Cursed girl still sane into her nineteenth year. Heretofore unheard of. The raw potential you could possess if you only tapped into those powers is immense. And your closeness to the queen would make it so much easier to have her removed."

Saiden sneered at him, baring her teeth like a caged animal. She knew that she shouldn't lower herself to his level, but his words were so full of hatred and clearly lacked recognition of a human life's value. He was everything she hated in the world. Everything she strived not to be.

"Now, now. Be reasonable. There is much in this world that you do not yet understand, death-bringer."

Internally, Saiden flinched at the old nickname.

"I imagine you're hungry. I can have food sent to you down here, and you can eat caged and filthy. Or you can surrender your anger, and I can find you a nicer room without the smell." He twisted his face into a look of distaste.

He took a step forward, and she grabbed for her chains, ready to swing them up towards him if needed, ready to defend herself. But he only stuck out a hand for her to shake. A peace offering from a man with no qualms about killing.

She kept her hands to herself. "How many of them did you kill because of me?" she asked instead, the venom in her voice clear.

"Four of them. Only the Giftless. I couldn't bear to sacrifice the other, so he was whipped instead. A hundred lashes. Should take the healers a few hours to stop the bleeding, and his back will never be the same, but he will live to remember his mistake."

Four more dead because of her, four new leaves. She had not taken their lives directly. Her blade had not been raised against them. But they were still gone because of what she had done.

When he reached out to her again, she growled at him and pulled herself closer to the wall.

She wanted nothing to do with him.

47
MOZARE

M ozare had disappeared during the crisis in the ballroom to avoid fighting against his fellow rebels or revealing his true loyalties against the Legion. He had to be careful, though. If someone noticed him disappearing all the time, they would eventually get suspicious enough to investigate.

He had not stayed to protect the queen as he had sworn to do when he had joined the Gifted Legion. The same day he had become Saiden's partner.

When the chaos had calmed down, he looked for Saiden. Revon had told him that their only mission was to capture the ruler. After the parade, they had decided to take her alive, to make an affair of her death befitting a Queen Chosen. Revon had wanted the people to see her weak, to see that she was unable to protect herself so that they would be more willing to come to his side even after he killed her.

It was a smart plan, but Mozare doubted Revon would truly give orders not to harm Saiden. She was a threat, and if she got in his way, the rebel leader would have no problem removing her.

General Nakti walked into the room with two other soldiers following her. He made his way through the still-crowded room, stepping over the bodies of the fallen to talk to her.

"Where is Saiden?" Nakti asked as soon as she caught sight of him.

He wasn't sure, and he let the General know. "We weren't positioned together. When the fight broke out, I lost sight of her." It was mostly true.

He was surprised to see how pale the General's normally dark skin had become, worry clearly written in her expression.

She dismissed the guards and left the ballroom. Mozare, having not been expressly dismissed, followed her. There was something she knew, and if it had to do with Saiden, then he would go anywhere.

Nakti pushed her way through the gathering crowds, people wondering what had just happened and what they were supposed to do now. Wondering what happened to their new queen. The General ignored them all as she headed further into the castle, closer to the queen's quarters.

Mozare wondered who she was truly looking for—Saiden or their monarch. He wondered if she would find either of them. If either of them would be left alive long enough to be found.

The doors to the queen's chambers were busted open, and splinters littered the floor. Mozare looked around, but the broken wooden pieces were the only sign of struggle. The sheets were tightly tucked into the mattress of her canopy bed, and the light of the setting sun filtered through the gossamer fabric hanging from the bedposts. The curtains hung perfectly from their rods. The windows were unbroken.

The General walked through the room, stepping over the larger pieces of the broken chest, to a panel in the wall. She pressed against it, and it popped open.

His eyes widened. A secret tunnel within the palace walls. It made sense. Kaizia had not always been peaceful, and previous monarchs would've needed a quick getaway route.

General Nakti stepped into the revealed, dank hallway and stepped back out, holding the shivering queen in her arms. There were tear tracks down her cheeks and dirt smudges on her dress. On *Saiden's* dress, the shoulder sagged down her arm.

"They took her." Considering her lack of training and everything she had experienced, the woman's voice was surprisingly stable. But her face showed the barrage of emotions she kept from her voice. "Those men who attacked the castle. They took Saiden."

Mozare turned and put his hand through the wall. He saw the queen flinch from the corner of his eye, and he left the room without being dismissed by either of his superiors. They had taken Saiden when Revon had explicitly said that she would remain unharmed. He knew what they did to prisoners, and he would not let them hurt her.

Though the horses weren't on loan for the Legion, he took one anyway. He could always return it later, and he needed speed to be on his side. He didn't particularly care about stealth, though he should've, but his anger about Saiden being kidnapped clouded his judgment. He couldn't think past the fog it had created in his mind after hearing that she was gone. After seeing Loralei in the dress the queen had forced Saiden to wear.

He didn't bother knocking this time, instead forcibly pushing open the latch door and throwing out a veil of shadows to prevent the guard from striking. He pushed the man into the wall as Mozare pushed the next door open, striding through the underground halls with purpose. He grabbed the first rebel fighter he found by the collar of their shirt, shoving them up against another wall.

"Where is Revon?" he ground out through gritted teeth. He was so angry that he could feel the shadows swirling around him. His powers were out of control, but he couldn't be bothered to try to rein them in. He wanted the rebellion's leader to have a reminder of how much more powerful Mozare was than him. How much more the gods had favored him, a legionnaire, than the weak Gift he—the leader of an uprising—had been given.

The young girl, a recruit, he was guessing, gestured down the hallway. He let her go, and she scurried off, running in the opposite direction of where she had pointed. He burst into their makeshift mess hall, slamming the swinging doors against the wall. Everyone in the hall turned to look at him.

Revon stood from the decorated table he had claimed for himself in the corner.

"You promised," he yelled, spit flying from his mouth. "You took an oath that she wouldn't come to harm. That you would take the queen and leave Saiden alone."

The people around him turned to their neighbors and began whispering, but he couldn't hear what.

The man to blame walked towards him, his hands up and palms out toward Mozare as if at any minute he might step forward and attack the man.

He was considering it.

"Your friend is okay, Mozare. She was taken by accident. By soldiers too new to pay attention to the details of their mission."

Another wave of anger pulsed through Mozare. Revon was putting the blame onto someone else, absolving himself, thinking that made things better.

"You are going to let me see her now, and then you are going to free her." He was directly in Revon's face now, and he realized for the first time that he was taller than the older man.

The leader always carried himself with so much importance, Mozare had never noticed the discrepancy before.

"You know I can't do that. She will be given the choice to join us. If she does not, she will have to die. It is for the good of the cause."

He went to swing at his mentor, at this man he couldn't believe he had trusted, but his fist never hit its target. Two other fighters had jumped from their seats to grab his arms and pull him back.

"Seeing that you are in distress, dear Mozare, I will not have you punished for this insubordination. But you will not be allowed to see the girl until I am done personally interrogating her. That is an order." Revon waved a hand, dismissing him.

The two fighters holding Mozare dragged him away from the table and out of the room.

48
LORALEI

Loralei paced the length of the hall. Despite the standards set for her by her council, despite the fact that it was improper for her nerves to be displayed in such a manner, the queen had too much energy coursing through her to possibly sit still. They had been there for hours, yet none of the soldiers or advisors gathered before her could tell her how they were going to find Saiden and bring her home. Any time one side of the room would suggest something, the other would shut them down, resulting in a perpetual cycle of hope and disappointment.

And she was frustrated. She had been crowned, yet couldn't do something as simple as run a search and rescue mission for one of her most elite guards. She couldn't protect the people she cared about. And the people she had with her were incompetent. Anger slowly burned away her fear. She hated feeling useless, hated that they made her feel so small.

She walked back to her seat at the table and surprised the room by slamming a fist against it. She surprised herself as well. If she had done something similar weeks before, she would have likely broken every bone in her hand. But with Saiden's training, she felt only a mild sting. And now she had everyone's attention.

"You are all hopeless. Get out of my sight."

Half the room listened, standing and obeying their queen as they should, while the others took a minute, waiting to see if she was only being temperamental. When she didn't move to call them back or change her mind, the rest finally left. She didn't know where they were going, and to be honest, she didn't care as long as they were gone.

One of the legionnaires came up to her and tentatively rested a hand against her shoulder. "We'll find her, Your Majesty. And Saiden will be alright, she's the strongest person I know."

Loralei wanted to rip the offending hand from the soldier's body. She turned around to face whoever dared touch her, ready to admonish his empty attempts at placating her. But it was Mozare. Saiden's partner. The rage swirling through her chest cooled slightly, though it never completely went away. She wondered what it was that made him so ready to believe that their mutual friend would be returned to them whole and unharmed. She remembered he had been raised in the temples from when she had invited her selected legionnaire guards to eat before the parade. But she couldn't imagine anyone being *that* pious.

"Perhaps you'd like to accompany me for a walk in the gardens?"

In all honesty, she didn't have to ask. He was her soldier to command. But her rage felt out of place here, and asking him helped center her in her own body.

He answered her by sticking out an arm for her to grab. She had seen him with Saiden enough times to know he was being uncharacteristically quiet, though she couldn't quite tell why.

Loralei waited until they were outside before she even considered her next question, letting the fresh air soothe her nerves. "Do you really believe she will be alright?"

"If anyone would be alright, it would be her." The way he said it made Loralei feel as if he knew more than he was letting on.

She couldn't tell if her doubts were true or simply a symptom of her paranoia. And since Mozare was the first person all day who didn't make her feel incompetent, she didn't want to alienate him by pushing the issue.

They were only outside for a little while when another of her guards, dressed in palace livery, came to deliver a message to Mozare. He was requested back at base.

"Sorry to cut this walk short, Your Majesty," he said, bowing to her.

Before he could turn away, she grabbed his fist, her hands steady for the first time in days. "You have my permission to do whatever is necessary to find her."

Despite the cold look on her face, Mozare didn't flinch away from her. He simply nodded and went on his way.

49
SAIDEN

Saiden had been forced to stay in the cells with no light and very little food for at least eight days. It was hard for her to tell if her numbers were exact. The meals came at times too random for her to use them as a marker. She had refused her captor's peace offering, and this was his way of making her regret it.

Eventually, someone had removed her chains, had led her somewhere to shower, and had given her new clothes. She heard yelling that reminded her of the legionnaire mess hall on a good betting night. They led her away from the sound and into a small room. There were no windows there either. And she hadn't seen any even as they led her through the halls without a blindfold. Her captor was getting cocky, not realizing she now knew they had to be underground.

He clearly thought he had something good to offer her, something he was sure would bring her to their side. Or he was going to kill her. Either way, he was sure she wasn't getting out of there to give their secrets away.

She heard the door click behind her as her escort left her in a mostly bare room alone and knew there was no point in trying to get out. If she were going to escape, she would have to do so when she was out in the hallways. And even then, she had no idea which way to go or how many people she would have to fight—without a weapon—in order to be free again.

There were two chairs and a table in the room and nothing else. She wondered if it was an interrogation room they used often, or if the mismatched furniture had been brought into the empty room just for her.

She paced too much energy running through her body for her to stay still. She was glad they had given her a long sleeve shirt when she requested it, even though her escort had looked at her like she was crazy.

There was a knock at the door, two soft taps against the wood, and then the sound of the lock clicking open. Her captor walked in, followed by a young girl carrying what looked like a heavy tray of food. There was meat on it, fresh meat and not the dried stuff they served at the barracks. She'd had finer food at the palace, but she wondered how rebels were getting better cuts of meat than the kingdom's finest soldiers.

The man took the tray from the girl who left without even having to be dismissed and set it in front of Saiden. She looked at it, smoke rising from the meat, and pushed the tray away from her. One should never eat food during an interrogation, especially without understanding the captor's motivation. There was no way she would trust anything he gave her.

"Who are you?"

"It is not time for your questions. It is time for mine," the man said. "But because I am feeling generous, and it might make things more palatable for you if you knew my name, I am called Revon."

There were old stories of generals before the first King Chosen that went by that name. She wondered if he had chosen it himself as a desire to emulate them, or if his parents had just had high hopes for their son.

"Where is the queen?" he asked, pulling her tray of food towards himself. Clearly, if she wasn't going to eat it, he would take it for himself. She wondered if that meant they weren't actually in possession of a good supply of fresh meat.

Saiden didn't speak but sat watching Revon eat the meal prepared for her, and wondered if it had been for show, or if there was still something in the meat, something he knew wouldn't affect him. She spent the minutes of silence trying to read him—and coming up blank.

He sat forward in his seat leaning towards her, and quicker than Saiden could keep track of, he pulled something sharp from his sleeve and cut a slice into her palm. She hissed, pulling her hand back and cupping it towards her chest. Her blood spilled onto her shirt, and she felt some satisfaction that at least he would have to deal with the stain.

He knocked on the table twice.

The girl came back in, going over to Saiden and resting a hand on the side of her neck. She wanted to pull away, but she noticed the skin on her palm knitting itself back together before she had a chance to.

The life-Gifted girl left, shutting the door again behind her, but Saiden imagined she would be waiting on the other side of the door for her next summons. She wouldn't be called again if Saiden could help it. She now understood his interrogation tactics, if not his intentions, and she did not plan to let him take another blade to her skin.

"Where is the queen?"

"Safe from you," she spat at him.

He raised a hand to slap her but stopped himself, pulling the hand back into his lap. He took a small piece of cloth from another of his pockets and wiped his face.

"Now, you really don't understand what is going on here, do you?"

Saiden didn't answer. It wasn't a question she could answer. There was so much going on. She didn't even know if Loralei was safe, or if she was also there, being beaten and tortured. But Saiden doubted he would have asked about her whereabouts if he had her in custody.

He was undoubtedly the kind of man who would show off if he had managed to kidnap the queen, especially in front of her personal guard.

"I think it's time you learn more about the kingdom you are so willing to die to protect."

50
MOZARE

With Saiden hidden within the rebellion hideout, it would be idiotic for Mozare to be there, too. While the sun still shone, he needed to be present where people could see him. Even so, he had convinced Rhena to eat breakfast with the other recruits this morning with the promise of a private training session when he was done because he didn't want to spend the meal pretending to be okay when he was worried about what could be happening to his partner in his absence. He couldn't let any of the legionnaires suspect he had any information on her location. He ate, but only because his body demanded it. And he couldn't help but fear that Revon would use this time to hurt Saiden, despite whatever promises he had made before. He knew their leader would do what he thought best, no matter who it hurt.

After the meal, Mozare went to a different training room than his and Rhena's normal meeting place. The walls here were stone, but underneath they were reinforced with metal. It could be a very dangerous thing when someone was just learning to harness and control their Gifts, and this space had been designed with that danger in mind.

He remembered what it was like when he was first learning to use his own powers. His parents had dropped him off so quickly after he started showing signs of the gods' favor that he didn't even know what skills he actually possessed. He remembered being scared when he woke up with his room covered in a darkness so deep no candlelight could penetrate it. And it was years later that he learned that he could also tell when women were pregnant and give predictions on the child's sex. It was a rare talent, but the space in between life and death where babies existed before being born fell into Ilona's territory, not Keir's.

Rhena skipped into the room, wide eyes taking it in with excitement. "So, when are you going to teach me to kick ass and wield shadows?"

Her joy was contagious, and he felt his own lips tug up in a small smile despite the worry swirling through his mind. "Not everyone Gifted by Ilona can wield shadows as I can, little one," he replied. "There are lots of abilities that come from her blessing."

"How am I supposed to figure out what mine are?"

"You'll feel the calling, and they'll show themselves. It can be a process sometimes, but I've never seen anyone unable to manage it. There is nothing to worry about."

Rhena was a true ray of sunshine, and she excelled at anything she put her mind to.

He sat down in front of her, crossing his legs, and motioned for the recruit to copy him. "You need to tune into the Goddess—in whatever form she has taken inside you. I'm going to trigger my Gifts, and you need to feel for the reaction within you that reaches out for it."

Without waiting for a response, Mozare closed his eyes. He had trained relentlessly to master his shadows, and calling them was easy now. He pulled them from inside himself, weaving different creatures that he sent running around the training room. He heard Rhena laugh and opened his eyes to watch her interact with his shadow creatures.

He kept an eye on her and waited for recognition to spark across her face. This was how he had been taught. A much older recruit, Catrina—now stationed in a village a few days' ride from the barracks—had sat with him and showed him how she could call upon the dead. She had spoken to dead queens and generals, and he had been amazed while watching the interactions.

When he had finally found that part of himself that connected with the power she had been using, shadows had completely filled the room. He had been terrified, but Catrina had talked him through how to pull it back into himself. She told him stories of how her family hadn't even realized she was Gifted, believing that she had simply not outgrown her imaginary friends.

Back in the present, Rhena's hands started shaking as panic ran rampant over her face.

He reached out, gently placing a hand on her knee, letting her know she wasn't alone. "What are you feeling?" he asked, keeping his voice low and even. He hadn't had the opportunity to train someone in their Gifts before, and he was curious to see what would happen now.

She grabbed his hand, fingers squeezing hard. "There's something inside me. It's cold, and—the feeling—it's spreading."

He felt her panic growing and stood. It was a mistake to trigger her powers so suddenly, without any contingencies to comfort her. As he moved to get closer, ice coated the floor. He slipped and fell on his ass, catching himself before he cracked his head on the stone floor.

"Water," he said, "and sometimes ice, is a strong elemental talent." He moved up to his knees and carefully slid his way over to Rhena. "Elements are very dependent on emotions. You will need to learn to control them in order to manage your Gifts."

The recruit took a deep breath, her shoulders relaxing. As calm settled in her bones, he watched the ice clear from the floor.

"What is it that controls shadows?"

"Personal understanding and balance of oneself. If you are unsure or your thoughts are tumultuous, the shadows stop listening."

"How does a teenager manage to be so sure of himself?"

He shrugged. He knew he had a mastery rarely seen at such a young age. But it hadn't been an issue. He saw the world so clearly because his religious childhood had given him a strong foundation.

When Rhena stood, the trembling in her hand now calmer, he reached out to hug her. "I'm proud of what you've accomplished today, little one."

"So we're on for another session tomorrow?"

He laughed. He was growing very attached to the young recruit, and he was glad to have this distraction today.

51
SAIDEN

Saiden sat across from Revon and watched him talk. He sat in a way that it was clear he had been raised in a proper household, and not on the streets like many of his soldiers.

"You know about the King Chosen and the origin of magic in Kaizia. But you know only what the crown has deemed appropriate for you to know. You know what they tell you to keep you docile and obedient. The rebellion—we know the truth—and we seek to reinstate our kingdom to its former glory."

She stared at Revon, daring him to kill her and get this over with. She already knew there was no way that she was going to leave this place alive. Not when he was sharing secrets with her.

He continued. "At the Battle of the Fallen, it wasn't the normal soldiers who won the war. The first King Chosen had very few men supporting his cause. Many in his kingdom were too afraid of the born king and what he might do if they lost the war the people knew was coming. He should've been absolutely crushed by the reigning king's forces. Yet, somehow, he survived the onslaught and emerged victorious. A curious story, is it not?"

She sneered, pulling at the cuffs that kept her strapped to the table. Her wrists were raw from wearing them while stuck in the dungeon, but she wasn't surprised that he had forced her to keep them on. She was sure she could kill him easily if freed, and she was angry and frightened enough that she likely would do so without hesitation.

She knew this history. It had been drilled into her mind countless times during her years in the Legion. They had never had a student as young as her, so most of her schooling had been dependent on what Nakti taught her. The sacred war was a favorite of the General's. "Keir and Ilona Gifted the soldiers of the King Chosen," she finally replied. "They sent their magic to earth to serve their cause."

"A religious soldier," he said, a touch of respect coloring his voice. "There seem very few of you left who study the scripture."

She thought about Mozare, who was even more pious than her. She trusted the gods, but not in the way he believed in them and their will. She shuddered and hoped her partner made it out of the uprising's ambush okay.

"As I was saying," Revon continued, "if it hadn't been for the divine intervention offered to our King Chosen, he would have been killed. The reigning king would have passed his crown to his son, and a corrupt line would have continued."

Saiden silently watched him as he did the same. He wanted her to ask questions, wanted to have something she wanted. But she wouldn't give him the pleasure.

When she didn't speak, he kept going. "What's more important are the Gifts our gods granted their Chosen champion."

"Chosen monarchs do not bear Gifts," she hissed, slamming her once-injured hand against the table. "Do not think me a fool, Revon." She thought briefly of Loralei, and the Gifts she kept hidden from the kingdom under threat of death.

Her captor reached forward, faster than she had expected him to move, grabbed her by her hair, and slammed her head against the table. Fingers still wrapped in her unraveling braids, he pulled her back to look at him. She could feel blood seeping out of a thick cut on her forehead.

"You would do well to remember who has the power here and not interrupt me again. Do you understand?"

She stared at him, refusing to answer. He wanted ultimate authority. It wasn't the first time she had dealt with a man who acted the way he did. It was, however, the first time she had done so while in chains.

Revon stood from the small table and knocked twice at the door. A small, stocky man walked in this time and used his Gift to seal the cut on her forehead, then left the room. She wondered how many healers were waiting on the other side of the door. She couldn't imagine what Revon stood to gain from having her healed, but she took the information and stored it in the back of her head.

Her interrogator sat back down. "The King Chosen was granted Gifts from both the side of life and that of death."

She felt her face mirror the shock she felt.

"He was what you would consider Blood-Cursed, though people like him used to be called the Anointed. Those truly and purely blessed, possessors of the greatest Gifts and aware of the gods' path. Those on the battlefield said they saw his hair burn like fire as he charged through the gates and led them to freedom."

Words kept coming to her mind, but none of them made enough sense to speak out loud.

Revon continued. "He was Gifted, and he brought balance and prosperity to the world. He showed the people what it was like to live under a just and kind ruler. The kingdom flourished for many years, trade grew with their neighboring kingdoms, harvests were bountiful, and the people were happy."

He paused, keeping a watchful eye on her as he stood to pace the room. It was another interrogation tactic she had used it many times when she and Mozare knew someone was withholding information. But she wasn't thinking about outsmarting Revon at the moment. Right now, she couldn't think past the fact there was once a king Gifted like her, and yet her contemporaries wanted her killed. Had wanted to kill her when she was just a defenseless baby because they thought she was cursed.

"Decades passed, and there were two more Chosen. Another king and a queen, each Anointed like the first. When the first Queen Chosen sat on the throne, she made it her path to conquer the realms beyond our borders. She thought she was sharing the prosperity of the lands, but her actions brought devastation. Not only to their lands but also to our own. She turned away from the gods' path, and so they turned their destruction towards her. Her Gifts raged out of control, and she killed many of her own subjects. Blood soaked the land everywhere she went."

Dread slithered through Saiden's muscles as she sat and listened. A captive audience to a madman's ravings.

"The people turned away from her, and when they learned of what her greed and pride had done to their lands, they called for her removal. The people started spreading stories that no mortal flesh could contain that much of the gods' likeness without going mad. So, the hunt began. Any child born with the telltale red hair was sentenced to death long before anyone even knew what would become of them."

Saiden sat, frozen with the knowledge Revon was presenting her. She couldn't believe him. Everything he was telling her could be a lie, something to try to sway her to his side, to whatever rebellion he was leading.

But he was also giving her everything she could ever want. A world where she could have been accepted for who she was. Somewhere where people wouldn't look at her and be afraid.

She couldn't trust him, but she also couldn't help wanting what he offered.

52
LORALEI

Once crowned, Loralei had been given unlimited access to the kingdom's Archives. It made it a lot easier to get answers when she didn't have to sneak around her own guards to get to the basement library. And since she had no way to help with the search—they told her she was too valuable to be picking through people in the streets—she spent her days reading through the old knowledge of her kingdom.

This time, she didn't bring Cara with her.

The Archives were quite extensive, and she enjoyed the quiet protection of their stacks. No one came to bother her. She wasn't sure if it was because of her breakdown, or because they still valued her input so very little.

She started by looking through the information on her advisors. Each had inherited their seat on the council. Once Saiden was returned, Loralei would likely remove them from their positions and reinstate a new board of people who had earned their seats.

There were protocols for removing a corrupted board, and she could work through some of the loopholes to change her advisory board to more suggestible people. Those loyal to the crown and the people it served, like General Nakti.

She had spent hours searching through the paperwork, reading everything she could find about Kings and Queens Chosen and the history that came before them. She had not been raised religiously because it was improper for the monarch to be too closely tied to the temple for fear they would choose the gods over their subjects. But she remembered nursemaids telling her stories of the rulers before her. They had been her favorite bedtime stories, and revisiting them now was like revisiting a dear friend.

As one of the Gifted, the temple had always felt like a place of solace. And it was where history had been recorded since the first King Chosen. Since his army rose with the might of the gods and removed the corrupted line of kings from power. They had served both the gods and the people. She would follow their lead and do the same. Even if she wasn't entirely sure how to do either, she could—would—learn.

Loralei picked up one of the scriptures and flipped it open. This copy was old, the leather binding was worn and creased in places, and the insides of the pages had been marked with red ink.

She read the first page. Then read it again. Whoever had owned the book had been correcting it, layering a new story on top of the old of the first King Chosen. This story was more violent, the blood shed by her people more grue-some, and the death toll much higher. Loralei couldn't put the marked version down, reading through to the truth of a man-made ruler.

The king was like Saiden.

Loralei shut the book, calmly putting away the rest of the papers she had been planning to look through that day. She went to her advisory room and found Oscan, who she sent to gather the others. When the seven of them were standing behind their chairs, she pulled the book from her robes and threw it down on the table. She looked at each of them, gauging how much each of them knew about the secrets that generations of rulers had kept.

"Your Majesty, if you could explain to us the nature of your grievance," Agneus said, "perhaps we would be better suited to help you."

"There is a history of our kingdom unknown to those who live in it." She did her best to maintain her composure, but as the minutes wore on with little explanation given, she could feel herself running out of patience. "I expect an explanation as to why the scriptures in the temple have been redacted."

"Your Majesty, there is much you are still too young to understand about governing a kingdom as grand as Kaizia," Oscan spoke.

"When people are afraid, you must give them somewhere to target their fear," another one added.

"So we murder people—to assuage the fear of others? You might be okay with that blood on your hands, but I am not. We are not killers."

"We are not the ones doing the killing, Your Majesty."

"There have been generations of children murdered for nothing but the crime of their birth. By allowing that practice to come into existence, by not fighting with every breath in your body to stop it, you become personally responsible for those deaths. Each of you is soaked in the blood of the innocent."

"Good riddance!" a third spoke. "Our kingdom is much better without them invoking the gods' wrath."

Loralei jumped from her seat so fast that her chair flew back, exploding into bits of wood as it hit the wall. Her advisors flinched away from her and it took her a moment to realize, in her anger, she had summoned Keir's light to her hands. She shook them, and the light returned to the god, but her anger remained her own.

"Guards," she called.

Two of them walked into the room, hands casually hanging by their weapons.

"Arrest this man," she pointed at the last advisor to speak. The others moved to stand in front of him. But when she shot them a glare, they stepped aside. "Have him thrown in the dungeons until I can come down to interrogate and sentence him."

The guards bowed and spoke in unison. "Yes, Your Majesty." They took the man away.

She took his vacated chair and moved it to become her new seat at the table.

"What else is there that I do not know about the kingdom?" She was prepared to sit there all night if that was what it took.

"The most important part, Your Majesty," the youngest of her advisors started, "is what was done to bind the Blood-Cursed and keep them from their powers."

She watched him and waited for him to continue speaking.

When he didn't, someone else took up the conversation in his place, and she wondered if perhaps he, too, was not completely enlightened to all the wrongs that had been permitted.

"The temple joined with those who thought the Anointed had too much power. Believers had started to turn away from their connection to the gods, instead seeking out the Anointed for blessing and charms."

Another one continued. "So the temple bound their Gifts so Anointed individuals who were allowed to live past infancy would not come into their powers on their own until the last of their immediate family died. Should these family members die naturally, the Anointed would remain without their Gifts."

"What happens if they are killed?" Loralei asked.

"Should the family have their blood spilled in a violent manner, the Anointed one's Gifts would surface all at once, driving them mad with the sensation."

Yet another took up the narrative. "They became powerful weapons for a time, but then the magic burned out of them, and they became empty husks of what they once were. So, the Blood-Cursed title took over."

The revelation of how the Blood-Cursed got their powers brought more questions than it did answers. Thousands of thoughts flooded Loralei's mind, but she kept going back to the list of prisoners. To the list where there had been no crime recorded for keeping Magdalena captive. When she had learned the woman was Saiden's mother, she figured the crime had been keeping the birth of her daughter a secret. Loralei hated that the legionnaire's mother had been locked up for doing something so compassionate, but it appeared even that was not the reason she was held.

Her advisors had kept Magdalena in prison for almost thirteen years so they could kill her to release the magic in Saiden.

Loralei's chest burned at the idea of Saiden as a mindless killing machine, at the idea of Saiden becoming everything she strived not to be. The thought stopped all the other noise in her head, making her next decision clear and easy.

She ordered the guards to have the rest of her advisors arrested.

53

SAIDEN

Revon unchained her, and she didn't move, waiting for his next attack. "You will be given time to think this over, but I suggest you not take too long."

Saiden stayed sitting, still trying to piece together the story he was telling her with what she had previously understood of their kingdom's history, wondering if he was lying to her. If he was telling the truth, there had been a time when she wouldn't have been hated purely for existing. When people would have seen her as the gods' hand instead of a scourge to this world.

He was holding out everything she had dreamed of as a child to her since she learned why her parents had hidden her. But she couldn't trust him. It was too good to be true.

Revon raised his hand and a new light came into the room. One of the walls next to her had not truly been a wall at all, but a one-way glass.

Through it, she could see the slumped figure of a man who sat shackled to another table. She stood up and walked closer, pressing her hand against the glass, and tried to get a better look at the other captive.

She heard Revon say something, but she couldn't clearly hear what, and then someone was walking into the room and lifting the prisoner's face so he was looking at her.

It was Mozare. The recognition sank deep into her bones as she looked at him. There was blood all over his face from a multitude of small cuts, and his arms seemed to have fared about the same. Clearly, he was testing her, but this had been the wrong way to do so. She would make him pay for every drop of Mozare's blood that he had ordered shed.

"You will let him go, immediately," she said without turning around. Her voice was low in her throat, threatening Revon.

"You, see child, I cannot free the boy when he is clearly that which you wish to protect. It's called leverage. You will come to my side, of your own free will, or your partner will die a gruesome and painful death. It is your choice."

She felt Revon move, his feet stepping closer to the door as if he were trying to leave.

Her body started moving before she had even fully comprehended what she was doing. She was running towards him, though there wasn't much space in the small room, and she grabbed his arm before he could reach for the door-knob, twisting it back and pulling hard.

She heard his shoulder pop from its socket and threw her body weight into pushing him onto the floor. He reached for one of his knives, moving as if to stab her, but she grabbed his arm, slamming it down against the floor until he released the blade. She kicked it away and pressed herself closer against Revon, pushing on his injured shoulder. Fury tinged her vision red. She wanted nothing more than to take his own blade right there and cut his throat. Saiden grabbed one of the short knives at his waist and rammed it into his thigh.

He laughed underneath her, the sound so abrasive to her ears, underneath the rage pouring through her. She stopped. He was completely at her mercy, and yet he was laughing.

"There is the power I've been told about." He slammed his hand against the floor three times, and the door opened again, and three large men walked into the room.

They pulled her away from their leader and let the healer in to help Revon.

She pulled against their hold, but they were much bigger than her, and against their combined strengths, Saiden did not have a chance of pulling free.

Revon stood, his pant leg bloodstained, but he walked without a limp and he turned his shoulder over where it was once again resting properly.

"Let me tell you one more secret, darling," he said, stepping into her personal space. "Mozare volunteered for this." Then he, along with his crew, left her alone in the room, reeling with that revelation.

Saiden had slumped back into her chair, her brain devoid of reasonable thought.

Mozare had volunteered for this? To be beaten? How would he be in a position to volunteer unless it was an act? To *seem* like he was being held prisoner, rather than truly being in danger. And if that was the case, how could her partner do this to her? And for what purpose?

She took a deep breath, trying to center herself in a reality that was quickly shattering to pieces.

Her best friend, the only person she had truly been able to trust, had been lying to her for years. Maybe even the entire time they'd known each other.

He joined a rebellion that wanted to destroy the very thing she had fought so hard to protect. It was too much for her to think about. So, she put the information in the small box she'd stored her observations of Revon, and pushed it to the back of her head.

Instead, she thought over the other supposed secrets Revon had shared. She yearned for the world he described in their kingdom's secret, alternate history. But she also hated him for telling her about it. Because she would never be able to bring their country to love people like her again. Their fear was too strong.

The door opened, and Mozare walked in, his face clear of any marks beside the pre-existing scar from the Enlightened's mirror shard. She didn't get up from her spot on the floor. When he knelt in front of her, she raised her fist and punched him square in the nose with enough force to push him backward.

He caught himself on the wall, sliding down and clutching a hand to his face. She was sure she had broken it, but could not bring herself to care. She could do much worse. And since bones could easily be fixed by any competent healer, she might very well do so if he didn't start speaking quickly.

"I'm sorry, Saiden." He looked down at his hands. "I've wanted to tell you for so long, but I couldn't. I've been doing my best to protect you from the inside. You were never supposed to end up here."

"You lied to me."

"I had no choice. The truth would have put my mission in danger. It would have put *you* in danger."

Saiden watched him, judging how genuine he was. They had both mastered the blank face of a mercenary, but he wasn't trying to hide anything from her right then.

She knelt in front of him and put one hand on the side of his face. "If you ever lie to me again, I will do so much worse than breaking your nose."

Mozare laughed and leaned forward to hug her.

She didn't resist as his weight pulled her fully onto the ground next to him.

They sat like that for a while, enjoying the silence and relative peace after days of constant worry. She tried to push away the doubt about his true feelings towards her.

"You better get that thing healed before you have a crooked nose to match that ugly face," she said, pushing against him. He laughed again and then stood up, pulling Saiden with him.

"Let me give you a tour, then."

"I'm sure Revon wouldn't want that. I'm not joining a rebellion. I am loyal to my queen."

Mozare stared at her, shock plain on his face. He must have expected that she would learn about the history, about what they wanted to bring back to their country, and she would join them.

But Saiden had sworn an oath to Loralei and to the kingdom and she would not go back on it.

"Sai, he'll kill you. He won't hesitate."

"Then I will die an honorable death. There is no more I could ask for of this life."

He grabbed her arm. "We serve the people, the subjects you are sworn to protect."

She shook her head. She knew that Mozare only saw things as black and white. This cause was everything he believed to be right, but she didn't see the world like that. She couldn't, not when seeing it that way would erase her from being. He couldn't understand that.

"Don't tell them, Saiden. Just wait a little while longer. You'll see that this is where you are meant to be, with us. With me. We're partners. There's nothing we can't do together."

When we have each other's backs, Saiden thought to herself. *And that requires trust.* But she didn't say anything.

He took her silence as agreement and took her from the room.

She went with him to be healed. She could almost pretend that this was normal, that they were just on a mission and Mozare had gotten into some kind of fight. Almost. There was no natural light in any of the rooms, and it kept reminding her that this was not where she belonged. No natural place hid so thoroughly from the sun.

Once his nose was set and healed, they went to get food. She had refused almost every meal that had been brought to her, and she felt the hunger tighten her stomach. Even so, she was hesitant to eat when she didn't know where it had come from and if the group who made it could even be trusted. But the weakness in her legs as she walked told her that she couldn't go any longer without food. Her muscles were tired just from walking. If it came to a fight, her self-imposed starvation would put her at a severe disadvantage. So she took a tray and followed Mozare, only picking from the food he was willing to eat from.

He had lied to her about being part of the rebellion, but he had also supposedly tried to protect her, and she couldn't cancel out years of trust. She understood how his brain worked, how he was raised. Seeing him here made sense. Even if she hated to admit it.

Two men came and sat beside Mozare. He smiled at them but didn't speak and just continued eating in silence.

She watched the three of them, tension sitting heavily in her shoulders.

Mozare was a friendly person, and yet he hadn't spoken a word since they had sat down. There was clearly something going on there that she did not understand. Politics of the underground that would take time to figure out. Time she very likely didn't have.

Between one second and the next, the two men grabbed hold of Mozare, pinning him in place at the table. She stood up, about to reach over and grab one of the men, prepared to throw them off him when she was pulled from her bench. Her attacker threw her to the ground, moving to stand over her with a fist already swinging towards Saiden's face.

She swung her legs, knocking the woman onto her back, and pulled her legs up so she was crouching, her side facing her opponent, but her arms still touching the floor.

The woman was quick to get back on her feet, fist raised for another punch.

Saiden threw herself up from her crouch, using the woman's momentum against her. She grabbed her arm, throwing her away and punching her in the ear.

The woman swayed on her feet, disoriented as Saiden had been hoping. Without giving her opponent time to recover, she kicked out at her, the heel of her foot making contact with the woman's lower ribs.

Everyone in the cafeteria was watching, and she saw a few of them cringe at the loud crack.

The woman fell to the floor, holding herself up on one arm, fervent hatred clear on her face.

It made Saiden wonder if she was the only one who had been privy to Revon's history lesson. Though why he would keep it from his army made no sense, and only made her distrust him more.

Others rose from their tables, clearly willing to step in where the woman was no longer able, but a loud voice rang through the room.

"That is enough. We are not barbarians here."

She had expected Revon, but the voice belonged to a woman.

Saiden turned, and shock coursed through her again. She was really getting tired of the feeling.

The woman who had stopped them from attacking was none other than Cara.

Loralei's lover was part of the rebellion.

54
MOZARE

Mozare shook off the two idiots holding onto him and went to check on Saiden. He wasn't sure what game they had been playing at when they had sat down next to him, but he certainly hadn't been expecting someone to attack Saiden so openly.

He couldn't have been prouder of his partner. Even without weapons, she had fought wonderfully.

She didn't need him to check on her. Besides the impact of hitting the floor, the woman who had attacked Saiden hadn't managed to land a single punch. Still, he was glad Cara had stepped in when she had. He hated being powerless to help his friend. Especially when so many others were lining up to fight her.

Cara came and sat at their table, bowing her head at both Mozare and Saiden. He had known that she had been placed in the palace, but he should have told Saiden. The shock of everything in the past few days had been enough. She must have been tired of learning how many secrets had been kept from her.

Saiden looked at Cara. "She loves you." It wasn't a question, but he knew Saiden was still waiting for an answer.

"I have a job to do. Being close to the queen means I can protect the people who matter to me."

Two small children ran through the room and jumped into her lap, illustrating her point.

Mozare smiled at them. Cara's little siblings were the only children allowed in the base. The rest had been sent to safe houses at the borders of the kingdom. Cara was vital to their intelligence network, so Revon had made an exception by letting her keep her brother and sister nearby.

Cara pulled both of them closer, not caring that they were getting too big to be sitting with their sister, tickling both of them until their faces were red with laughter. She whispered to them, and they ran off again, holding hands.

"I have something you need to know, Mozare. Saiden, I imagine you will want to know this as well." She tucked herself into the table, looking at both of them before continuing. "Loralei has had all her advisors arrested. They are set to be executed within the next few days."

There was no emotion behind what Cara was saying, just a plain statement of fact. She saw what the queen was doing, and she was reporting it back.

But the words hit Mozare like a blow. Innocent lives were not meant to be sacrificed in the fight to free their kingdom.

Saiden didn't look like she believed what she was hearing. "No." She shook her head. "No, she would never shed blood without reason. There has to be something we don't understand here."

"Sai, this is what we're fighting against. There is too much power in having a Queen Chosen. The gods are not selecting rulers for us anymore, and the power has corrupted their line. We cannot live with a leader like this."

Saiden looked at him, still shaking her head.

He watched the warring lines of thought flicker across her face. She couldn't believe that Loralei would be capable of such horrors. Mozare might not know the same side of the queen as Saiden, but it had to be different from what he was seeing now. Saiden wouldn't defend her if she thought she was unjust, queen or not.

"The people are terrified. There has not been a King or Queen Chosen who has risen up against her advisors and incriminated others unjustly since Queen Iola."

Mozare knew who Cara was talking about. Revon had made sure they all learned everything they needed to about their cause. In the Legion, they weren't taught about the true nature of the first Chosen rulers, so he turned to explain that Iola had been the last of the Anointed queens. That she had killed her guards and everyone who lived in the palace before she could be stopped.

But this news was too urgent to not be immediately addressed.

"Cara, we have to stop her. We have to go now," he said. They were not meant to leave innocents to the mercy of ruthless monarchs.

"I came to you because I think you will have the best chance of convincing Revon. He won't be keen on a rescue mission. Especially for those pigs."

He turned to Saiden, who was looking at her hands. He couldn't guess what was going through her head.

She looked up, wearing the mask she put on for the rest of the world, carefully hiding her emotions. Even from him. "I will fight with you," she said, her voice barely louder than a whisper.

He smiled, but he couldn't celebrate the way he wanted to.

He could see the decision weighing down her shoulders, another burden she had to carry. This one, he would not let her carry alone. He grabbed her arm. If she was fighting with him, he would treat her as no less than his partner. She deserved at least that.

Since the leader liked to be where people could watch him, Mozare checked Revon's office last. He hadn't expected him to be there. Revon liked the adoration, liked the praise and reverence. He always told Mozare he needed to be seen.

Of course, because he had assumed that was the last place Revon would be, it was where he found him.

He knocked on the door, and when he heard Revon's voice calling for him to enter, he pushed the door open gently and walked in. Normally he let Saiden go first, but he didn't trust Revon's motives when it came to her and didn't want to be ambushed again.

"Why isn't she still locked in her room?" Revon asked, by way of greeting. He wasn't big on *hellos*, but Mozare hadn't been expecting that to be his first question.

"She's agreed to fight with us. Seems only fitting she got to learn about how things work around here."

"And what was it you were hoping to show her?"

"Cara brought news from the palace."

"And yet she didn't see fit to come see me herself. She went to you first."

"She thought I would be the best to share this information with you, sir."

"Get on with it then, Mozare. The rest of us don't have all day to wait for your dramatics."

"The queen has ordered the execution of all seven of her advisors, sir. I think sending a rescue squad should be seen as an immediate priority."

"Now, why would I do that?"

"They're innocent men. They've done nothing to deserve their sentence."

"They serve the government we are currently trying to overthrow. Their obedience allowed for centuries of godless monarchs. Of oppression of those Gifted who lived among them. Their deaths will further our cause."

Mozare froze.

He hadn't been expecting Revon to react so coldly. How could he convince a man with no regard for these people to save their lives? How was he so wrong about how he thought Revon would react?

"They are innocent," he tried to repeat, but the words sounded weak even to him. His blood started to boil. "You can't let her kill innocent people."

"I will do nothing to stop her and neither will you. That is the end of this discussion."

Mozare swiped an arm over Revon's stuff, scattering papers and trinkets all over the floor. He stepped forward to challenge him, and he felt Saiden step forward so she was next to him.

"You are dismissed."

The door opened and someone else stepped in. Saiden grabbed Mozare and forced him to leave the room. He struggled against her, but she was stronger than he was, and he didn't have the heart to keep struggling.

They didn't speak as he led her away from his office. There was nothing for either of them to say.

55
LORALEI

Loralei stood in a blood-red gown, the color unintentionally mimicking Saiden's hair. She wanted people to stop seeing her like a child, and to understand that she was their queen, not some puppet to be controlled. No more flowers and pageantry, no longer a little girl being manipulated by men who presumed to know better.

One of her lady's maids had braided her hair so none of it hung down around her shoulders. The thick coils supported the small diadem she wore, a remnant from a long-ago queen. She felt light. Like a weight had been lifted off her shoulders, and she didn't think it all had to do with her hair. With her advisors gone, she wouldn't have to worry about ever being used or lied to again.

All seven of her advisors were walked out before her, chains running between them, led by her guards. She could see that there were plenty of people who did not agree with her, but she was the Queen Chosen—and now crowned monarch—so there was no way that they would disobey her.

Her executioner, a life-Gifted man with dark brown curls, stepped forward. His Gift gave him the ability to quickly take a life, and she had hired him for exactly that skill, to dole out quick deaths. They did not need to be drawn out.

One by one, the guilty men were led forward in front of the crowd, separated from the others who awaited the same fate.

Loralei stepped forward to read a list of their crimes and sentenced each and every one of them to death. She prayed that Ilona would have mercy on them in the life after this. That they could earn the forgiveness of the gods.

When they were finished, she retired to the seclusion of her throne room. With no advisors to pester her, she could be alone anywhere in her castle, and she enjoyed the way the light filtered in through the tall windows and painted the room in gold.

She didn't mind being alone. It gave her more time to wonder what else might have been kept from her in an attempt to keep her weak and controllable. They had wanted her to be oblivious to the actual ruling of the country, relegated to dinners and balls. She wouldn't stand for it.

Sometime later, she summoned a servant to bring her a glass of wine. Then had it refilled multiple times.

Her mind kept going over the executions, thinking of the long robes they were dressed in, and the priestesses' blessings. Thinking of the smell of blood as it permeated the hall. Seeing each of their heads removed from their bodies. The sight had brought her no joy or satisfaction.

Saiden was still missing, and with Magdalena away for her own safety until Lorelei could learn if anyone else knew how to release the curse, the castle felt far too big. She was grateful that Cara was still there. And, without the judgement of a council, Loralei had finally been able to free her from servitude. Keep her by her side.

As if her thoughts had summoned her, Cara walked into the room. She was wearing one of Loralei's dresses, the corset too tight on her.

The queen watched, entranced from her throne, as her lover swayed her hips and approached her.

She wondered what had made her get so dressed up today of all days. She hadn't expected her to be back at all, taking advantage of her new freedom to spend more time with her family.

"Your Majesty," she said, letting the words dance slowly from her mouth. She bent low, so she was spilling over the top of her borrowed dress. She walked up the steps and sat down in Loralei's lap. Cara traced her finger down the queen's cheek, going lower over her collarbones and lower still.

Loralei pulled her lover closer, kissing her neck, then moving to run her lips against the soft spot behind her ear. She loved the feeling of her underneath her fingers, her lips. She pulled back, smiling, and kissed Cara, dipping her back until she was completely supporting her weight.

Her lover wrapped her arms tightly around Loralei's shoulder, kissing her with equal abandon.

They stayed that way, kissing and touching each other from the throne of her kingdom until long after the sun had set, and the room was cast in the moon's pale light.

56
SAIDEN

S aiden had lied to her partner for the first time in her life. She knew without a doubt that it was necessary—she couldn't protect the queen if she was dead—but she also felt guilty about it. Even with the tangled web of deceit she was still unraveling, it was hard for her to separate this Mozare from the boy who was her first friend.

Their hideaway was close to the barracks. He had explained that much to her. It was how he had been able to relay so much information and sway the missions the Legion took on. They were taking on both enemies of the crown, but also people who Revon thought would stop him from taking over.

Saiden felt the betrayal burning deeper and deeper, coming at her from all sides to the point that she would have likely broken out of the base if Mozare hadn't finally agreed to take her outside. They didn't have horses, so they were just going to go for a run. It wasn't much, but it was enough to get her out of the hallways. She had waited for days in the underground bunker before she could no longer stand the claustrophobia of being kept so far from the sunlight. And it had taken her hours to convince Moze, but he had finally agreed to taking her out for a walk. If only a brief one.

She had an idea of how they could let her out, and she wanted to talk to him about it while they were out today, in the hopes that he could convince the others. While Revon seemed to head the entire operation, there were a few people he trusted that acted as a kind of advisory board. Mozare and Cara were two of those people, along with people named Vesta, Chiro, and Sympha.

If she could get them to see the merit of her being returned to the palace, she might be free of the base today. For good.

Saiden had been told to wrap her hair in the styles of the southern kingdom to keep people from seeing who she was. She had wondered if she could use the chance to escape, but she knew Mozare wouldn't let her get far, and she couldn't afford to give up her ruse so quickly.

When the guard on duty opened the hatch door for them, Saiden had to look away from the sunlight. She was still wearing a hood, but her eyes had forgotten how bright the Kaizian sun got. She climbed the ladder out and smiled as the warmth soaked into her bones. She had missed this more than she had missed anything else.

"You're going to have to hit me, Mozare. They need to believe that I actually escaped. That I've been held hostage all this time in an attempt to get information. They have to think that there was a good reason that I've been gone this long, and not just that I've been in league with you." She was trying to find a balance that let her return to the palace without getting Mozare killed.

"We're partners, Sai. We'll always be in league together."

She looked at him and she felt guilt swirl in her stomach. She knew that he understood what she was talking about, but that he desperately didn't want to. He didn't want to be forced to make Saiden look like she had been held hostage, but he was the only one she trusted to do so without any malice in his heart. The others would take joy in hurting her, and they would be careless with where their punches land. If she let them, she could be too hurt to leave, and then the beating would have been for nothing.

She didn't have anything to pack or anyone to say goodbye to, so once she had gotten permission, she stood facing Mozare. "Just do it." She braced herself.

It had been her idea, but she still didn't like the idea of standing there and not defending herself from his punches. It went against her every instinct, and she had to fight to not stop Mozare.

He swung at her. The first hit connected with her face. She could feel the bruises form as soon as his hand retracted. The second one hit her collarbone, then a kick to the side. She stopped counting after that, doing her best to maintain her composure through the pain.

Saiden knew, though she didn't tell the others, that she wouldn't have to deal with bruises for long after she was reunited with the queen.

This beating, the bruises blossoming freshly on her skin, these were her punishment. That is what she deserved for allowing the deaths of so many others without more of a fight.

She would not fail the gods now.

Cara was going to take her to the palace and tell Loralei that she found her half-starved in the forest on her way home from visiting her family. The story was that Saiden was delirious and calling out for help. That Cara had thought her to be dead when she finally found her. Loralei would trust that Cara was telling her the truth, but the lie tasted sour to Saiden. Cara had assured her that the queen had been distressed by Saiden's sacrifice, that she wouldn't question her loyalty.

From the palace, Saiden could do her best to topple the oppressive government without the loss of more lives. That thought was the only way she could live with what she was doing.

When they were sure she was bruised and bloody enough, Mozare helped her onto a saddle in front of Cara. She had to look like she was close to dying, so she couldn't exactly ride as a second or by herself. She was closer to the other girl than she had cared to be, but it was another sacrifice she would have to make to keep her alive.

When they arrived at the palace, the real show began.

Cara jumped from her horse, pulling a now slumped Saiden down from the saddle with her and calling for guards.

Two came running. Saiden wondered if they knew who Cara was to the queen, or if they were just so afraid of Loralei's wrath that they didn't dare step out of line. Even with a servant.

She felt one of them lift her up, and then they were running—Cara next to her while the other guard went to summon Loralei.

They brought her to Saiden's room, which felt now like a bite of poisoned fruit that had seemed juicy from the outside. She was as trapped there as she had been in the bunker.

Someday, she wanted to be free of it all.

The guard rested her gently on the bed. She was surprised not to just be thrown to the side like trash, but perhaps there were still people in the world with true kindness in their hearts. Or the fear of their Queen Chosen now ran that deep after the advisors' executions.

She couldn't know for sure.

Footsteps echoed through the room, and though she had only expected the queen, she heard a second pair louder than Loralei's likely slippered feet would be.

She opened her eyes as wide as she could and was surprised to see the General standing at her bedside.

Nakti knelt down next to Saiden on the bed and cradled the upper half of Saiden's body in her lap. "My beautiful girl, what have they done to you?"

She felt the woman's tears wet her own cheeks as she rocked Saiden back and forth. Warmth started to spread through the legionnaire, as the tears and small sections of skin contact allowed her superior to start healing her with her Gift.

Saiden felt another hand on her face, one without the General's weapon-worn calluses. She could move now, since the worst of her injuries had been healed by her surrogate mother's ministrations. She sat up, holding Nakti's hand in hers and squeezing.

"My child, you will be alright. I am here. They can't hurt you anymore."

Saiden had never heard the General speak that way to any of her soldiers, not even those lying in wait for Ilona. She was the closest thing Saiden could remember to having a mother, but she hadn't realized that perhaps Nakti had felt the same way. The woman smiled a shaky smile at her and waited to see what her newly rescued fighter would say.

Loralei sat next to her on the bed, fluffed the pillows, and sent Cara to fetch tea and fresh fruit.

"Where were you?" Loralei asked.

"The rebels who attacked your palace," she said, "they took me because I had dressed myself to look like you. They were angry when they realized that I had tricked them, but they thought that keeping me there would benefit them. They thought I would tell them how to get to you. They beat me bloody every day, and then they sent healers at night so I could sleep. Everyday. The same torture."

She took a deep, shaky breath for effect.

"But I refused to tell them anything. They started getting careless with locking my room, and I left one day before they sent the healer to me. They hadn't expected me to have the strength to leave."

She paused again, as if exhausted just from talking.

"If Cara hadn't found me, I doubt I would have made it back to the castle."

"Can you tell us anything about where they are hiding?" Nakti asked, the serious General once more.

Saiden would remember the love she showed her, even if seeing it had made her betrayal eat her up inside. She had not expected to feel so much grief at being back in the palace, but the feeling burned in her chest.

"I was delirious, half-starved, and in so much pain," she started, but Loralei rested a hand against her arm. She stopped speaking.

"I do not expect you to have any information for us," the queen said gently. "Please excuse the General's eagerness. We are glad of your safe return, and the rebels will be hunted down until each one of them is dead for what they've done to you."

Her skin paled, and she desperately hoped Loralei just thought she was tired of death and destruction. Because if Loralei's wish came true, Saiden doubted she would live to see her next birthday.

57

LORALEI

Loralei had spent the night at Saiden's bedside, wondering how she would tell the girl that her mother was still alive. That she had been kept as a prisoner in her own dungeon for all those years because of her own ignorance. She had wanted to spill everything to Saiden as soon as she had arrived back at the castle, but the words had gotten stuck in her throat when she had laid eyes on the legionnaire.

The queen hadn't wanted Saiden to feel alone, and she worried that the soldier would have nightmares. So, she had moved the chaise lounge over near Saiden's bed and was resting in it while her personal guard slept.

Upon her arrival, Saiden had been covered in bruises, her clothes stained a deep red with her own blood. And since her safe return, she had eaten a hardy meal, filling up on fresh meats and fruits from Loralei's own garden.

The queen couldn't imagine the pain her guard had endured to protect her kingdom. Loralei wondered if she would have been able to endure the same thing, and her doubt made her feel like a failure. Like she had failed at every aspect of being a monarch even before the crown had officially been placed on her head, and in the days since her coronation.

Nakti had continued asking Saiden questions. Any details she could remember about their location, identifying members, birthmarks, or specific bird calls.

Loralei didn't even know how many questions she had asked, before realizing that Saiden truly couldn't remember anything about where she had been. She hadn't wanted Nakti to continue questioning Saiden. The legionnaire was her guard, not a prisoner or a suspect, but she let the questions continue as a sign of good faith towards the General, one of her new advisors. She saw the fear in their eyes whenever she showed even a flicker of the temper that seemed to be growing inside her every day.

The queen stood over Saiden and brushed aside a piece of hair, wondering if perhaps it would be better to never tell Saiden the truth. Her mother was safe now. Somewhere no one could use her against Saiden. Loralei could ensure Magdalena lived a long life. And if her blood was not spilled, Saiden would live a peaceful life. One without the insanity of the temple-inflicted curse.

She leaned over and kissed her forehead, pausing when Saiden stirred slightly, and then left the room. She wouldn't go far, but there was something in her head that she couldn't resist looking into. She raced to the archives.

She read for a while, and morning came before she knew it. Before she'd had a chance to sleep. She would be tired, but it was nothing a bit of tea couldn't fix. She made sure to add it to her breakfast order, with instructions that she was going to eat with Saiden. In the guard's chambers. She didn't want to push the legionnaire too far on her first day without getting to gauge how she was doing first.

She walked in without knocking, thinking that Saiden would still be asleep. She was surprised to see her standing and clothes on the surrounding floor.

"I'm so sorry," the queen said, a flush burning her cheeks. She turned away, but not before seeing that the vines the woman wore on her arms didn't start there. They wove around her shoulder blades and her sides.

"Loralei. Good morning." Saiden punctuated the statement with a yawn.

"Perhaps you should still be in bed?" But she wouldn't push her. Saiden needed to be in control of herself. That was something Loralei could understand.

"I've been from your side for far too long. Don't you have rounds to go on?" the legionnaire asked.

When Loralei finally turned around to look at her, Saiden was pulling on her gear pants, her tattoos already covered by a dark gray long-sleeve shirt.

"If you're feeling up to it, we can go into the city. But I don't want to rush you. You've been through an ordeal. More than I could ever imagine going through. If you feel you need time to rest, then you should take it."

"Loralei—Your Majesty."

The queen turned to look her guard in the eye.

"I'm fine. Getting back to normal will be good for me."

She had to admit she was excited to take Saiden back into the town. And she had been so worried about where her guard was all this time that she had neglected the people she cared for.

She told Saiden that she would be ready in a few minutes, and to meet her at the front. She still had Saiden's gear jacket in her own quarters, as well as the new jacket she had commissioned for herself. It was more fitted, meant to be worn over a corseted dress. She was glad to be wearing it, knowing that Saiden wouldn't get hurt again because she had given hers to protect Loralei.

When she returned, Saiden was waiting patiently on the steps, a blade twirling through her hands. Loralei was glad that she had kept hold of the kindjal blades. Clearly, they were important to Saiden.

She handed her the jacket, and they left, heading into the city. Saiden hadn't braided her hair, and the red curls bounced as she walked down the steps.

The queen smiled to herself and followed.

The town was crowded, the market in full swing.

Saiden ducked through the crowd, trying to keep her head covered, but without her braids, curls kept slipping free.

Someone yelled, fingers pointing, as people backed away from her.

Loralei watched her friend try to shrink away from the sound, from the people cursing her and everything they believed she stood for. They didn't know her at all.

She tried to step forward, to do the brave thing and defend her friend, but Saiden grabbed her arm. She looked back, and the legionnaire shook her head slightly.

A man stepped forward and took a swing at Saiden, who easily ducked to the side so he missed, flying past her.

Free from her guard's grasp, Loralei stepped over and grabbed the man, forcing him to his knees in the middle of the square.

When people realized that their queen stood among them, they backed further away, bowing and whispering apologies.

She looked at the crowd, standing as tall as she could among them.

"Anyone who attacks the queen's protector is subject to execution. For your crimes against the kingdom, you will die. May Ilona have mercy on you."

She struck her small dagger through his chest.

58

MOZARE

Mozare saw Saiden waiting for him in his room when he came back from a run. He felt his heart speed up when he noticed blood splattered on the embroidered flowers of her official queen Guard's gear.

"What happened?" He shut the door quickly before moving to touch her. He put a hand against her shoulders, and she crumpled against him. He felt tears wet his shoulder, and shock froze him.

He could count on one hand the number of times he had seen his partner so vulnerable. Panic burned through him, pumping his heart faster than any run could.

"She killed a man," she said, voice quiet through her tears. She pulled back and worked her hands through her hair, her eyes red and her cheeks marred by streaks of tears. "She killed a man in the middle of the market because he attacked me."

"Saiden, you aren't responsible for any of her actions. You can only control how you respond to it."

She looked at him, and he waited to see what she needed next. This was new territory for him, and even though it was unfortunate, he was going to need her to guide him through helping her.

He helped her out of the gear jacket, throwing the blood-splattered garment into the pile of dirty laundry he kept in the corner of his room. He would clean it and then return it to her free of bloodstains.

"I need to move," she said, swinging down from his bed. "I need to hit something."

"You know I'll always volunteer to get my ass beat by you." He bumped his shoulder against hers. He didn't expect her to smile, but he was glad that at least she wasn't crying anymore. A good fight would center Saiden and give her time to clear her head before their meeting tonight. Besides, he always learned something from fighting her, even if he ended up being the loser.

Mozare chose to take her to one of the private training rooms instead of the main training room. If she was emotional, the fight could get messy, and he trusted she wouldn't want an audience for that. It was likely why she had been waiting in his room instead of going to meet him on the track.

They both picked up long swords. It was Saiden's weakest weapon, though he was never able to understand why. If she was going for a challenge, her mind was racing more than even he could tell. And they were adept at reading each other.

He swung, starting the fight on the offensive with a high strike towards her head. When she blocked, he readjusted and aimed for her legs.

She jumped, landing in a roll behind him.

He turned, and she forced him onto the defensive with a number of quick hits one after the other. Sweat built on his forehead and soaked into the back of his shirt.

Saiden twirled past him, switching sword hands as she turned and slapped the back of his legs with the flat side of the blade.

He fell back, letting go of his own weapon so he didn't accidentally impale himself. He had done so as a new recruit, handling a blade before he was meant to, and the healers and recruits had laughed about it for weeks.

She reached out her empty hand. "Loser chooses the next weapon." Her muscles were less tense despite the workout, and he could see her returning to normal.

"So, I get to choose the next weapon you wipe me out with?"

She nodded, stretching her arms while she waited for him to answer.

He didn't, instead charging at her.

She saw him coming and quickly leaped over his shoulder as he ducked down, clearing him with a simple flip. He almost instantly regretted his choice, but at least this way he would only be dealing with bruises.

She slammed into him from behind, knocking him over. She waited for him to stand again, feet spread apart so she could stand her ground if he charged, or move if she needed to.

He waited for her to hesitate, but he didn't get an opening.

She swung by, trying to knock him over again, but she missed, and he grabbed a piece of her hair to pull her back.

It was a cheap move, but they never played by any rules in here. They needed the practice—because no one played by any rules in a real fight.

They kept fighting until Saiden was tired, far past when Mozare would've stopped himself, but he knew she needed this.

Then they went their separate ways, planning to meet up at dinner before their meeting and Saiden's reluctant return to the palace. He knew there was one young lady who would be very excited to see her.

Hopefully, that joy would carry Saiden through until they were free of the queen.

59
SAIDEN

Saiden had not wanted to return to the underground rebel base. She did not want to continue lying to Loralei, despite her earlier actions. But the queen had believed her when she told her she wanted to visit her parents' graves, so she forced herself down the ladder and back into the darkness. They were running out of time to stop Loralei before she did something truly terrible and plunged her soul—and the kingdom—completely into darkness.

She had seen that hatred fill the queen's heart in the market as Loralei sentenced the Enlightened man to death and immediately killed him without ceremony. His body hadn't been properly and thoroughly blessed. His soul would remain locked between worlds forever because of it.

There were more people in the base than had been there last time. The rooms teemed with people running errands and passing through the hallways.

Saiden walked around until she found Mozare, who had assured her that he would be safe coming back. She had wanted him to stay out of it, but he would fight with her to the end. Besides, he had said to her, someone had to make sure she didn't get herself killed.

She was relieved when she finally found him. There were far too many people in a place that already made her feel claustrophobic, and having something familiar helped her feel calmer.

They went and joined a few others in Revon's office—Cara and three other rebels who acted as his advisors. Beside him was another young man. One she hadn't seen here before.

He reached out a hand to her, an action which marked him as a foreigner before he even had a chance to speak. "I am Cassimir, from the Southern Kingdom of Taezhali."

She shook his hand and watched as he placed the other across his chest and bowed to her. He had rich tanned skin and hair as brilliant as gold. It took Saiden a minute to realize that she was staring at him. For all the diversity in the Legion, Saiden had never seen anyone who looked like him before.

Mozare coughed slightly, though it sounded more like a laugh. She elbowed him in the side and turned to the map spread out over Revon's desk. They planned to attack the castle because her return to Loralei meant there was nothing they could use to lure her from her sanctuary. Luckily, she had been able to mark the secret passageways for them, which would grant at least some of them the benefit of surprise.

"I don't think the queen is beyond saving," she said, speaking the words she knew no one wanted to hear. "You could remove her from her throne and still let her keep her life. Send her to another kingdom, somewhere over the Zalfari Sea, where she can't come back."

Cassimir watched her speak, which unsettled her. He didn't seem to observe her with the hatred others felt for her due to her nature. Very few people looked at her with kindness, like he was now. Like he thought she had something valuable to say. She put it aside until she could think about it another time.

Mozare was tense next to her, and she waited for someone to yell at her, to draw their blade, to say that she could not be there. No one spoke. Not even Mozare, who she had hoped would back her up even though her partner knew how hard this was for her, encouraging what would likely be the death of many innocents.

When no one spoke, she left the room. In this world, where she had so harshly been judged for who she was, she had tried so hard to be good. She was tired of fighting and taking lives. She was exhausted.

She heard the door open behind her, and familiar footsteps make their way across the hall until Mozare was standing next to her. She didn't look at him, even though she knew that was what he was waiting for.

He eventually sat down on the floor of the surprisingly empty hallway.

She didn't understand how there weren't people in the hall here when there were so many more people inside the base than it was likely able to house.

"He's never going to let her go free." His voice was not unkind, but the words were harsh in her ears, nonetheless.

"She's no older than we are. Should we all be judged so harshly?"

"We've tried all our lives to do what is right, Saiden. The same cannot be said of the queen."

"How do you know? How do you know we're doing the right thing? How do you know Loralei isn't?"

"Because I trust in a higher power than us. She has stopped having any regard for where we come from, or where we return to. She has become the ultimate and sole power of the court. That cannot stand."

"How are we any better if we decide whether she should die?"

Mozare didn't have an answer for her right away. "I guess we just hope that the gods have mercy on us. Because we want to stop more people from dying. Peace cannot be bought without bloodshed."

"Then we are monsters no better than her," she said, standing up from the floor and walking away.

Saiden stormed out of the bunker. She knew it was childish, but there was too much doubt swirling through her head for her to stay there, surrounded by so many people. She knew there was only one place she could go where she would get the answers she needed. She set off in the direction of the temple.

She didn't speak to anyone, retreating to one of the single prayer rooms before she could even be approached by the religious attendants. She lit her candles, raised her hands, and waited for the world to shift. It didn't take long. Perhaps they had been waiting for her. Or perhaps they were bored. She didn't really care which. What mattered was they had answered.

Ilona and Keir stood next to each other, surrounded by darkness. They had not tried to bring her somewhere this time, which led her to believe that there was something going on that they did not want her to know about.

But she liked the blank background, liked that there was nothing to cloud her focus or distract her.

"Sweet girl, what is it you have come to speak to us about?" Ilona asked, stepping closer to where Saiden was still kneeling.

Keir moved to touch her hair, but she pulled away from him.

"I need you to guide me to the right path. There is a war coming, and my heart is torn between my people and my queen."

"You are right to be torn," Keir said, having returned to his spot next to Ilona.

She noticed that the hems of each of their outfits were bleeding with color, red like her hair. She had never seen them in any color besides their signature black and white.

"It is not as simple as there being only one right path," the god continued. "We see many paths set before us, but you will be the one to decide which one is truly yours."

She frowned, but waited for one of them to continue.

Ilona spoke up next. "We admire the value you place on life, but you must ask yourself if one life is worth so much when compared to many others."

"Loralei's—" Saiden started.

The goddess interrupted. "I do not mean her life. Her path is clear."

"The people should not live in fear," Saiden responded. "I swore to protect them. To take out whatever threatened them, queen or not."

"And you must be aware of the cost of such bargains," Keir added. "About what that will do to your life."

"Choosing the fate of a country is no easy burden. That is why we Anointed the Kings and Queens of old," Ilona added.

Saiden was tired of their cryptic answers. She knew they had a plan, that everything that happened had their hands in it, but yet they wouldn't tell her what she should do.

She pulled herself from the vision rather than waiting to be dismissed by them, upset that the visit had done nothing to ease her anger and nerves.

She went instead to find Rhena, to remind herself what was worth fighting for.

The recruit was sitting at a table surrounded by the other recruits in her class. She smiled when she saw Saiden and bounded over to hug her.

She loved that about the girl, the way she exuded goodness. Perhaps she had needed that more than she had ever needed the temple.

It was the people around her that mattered more than the divine. They might influence their paths, but they could not choose which one would be taken.

"I just wanted to say hi," Saiden said. She hadn't seen Rhena in weeks, and she was so proud to see how the recruit was fitting in and excelling in training. She had no doubt that she would be as good as Saiden herself one day, as long as she kept pushing herself.

"You should come meet my friends," she said, reaching for Saiden's hand.

"I can't today. I just wanted to see you quickly before I head back to the palace."

Rhena hugged her again and then went to rejoin the group of young fighters.

Watching them together, Saiden knew what her decision had to be. She had to choose whatever path would make this kingdom a good place for Rhena to live in.

60
MOZARE

Mozare was following Saiden through the palace. He wasn't supposed to be here. A thought that produced both anger and anxiety within Mozare. His hands shook, even though he should have nothing to worry about. No one was looking for him. No one knew the secrets he was hiding.

Except her, of course. But he wasn't worried she would hurt him. Maybe give him a good bruising in training, but there was likely no one in the entire kingdom that he was safer with than his partner. Even when she was angry with him, the way he knew she was now.

He had no doubt that Saiden knew he was behind her, that she was keeping just far enough away from him that he would have to yell to speak to her, alerting the entire castle to the fact that they were sneaking back in well after midnight. Knew that she was just clever enough to avoid this conversation entirely if he couldn't get to her before she managed to close herself in her palace rooms.

His partner was still in front of him, and the entirety of his attention focused on her.

When the shallowest of breaths exhaled behind him, he turned. Just in time for a blade that had been aimed at his heart to lodge in his side. His brain couldn't even catch up to the idea, despite the fact that his body reacted, one hand reaching to put pressure on the wound, to try to stop the blood from pouring out of him.

The queen was pale to begin with, but her face now was so light he thought he might have been seeing a ghost. His blood left tiny red droplets on the silky gown she was wearing. His brain tried to focus on the details, tried to keep his eyes locked on her face and the guilt she was wearing, but his vision blurred.

He felt Saiden's arms around him, despite the fog in his ears that had hidden her approach. He hadn't even realized that he had started to fall until the warmth of her chest pressed into the side of his face.

"I...I didn't mean to," Loralei stuttered.

"Go get a healer," Saiden's voice was hard, even in the faraway place where the words drifted from. To someone else, he knew the look on her face was emptiness. But he could tell from every blurred crease on her forehead that she was terrified.

He watched through the black spots in his vision as she pulled her jacket off, and the long sleeve she wore underneath it despite the heat, pressing the fabric to the wound in his side. Her fingers trembled as she applied pressure, trying to keep him here with her.

"I'm alright," his voice shook as he tried to reassure her, the sound weaker than he thought it would be.

"You're an idiot is what you are." The words were hissed, as if every wall around them were trying to hear what she had to say. "Following me into the palace in the middle of the night. It's like you were trying to get yourself killed."

He felt the blood trickle from his mouth as his chest shook with the barest hint of a laugh. Saiden gave him a stern look, reprimanding him with her eyes for disrupting the wound.

He leaned his head back onto the cooling marble floors, his eyes barely drifting shut for a second. "Your fault."

"Keep your eyes on me, you fool," Saiden snapped, her voice growing louder with every word, fear punctuating her insults. She never meant them anyway.

Louder footsteps sounded from the way Loralei had run off, a set of healers following after the queen. His blood was smeared on her forehead where she must've tried to keep her hair out of her face. He couldn't stop staring at her, at the smudge against her pale skin, the color an even greater contrast with the darkness of her hair. Didn't stop looking at her even as Saiden sank back on her feet, as the healers gingerly pulled the blood-soaked cloth away from his chest, hissing at the sight of his injury. Didn't even care to stop staring when he felt the warmth from one of their hands pouring into his side, the skin and muscle itching as the healer coaxed it to stitch back together.

"Try not to do that again, you reckless idiot," his partner said, pressing her forehead against his once the healer had returned to the queen's side. "Do you think you can make it back alright?"

"He's more than welcome to stay here." Loralei still spoke with authority, despite the tremble in her voice.

Mozare had to work to prevent a snarl from escaping.

"It wouldn't take long for a room to be made ready," the queen continued.

Mozare kept his eyes on Saiden, weariness and exhaustion coursing through him. The healers could fix his skin, but despite stimulating his body to produce more blood, they couldn't replace everything he had just lost.

"I think I'll just bring him to my room," Saiden said, answering for him.

Loralei curtsied behind him, as if *they* were royalty, not her, and escorted the healers away without argument.

"You really are one of the dumbest creatures I have ever met," Saiden mumbled as she helped hoist him off the ground.

They were already closer to her room in the palace than he had originally noticed, which was fortunate, considering his brain didn't seem to be communicating with his feet.

She left him seated on a plush sofa while she fetched water and a rag for him to clean the blood from his skin, and a pair of clean pants for him to wear to bed. "You already stained the lounge. You aren't allowed to stain the bed, too."

He was grateful, as a full laugh shook through his body, that this time it wasn't accompanied by blood.

Mozare woke up, heart racing as he took in his surroundings, and his brain remembered what had happened last night. Without a shirt, it was easy for him to trace his fingers along the new scar on his abdomen and freshly admire how close he had gotten to death.

Saiden was already gone, the side of the bed where she had slept last night neatly made, making him think she had already been up for quite a while. If she had ever gone to sleep in the first place.

There was no reason for him to stay in the palace, but he wanted to talk to Saiden about last night. Both their meeting and their encounter with the queen. But he had other responsibilities that were more pressing now.

Saiden didn't make it back to the rebel bunker until it was already well past sunset. Mozare heard the door open and sat up. He had volunteered to guard the door, even though it had never been one of his responsibilities before. Most new recruits spent their first months on rounds of guard duties, but Revon had claimed he was too valuable for that. He only stood watch tonight because he wanted to know when his partner came back. He wanted to apologize for not being able to stand with her. He couldn't change his stance, but he hated that they were once again on opposite sides.

"Saiden," he greeted her.

"You know this isn't what I want. You know that this isn't anywhere near right. But I can't believe what she did to you last night, and I'm trusting you know what you're doing."

His planned apology died on his tongue. There weren't enough words to sum up his feelings for forcing Saiden into such a choice, even if he believed with all his being that it was the right one. He couldn't express how much her continuing trust meant to him, even after his epic betrayal.

"I will do what I must to protect the people. They are what matter. But I will not shed innocent blood," she said, her tone brooking no argument. "There has to be a plan in place that results in the least amount of innocent death."

"I can talk you over what Revon said. He values your opinion, though he wouldn't admit it. He said he would appreciate you looking over his plans."

She crossed her arms and raised a disbelieving eyebrow. "No, he didn't."

Mozare laughed. "No, he didn't. But he should have. The others—they trust your judgement on this attack more than they do with Revon because you've lived in the palace with Loralei. He hasn't been there since he was a little boy. They want to know what you think. They want to follow you into battle."

His partner didn't answer.

Mozare would have thought that to be an honor, but there were some things they saw so differently, on a fundamental level, that he couldn't understand what she was thinking. Still, she was here, which meant that she was willing to fight with them.

He led her down the hall to where the others were once again gathered in the office room, staring at maps, directions, and plans.

When Saiden stepped into the room, everyone turned to look at her. She commanded their attention without even having to speak. He didn't think she even noticed it.

"This is what you need to do," she started, laying out a different path on the maps they were looking at.

"Who said you were in charge?" Revon asked her. He clearly had noticed how the room had gravitated towards her. How, even now, they were circling around her.

"You wanted an army. Armies need generals. That's why you have me."

Tension flooded the room as Saiden stared at Revon and dared him to counter her. No one spoke for what felt like hours, but in reality, was only a few minutes.

And then Cassimir started clapping. "It is not often we see someone as war-tested and true as you are, Mistress Saiden. It would be an honor to follow you into battle." He had a rich accent, though he spoke their language with ease.

Revon looked at the diplomat. His foreign aid was invaluable to their mission, and so he didn't argue. But he didn't look happy about the turn of events. The turn of allegiance away from him, even if it was for the sake of the mission's success.

Mozare knew that there were other things going through their leader's mind, ways that he could take Saiden out at the same time. Revon would not tolerate a threat to his authority, no matter where it came from. The man would let Saiden be as long as it suited him, but Mozare knew she was in danger the second she stopped being useful to their cause.

For all that Revon might disagree with her, his partner's plan was a good one. With a smaller group of soldiers, they were less likely to be intercepted. And Saiden knew the palace's security schedule well enough to attack when the guards were few and far between. She seemed completely in her element, which was frightening. He knew there was nothing about this that sat comfortably with Saiden, and the wall she was putting up now to look in control—it was something that would get her killed if she wasn't careful.

He couldn't let that happen.

When the battle meeting adjourned, Mozare followed Saiden out of the room. He wanted to apologize again. Saiden was the truest, most honorable person he knew, and he felt like he was forcing her into a corner. He didn't want her to hate him when this was all over.

"Saiden, listen—" he started, trying to say what he had failed to earlier outside the entrance to the hideout.

She cut him off. "I know you're sorry. I just hope we don't all live to regret this."

"Not all of us see you as cursed, you know. Some of us still think you are Anointed."

"Temple-raised idiots think I'm Anointed," she said, knocking her shoulder against his, indicating she didn't think him among the religious fools she just insulted. "The rest of them think I'm leading them to early graves."

"But they would still rather die fighting than live their lives hidden and afraid."

"I know that. I know what it's like to be hidden and afraid. To have enemies waiting for you behind every turn." She stopped walking and turned to face him. "That is what I've lived with my entire life, Moze. You are the first person I can remember looking at me without an ounce of fear, without disgust and hatred in your eyes."

"You are worth so much more than fear or hatred, Mistress Saiden," Cassimir spoke from behind Mozare.

He hadn't heard the other man approach.

Cassimir reached forward, grabbing her hand and kissing her knuckles.

Confusion spread over her face. She had little experience with traditions outside of Kaizia, so the respect Cassimir meant to show her was lost in translation.

Mozare interrupted the silence with an offer of food. It was late enough in the day that the cafeteria wouldn't be open, but he had flirted with the chef enough that he knew where the key was. He figured between them, they would be able to whip up something to eat.

In the end, he and Saiden were of little use in the kitchen. But Cassimir was surprisingly very talented.

He pushed them both aside to run the kitchen. "I'll do my best," he said, "but your kingdom has significantly fewer spices than I am used to."

Mozare moved to sit next to Saiden on the opposite counter. "What's it like in your kingdom?" he asked.

Saiden pulled an apple from one of the baskets and rolled it back and forth in her hands. She was still upset, her shoulders were tense, but her silence was a bigger key than anything else that today's events were bothering her.

"It's much warmer. I truly can't understand how anyone deals with the cold here."

Saiden laughed quietly, as if to herself.

"The people there—they don't have Gifts like you do," Cassimir answered. "They pray to different gods, and they believe in the power of nature and nature serves them in kind."

"What do you do in your kingdom?" Mozare asked, looking between his partner and the foreign advisor.

"My uncle is the king. I help with my cousin's princely duties, and of course, I act as foreign aid to rebellions." There was a joke in his voice.

Mozare smiled at his back as Cassimir flipped ingredients in the pan he was using.

"It's peaceful there?" Saiden asked, longing in her voice.

The man turned around to look at her, leaving the food on high heat. "Peace must be fought for, Mistress. That is true in any kingdom." A few moments later, he turned the stove off, plating three servings of whatever he had just made.

Even without the Taezhali spices, the food was different from anything Mozare had ever eaten before. Rich with so many more layers of flavor than he was used to.

The man was a good cook, and it made him wonder what Cassimir was doing, lending aid to foreign rebel fighters.

He wondered if they should even trust him.

Even if they couldn't, the food was delicious. And though it wasn't like the food he used to eat, it made him think of home. It wasn't something he did often.

His parents had been quick to deliver him to the Legion. They had considered it the gods' will and had not contacted him again. He never got letters or visits from them. They had abandoned him—gods' will or not.

Thinking about it made him feel heavy, and he tried to think of other things to bury it in his mind. There was too much happening in the present for him to be sucked into the pain of his past.

M ozare rolled onto the balls of his feet, feeling the adrenaline coursing through him. Their day had finally come, their freedom within his reach. Weeks of planning had passed where their small council went back and forth before finally agreeing on Saiden's plan.

She waited in front of him, listening for their cue. She had kept the strike attack assignment for their group. They would sustain the most damage, and so Saiden had been unwilling to let anyone else take that risk. And because she put less value on her own life, she ran point.

He stood beside her, ready to defend her blind spot. Even with the tension between them, they were still partners.

She had her kindjal blades unsheathed, and multiple throwing stars were strapped over her chest. Her stiletto blades were still sheathed in a new gear jacket from Revon, reinforced with stronger material that had been sent to him from far away allies to the cause.

Mozare wore a similar outfit, though he carried a double-edged sword. He had other weapons sheathed on his body, including his axes, but the sword was dramatic. In a battle, he needed something strong and fast. But if he were over-whelmed by people, he could pull out shorter-range weapons and fight with both hands if he needed to. Especially if he was going to be following Saiden, making sure she didn't take a knife to the back.

Their group was small, a ploy to get the guards to underestimate their strength. Cassimir stood on the other side of Saiden, each hand holding a sharpened chakra. There were short daggers strapped into elaborate harnesses on his legs, and the kirpan blade sheathed at his waist. They took only eight others with them, all trained fighters, and split the rest of their forces.

Cara and Revon were leading a small group to find Loralei. Their plan was to have Cara lure her into a false sense of security, or even pretend she had been taken hostage.

And Revon needed to be there. If Loralei surrendered, or if she died, tra-ditions of the country would dictate that her successor must be present. It was the only way a Chosen ruler could be removed from their throne. Otherwise, they would need to wait for the next cycle.

On the other side of the palace, aiming to attack the guard's barracks, were

Revon's other trusted lieutenants. If they managed to take out the majority of the palace forces before reinforcements could be called, then the battle would be won with minimal bloodshed. If each piece played out correctly, the country would be theirs in a matter of hours.

On a personal note, Mozare was glad for the different groups' placements. Their spread-out nature meant that he didn't have to worry about Revon or his other generals taking advantage of the impending chaos to remove Saiden from the equation.

He followed his partner as she pushed through the front door. An alarm sounded from the rebel barracks, their cue that it was time for their attack. The barracks fighters would keep the royal soldiers from forming a protective barricade.

The queen would fall, no matter how much they fought against it.

Saiden was the first to raise her weapon, and the rest followed. When she lowered it again, the eleven of them charged into the fray of guards, Saiden as their arrowhead.

He watched her plunge the shorter of the kindjal blades into the first guard, doing her best to avoid anything sensitive, and then he was swinging one side of his sword towards the guard closest to him. Their deaths were honorable, and that is how he was able to carve through them free of the guilt that he knew Saiden felt. She didn't want them to die, honorable death or not.

He sliced through the men, but they kept coming. Saiden hadn't been able to give them an exact number of guards stationed at the palace. While they had assumed there were a lot, they had not expected this many of them to be fighting their group.

Two soldiers charged toward him, and he stopped, freezing, letting his eyes go wide. He knew what they would see, a frightened rebel fighter in over his head. By the time they recognized him, he had already plunged his blade through the first, swinging around to slice deeply through the chest of the other soldier.

He saw Cassimir swirling through the crowd, his mouth moving as if he were speaking, but Mozare was too far away and there was too much noise for him to understand what the man was saying. He couldn't stand there watching him either—unless he wanted to bleed out on the palace floor.

Mozare wove his shadows through the air, keeping the guards closest to him from being able to find their targets. He stabbed them through, rushing through the group before any of the others could come to their aid. Blood soaked the blade, dripping on the floor in front of him. He stepped around it, careful to keep the puddle from tripping him up.

A guard came up behind Saiden, and she was too busy fighting another in front of her to notice their approach.

He raced towards her, pushing through others with his blade swinging around him in furious circles. On her other side, another of the rebellion fighters charged toward Saiden, but neither would make it in time. Mozare stopped, pulling a throwing dagger from his belt, and hurtled it through the air. He held his breath, watching the blade fly and land hilt deep in the guard's back. The man toppled over a second before he would have reached Saiden.

She dispatched her guard. She turned around to see how close she had come to death and gave Mozare a short nod before jumping back into the fight.

The smell of blood was filling the room, and he could feel it making the floor slippery under his feet. Something about this wasn't right, but his brain couldn't focus enough past the fighting to figure out what felt so wrong.

61
LORALEI

Loralei perched on the side of her bed, listening to the sound of fighting echoing up the stairs to her chambers. Her hands shook in her lap, fear paralyzing her to the spot.

She heard her guards whispering in the hall that Saiden was the one leading the attack. She had thought they were friends, but she understood the truth now. Understood that Saiden had used her, gotten close to her, just so she could bring death to her door.

The secret door in Loralei's room opened with a soft hiss. Her mattress was soft underneath the layers of her skirt. Terror kept her from picking up a weapon, from fighting for her own safety. She turned to watch the door the legionnaire had once used to protect her open to further betrayal.

She felt her heart break in her chest. Quiet tears streamed down her face as she watched another close one turn against her.

Cara stepped forward, dressed in fighting gear. It was a good look on her, though Loralei barely had the energy to care. Cara had never been told about the secret passageways. Even when Loralei had wanted to use them to make their late-night rendezvous easier, she had restrained from showing her the pathways. *Yet another person she cared about fighting on the opposite side of a war.*

A man stepped out from the wall behind her. He was tall and well dressed, forgoing armor for a slim fitting black suit, and she knew just from looking at him that he was the one who had to be in charge of whatever rebellion had been responsible for all the recent attacks. They were the ones who had taken Saiden, which left her confused as to whether her guard had ever been in danger to begin with.

"Your demands, then?" Loralei asked, her voice smoother than she had expected. She sounded heartless, and wondered if perhaps a heart could only take so much pain before it completely died, leaving a person hollow and emotionless. If it was possible, she suspected that was what she had become today.

The sound of battle rang through the castle, but there was an overwhelming silence in her room as she waited for an answer. With each second, she felt dread settle in her gut, her brain trying to warn her, to remind her of the policies of the kingdom she'd given her life to serve.

"You understand we can't let you live," the man said. "We can't let the shadow of your reign and everything you represent stop the light from shining on this kingdom again."

She didn't care about what he was saying, didn't care that death stared her plainly in the face.

"Did you ever love me?" she asked Cara. "All those nights you laid with me, did you ever love me?"

The woman shook her head, but the tears on Cara's face made Loralei think she was lying.

She should've been more careful not to believe her lover before, and now she couldn't trust her own judgment. She couldn't trust that Cara hadn't loved her, but she didn't want to think that she had and was still capable of doing this.

She stood from her bed, and the two invaders watched her warily. Other rebel fighters had started fanning out of the secret passageway into her bedroom, so she had very little time if she was going to get out of her room without dying first.

After Saiden had been taken, Loralei had commissioned for herself a few different weapons. Most important was a sword, the pommel fitted with amethyst stones. But she had also requested a set of daggers, one of which she kept under her pillow at all times.

In a flurry of motion, she reached for the dagger and threw it, watching as it sank into Cara's chest. She could've killed the man behind all of this, but she knew that it would be pointless. In the end, she would likely still be dead. This way, at least she would see Cara in the afterlife. She would have someone there who had once loved her, even if their love had also died today.

She ran from the room, bolting the door behind her and shoving the heavy chairs from her receiving room against the handles. They would be out of there soon enough. She knew from experience that doors did not stay barricaded long against soldiers, especially Gifted ones, but it would buy her the few seconds she needed.

She charged up the stairs, away from the fighting and the noise. There was something she needed to get before she could join this fight if she was going to have any chance of making it out of there alive.

62
SAIDEN

Saiden saw the room in terms of colors and movement. The guards' bright uniforms and the glint of sunlight on their weapons. But she could not discern their individual faces. Each of them was just another number, another leaf for her to mar her body with. She tried not to think about it. She would need to scrub her hands for hours later to stop feeling the sensation of it sinking into her skin.

She stabbed again, the unlucky guard's blood spraying from the wound and mixing with the blood of his comrades and dripping from her hand. She sliced through the armor of another. She stopped only when she finally recognized one of their faces.

She froze. *Nakti.*

Did that mean the Legion was here now? They didn't have enough fighters to face the elite soldiers, which is why they had needed a quick victory. But there were no more soldiers behind her. She couldn't see any other legionnaires. Then she remembered that Nakti had been appointed to Loralei's new advisory board. A detail she had completely forgotten during all of her planning.

She looked around, trying to find the others, trying to find a way out of having to fight the only mother she had ever known. But Mozare was surrounded, an ax in each hand and his sword covered in blood, lost on the floor beyond his reach. Cassimir was across the room from him, fighting to get to his side.

She was on her own. Perhaps it was better this way. If she was honest with herself, she was the only one here who had a chance at beating the General in a one-on-one fight.

Nakti stood on the landing that joined the two higher flights of staircases. She was holding a staff, the carved wood ending in a sharpened chunk of metal. Saiden had seen Nakti fight with it before and knew it was the woman's best weapon.

She knew the woman was waiting for her, and yet she still hesitated. She took a deep breath and then another, then started walking forward.

Nakti had the high ground and, like any experienced General, she was not going to give it up. But she could feel the woman's hesitation run as strong as her own. She didn't want to attack Saiden.

Fear made her limbs heavy as she stepped up to the landing, making herself even with the General.

"How could you turn against the oath you made, my daughter? We protected you. I took you in when they said that you were worth nothing and should be killed. This is what you do with that Gift? You waste it on hot-headed revolutionaries. Do you know anything about them?"

"I know that the people are better than those who suppress them."

Nakti laughed, the sound harsh against the ring of battle. "You know nothing about the people you fight for. The days to come will see more suppression than any that have come before."

"They want a free country, one where everyone has an equal voice," Saiden said, but the words sounded hollow to her own ears. She'd thrown her support into this cause because she let her fear of death be more important than her own purpose. She had let Revon and even Mozare push her into this even when her heart hadn't been behind it.

Nakti stepped forward. "Despite everything, it has been my honor to see you grow." A single tear ran down her dark skin before her face hardened, the mighty General once more. She swung at Saiden, no hesitation in her attack.

The stairs made it hard. There was nowhere to back away from the swing, so she was forced to duck under her, adjusting her balance so she could roll from the swing. Nakti had trained her, Saiden knew that she couldn't win through technique alone. She needed the gods to be on her side—and a bit of luck—if she was going to make it out of this fight alive. She raised the shorter of her blades to block the next strike, swinging the other out to nick Nakti in the leg. It was a dirty move, but she needed any advantage she could get. Her blade cut a divot in the wood before the General pulled back. She feigned to the right, then spun, striking at Nakti's bicep.

With every move, every drop of blood she drew, she pulled another piece of armor around her heart, burying the pain this fight would cause, no matter the outcome.

Noticing the weakness in the wood, Nakti easily snapped her staff in half. She kept the speared end in her uninjured hand, letting the other fall back into a defense position. She swung forward, but they were now balanced, each strike hitting against the other's weapon.

It was the first time that Saiden felt the sweat dripping down her back. Nakti was the only opponent who could push her hard enough that she felt exerted. Then she saw an opening, a brief flash where she could get past the General's defenses. She pushed forward, and she drove her blade through the woman's chest. Warm blood splattered across her face and pumped from Nakti's chest to soak her hand where it was still stuck on the hilt of her blade.

The General dropped the two pieces of her weapon, eyes wide as she felt Ilona's hands reach for her from the afterlife. Saiden let go of her blade, reaching for Nakti, the armor around her heart cracking as they slumped to the floor together. As her tears flowed freely, the fighting around them carried on. But pain dulled the sound of it, as if she were underwater.

Her surrogate mother reached a shaky hand up to touch her face, leaving streaks of her already cooling blood. "I loved you," she whispered. Blood trickled from her mouth. Then her body went limp in Saiden's arms, head pulled down to the floor.

Saiden bent over, sobbing as she pulled the General's lifeless body closer to her, not caring how her blood stained through her jacket. She screamed, and she didn't care who turned to look at her.

There were footsteps next to her on the stairs. She should have looked up, should have pulled her blade from Nakti's chest to defend herself, but she didn't care if her life ended here on the stairs of the palace. If her blood spilled and mixed with the blood of the woman who had raised her.

"Mistress," there was a hand on her shoulder, "the fight isn't over. The time to mourn what's lost will come, but it hasn't come yet."

He grabbed her under her armpits and carefully lifted her from the floor. She pulled her blade with her, watching Nakti's body pull and sag as it released from her chest. She rejoined the fight, Cassimir at her back, moving towards Mozare.

She only froze again when she saw Loralei.

Even with the rebellion, the queen still commanded attention. And she was holding a woman in front of her like a shield, a blade at her throat.

63

LORALEI

Having successfully escaped her room, Loralei wasted no time and raced up the stairs, running past guards who barely looked at her before going to join the battle in the castle's front chamber. Loud footsteps echoed on the steps, but she doubted the rebels would be able to follow her as she deftly moved between her guards. They would make room for her, but never for an unknown intruder.

She'd had Magdalena moved to one of the rooms in the west tower, far enough away that rebels wouldn't have been able to reach her if there was another attack like the one at the ball. She had wanted to protect Saiden, even if the other girl hadn't known about it. Now, she wished that she had given Magdalena a room much closer to her own.

She was glad that at least the training exercises she had been going through had made it so she could run up the stairs without being completely winded by the exertion. At the landing, she paused briefly to kick off her slippers, worried that she might slip on the marble staircase and get herself killed before any of the rebels even got a hand on her.

Magdalena was alone in her room. The queen assumed that any guards she had assigned to watch over the woman had left when the chaos started. She would have to have them punished if she got out of this. Direct orders were direct orders, and clearly too many people thought she could be walked over. That her commands could be easily dismissed.

"Your daughter is here," she said. "I need you to help me save her from the darkness that threatens her." She reached out to Magdalena, the lie easily spilling from her lips. She was too far gone to care about anyone else getting hurt in all this. To care that she had wanted to reunite the innocent woman and former prisoner with her daughter. To right the injustice done to both of them. They would still get their reunion. But only if Loralei could get out of here alive. That was her asking price.

She thought she would be a good queen, but she was willing to give up her kingdom today. Willing to turn over her throne and her people. The weight of her crown was too much for her to bear anyway, and she would be grateful to be free of it.

Magdalena grabbed her hand, her fingers bony and thin in the queen's pampered hands.

She hated the difference between them, hated what her kingdom had done to both of them.

They took the stairs more slowly. Years of being underfed and confined had left Magdalena weak, and she had to be careful on the staircase. Loralei couldn't afford to lose her one bargaining chip.

When they finally reached the bottom, the sounds of battle raged around her. She pulled Magdalena close and apologized. Then she slipped the dagger from the sleeve of her dress and pressed it against the old woman's throat.

Soldiers and rebels alike stepped aside so that Loralei could move through the room. She saw Saiden's partner, arms covered in cuts, looking for someone. Probably his leader if she had to guess, but neither of them was who she was looking for.

She adjusted her grip on the blade of her new knife. She hated what she was doing, but it was the only way that she would be able to say what she needed to before one of them killed her.

With Cara dead or bleeding out in her chambers, Saiden was the only

260

one left who still needed to pay for her betrayal. She had sworn to protect the queen, and yet she was fighting against the crown. It was unforgivable. She had killed multiple times for Saiden, let her soul be darkened because she had believed them to be friends.

Loralei now knew she was pathetic for having trusted either of them. For having loved either of them.

The room split and the Blood-Cursed legionnaire walked forward, her partner and another man keeping any of the guards from reaching her as she made her way closer to the queen.

"Loralei."

"You don't get to speak, Saiden. You only get to listen." She took a deep breath, careful that her hand didn't shake. She didn't want to hurt Magdalena by accident. She was the only leverage she had now. "I have seen you for who you really are. I trusted you. I brought you into my confidence, and let you into my life." Though her hand remained steady, her voice shook.

"You've hurt innocent people and used your relationship with me to justify it," Saiden replied. There was nothing cruel in her voice, though that didn't exactly surprise her. Saiden was a defender of those looked down upon. She wouldn't judge Loralei.

"You were my friend."

"You were my queen, and now you're holding another of your people hostage."

She waited for shame to fill her, but it never came. She couldn't tell if she was too far gone to care.

"A very important hostage, Blood-Cursed girl."

In her arms, Magdalena went stiff. To anyone else, she was just insulting Saiden, but to Magdalena, Loralei was identifying her daughter.

She saw Saiden flinch at the words she flung at her. It was the first time she'd ever used the derogatory term.

"Little Maus," her hostage said, shaking in Loralei's arms.

Saiden's face paled under the blood streaking it. "Mother?"

"Your mother has been a prisoner of the realm far longer than I've been Chosen. As long as she has been missing from your life, I'd assume."

"Let go of her." Saiden's voice was just loud enough to be heard over the battle that still raged around them.

"I can't do that. They're here to kill me. And I can't allow that to happen."

64
SAIDEN

Time stopped as Saiden watched Loralei. Watched the small drop of blood drip down her mother's chest and soak into the collar of her dress. Her mind couldn't wrap itself around the fact that she was in front of her again. Alive, even if not completely unharmed.

Even from a distance, Saiden could see that there was barely any muscle left on her body, her bones stuck out at the joints, her collarbones on full display. Even cinched at the waist, her dress was far too big for her frame. Her hair, once a deep chestnut brown that fell to her waist, was now cut short and liberally streaked with gray. Wherever she had been kept all these years, they had done little to care for her.

Her face was sullen, but her eyes looked like Saiden remembered. Bright and full of love that no number of years could ever dull.

Saiden's heart was heavy. Grief over Nakti, the woman who had raised her all those years her own mother had been taken from her, still pressed against her heart. But it did nothing to dim the astonishment that bloomed in her chest at seeing her own mother again.

Memories of their small cottage flooded through her, the noise of the hall fading in the background. They had been happy there with her father. The three of them had been a family. And this kingdom had taken it away from them. Maybe she really was cursed, just not in the way everyone else had expected.

She wondered what her mother would think of her now. A killer who lived in the body of the daughter she had once loved. She didn't doubt that she would be disappointed, that she would regret the pain she had endured for the sake of the monster Saiden had become.

As Saiden looked around the room, she realized this wasn't who she wanted to be. Her whole life, everyone had pushed her to become the best, convinced her that succeeding in the Legion was the only way that she could prove that she wasn't a monster. And they had still turned her into one.

Everyone except her mother. She had kept her safe in that cabin. Until she had accidentally drawn the neighbor's attention and Nakti had brought soldiers to kill her. She didn't want this life anymore.

She dropped her blades, and the echo of metal on the marble floors of the castle rang through the whole room. The people closest to her stopped fighting, arms and weapons hanging at their sides. The sudden silence was deafening.

"Whatever you want, Loralei. My life is yours."

"I want to be free of the castle. I want to leave here with my life. The castle, the crown, the kingdom, give them all to your leader. I don't care about them anymore."

"And my mother?"

"If you swear to protect me, to help me leave the kingdom unharmed, then I will give her to you. I have no desire to spill any more blood because of you." She spit the last words, and Saiden felt each of them hit her like a physical blow.

"I will offer my life to you in protection."

"You've made that offer before. I'm not going to trust your word this time. It means nothing to me."

"What do you want me to do?" Her nerves were frayed, and panic was building. She knew that made her unreliable, but she couldn't bring herself to that calm that usually fell over her in a fight.

"A blood oath."

Mozare's voice sounded behind her. "No one has sworn a blood oath in a thousand years, Loralei."

Saiden had no idea what he was doing, but the guards were letting him closer. She couldn't let him stop her from getting her mother back. Couldn't let anyone else stop her from being a better person.

"Tell me what I have to do."

"Take your blade, cut it across your palm."

There were footsteps on her other side, but she didn't dare turn around to see who else had come to stand with her.

She reached for one of the small daggers on her thigh, the blades she had sharpened just that morning. The pain was nothing compared to everything else she had endured.

Loralei moved her blade from Magdalena's throat, though she didn't let go of Saiden's mother, and she cut deeply into her own palm. She reached out, her other hand across her mother's chest. Saiden pushed herself out of her reverie and walked to the queen, clasping her hand, their blood mixing between their injured palms.

"I will give my life to get you free from here, in return for the safe release of my mother."

She heard Magdalena whimper in Loralei's arms, and then she was released.

Her mother was suddenly hugging her, bone-thin fingers running her over for injury. She didn't even seem to care that Saiden was covered in blood, that she had killed countless people today.

Eyes wide, she looked at her mother, and the older woman was crying, tears racing down her cheeks and dropping to mix with the blood soaking the floor. Saiden pulled her closer—whatever conflict still burning inside her pushed aside with wondrous joy at having her mother returned from the dead.

She passed her to Mozare, trusting that whatever else happened, he would get her mother to safety. The tentative truce that had stopped the fighting was already growing thin. Fighters on both sides lusted after the bloodshed, the freedom to fight and kill without restraint.

She needed to free Loralei before the hall broke into uncontrollable chaos once more.

Saiden picked up her kindjal blade, taking her eyes off Loralei for only a brief second. But it was long enough to be an irreparable mistake.

She heard the queen scream.

65
MOZARE

Mozare held tight to Saiden's mother. He was astounded to find the woman alive, to find out that she had been held captive for all these years. And he was happy for Saiden, that she would have the chance to know her mother and the love that only mothers could give. But he knew that as much as Saiden wanted the young queen to make it out of here alive, Revon would never let that happen. He would never rest until she was dead because the man could hold no legitimate claim over her throne if the Queen Chosen still lived.

Saiden was too far away from the Loralei, too distracted by the day's events to notice that his leader had entered the grand hall. Mozare couldn't think, torn between his loyalty to the rebellion and the dangerously fragile trust between him and his partner. He had done so much to hurt Saiden, but he couldn't let the queen get away, regardless of what her death would do to Saiden. He would just have to find a way to make it up later.

Mozare didn't say anything as Revon crept through the hall, hidden by the small wisps of shadows that required all of his Gifts to summon. He said nothing, as his leader pulled his blade and used it to run the queen through from behind.

Loralei screamed, the sound piercing the silence.

Saiden moved to step forward, and he let go of her mother to grab her. His partner was already on Revon's list of people to watch after the way she had commanded his rebels. Fighting him now would likely only get her killed.

She was screaming herself, pushing against his arms, so Mozare had to put everything he had into restraining her, forcing her to watch as the young queen's blood fanned out from the knife that protruded through her chest. Her dress was quickly stained with it, and her knees hit the floor with a loud thud.

Loralei spoke, her voice soft. "Beware the secrets of kings, world-ender."

Mozare pulled Saiden tighter against him, falling to the floor with her in his lap when her body collapsed. Her blades had fallen to the floor again, but he knew she wasn't weaponless. Still, she chose to pound at him with her own fists, hurting both of them in the process.

He had never hated himself more. Her tears streamed through the dried blood on her face, and he couldn't endure the look of pain. He tucked her face against his chest as she cried, granting himself a reprieve of seeing her pain.

Revon pulled his blade free, casually wiping the blood off on the train of Loralei's gown. He ordered her men, now his, to have the body removed from the hall. There would be time for mourning, but right now, the rebellion leader needed to stake his own claim. He had managed to kill the Queen Chosen. Those here would have no choice but to turn to him for orders.

"Too long have the strong bowed to the weak," Revon spoke, stepping over the streak of blood from where Loralei's body had been dragged across the floor.

This time, when Saiden pushed against Mozare, he let go. She punched him square in the jaw before standing to look at Revon. He knew the hate that likely marred her face, knew that many strong people had fallen to that look.

Revon didn't even spare her a glance.

Saiden's mother came to stand next to her, holding her hand and leaning against her daughter. Saiden had outgrown her, almost a head taller than her mother. He watched as she stretched up to kiss her daughter on the cheek. And he was relieved when Saiden turned away from Revon and her anger to focus on what was possibly the only good thing to come from the day.

66
SAIDEN

A week had passed since Saiden had failed to keep her promise. A week of scrubbing the blood from the hall of the castle and trying to forget the sound of Loralei's scream. They haunted her while she was awake and plagued her dreams.

Since the assassination, she'd barely slept more than a few hours. The smell of blood consumed her whenever she was anywhere near the front hallway, despite the cleaning that had taken place.

It turned out that while Revon had trusted his three lieutenants, he hadn't done a very good job training them. Their attacks on the barracks had been quick, and they had been killed, along with the small group of rebels they had brought with them. That was why they had been faced with so many guards in their battle. Two of their eleven had also fallen to the queen's forces.

"A small cost," Revon had said when she and Mozare had reported the loss.

The man was now holed up in the queen's quarters, already redecorated for him, while he waited for someone to come challenge him, as tradition required. But when the week had passed without an attack, he had decided it was time to make it official.

Saiden, Mozare, and Cassimir were meant to stand as witnesses to his coronation, which would be held in the palace instead of the temple.

She could barely contain her constant rage. Every time she saw him, she was reminded of how she had failed. And he hadn't even given her leave to return to the barracks. She wanted to be free of the castle and the death that still clung to it. She wanted to see Rhena again.

Her mother, at least, was allowed to remain in the castle. And Revon had done her the courtesy of giving them adjoining rooms in the hallway he had designated for his closest confidants. Saiden didn't want the title, nor did she think he believed she had earned it. She knew she was there because he wanted to keep a close eye on her. She couldn't blame him and would have done the same if their positions were reversed.

Saiden was angry again today. He had taken away yet another of her choices by sending the garment she was required to wear for the coronation. Just as Loralei had. He had left a note, claiming that they had to present a united front to their new kingdom. The dress he had provided for her was bright white, though she didn't care about the color.

What bothered her was that the dress was sleeveless, the back hanging down in a way that would show most—if not every single one—of her tattoos. She felt more vulnerable in it than she had ever felt in her life. She wasn't even sure how he had found out about the tattoos in the first place. Probably Mozare. Yet another betrayal from her partner. And she wondered if Revon knew what they meant to her.

She stood to the usurper's left. On the other side, Mozare stood dressed in a completely black suit. It complemented his coloring, and she wondered if Revon did that on purpose to represent both Keir and Ilona as was the kingdom's custom.

Cassimir was next to her. He had been allowed to dress in clothing of his own choice. A beautifully colored suit she imagined came from his own country. She'd never seen anything that colorful in any shop north of the southern border.

Standing tall between them, Revon wore a black and white suit split down the middle to separate the colors. His way of reinforcing the idea that the Gifted were better, and therefore deserving of crowns and authority.

She hated looking at it, but she cleared her face so that no one in the audience would see it.

Her mother sat in the front row. Already, Saiden could see an improvement. Her cheeks weren't as sallow and they had regained some color. She'd had a proper haircut, and there were flowers woven in her hair. Her mother had taken one of those flowers and tucked it behind Saiden's ear, which had made Revon smile when he saw it. She loved that her mother had given it to her. She never thought she would get anything from her parents again. But seeing him smile had made Saiden want to crush it under her feet.

The ceremony was nothing like the one Loralei had, all other traditions aside from their colored outfits thrown aside.

Revon gave a speech about the gods' will and crowned himself.

Saiden was certain Keir and Ilona would've hated the words of the new ruler, spoken in their honor after so much bloodshed. She felt it somehow boded poorly for the future of his reign, but she was so numb to it, she didn't even care. She had herself and her mother to worry about. As far as she was concerned, they deserved whatever Revon did to this country.

She was done being a weapon for other people to use.

She wouldn't be anyone else's monster.

NAKTI

HARDCOVER EXCLUSIVE SCENE

13 YEARS AGO

Nakti was not entirely sure she was prepared to be going on her mission today. She'd been on plenty of patrols. After all, her team had been sent to calm villages and help rebuild after disaster.

But this mission was nothing like that.

This was a raid.

They were a hunting party.

Rumors of a Blood-Cursed child were something the Legion could not ignore, not when they had been outlawed for centuries. Anyone born with the sign was put to death. They weren't at fault for what they were, but the Legion couldn't let them live, either.

She did not relish the thought of hunting a child, but she'd never disobeyed orders before, so she stood by the other legionnaires and armed herself.

Their target lived on the outskirts of a village so small it wasn't even named. Nakti wasn't sure it was close enough to be technically considered part of the community, though it had been the villagers who had tipped them off to the young girl.

Her mind was muddled. Not even syncing her steps with the other soldiers was able to clear the mental fog.

Grunt soldiers weren't meant to have independent thought. She wasn't meant to be debating the morality of her mission or the righteousness of the kingdom's position against the Blood-Cursed. And yet, the tingling at the back of her mind she always associated with Keir burned with forceful condemnation.

Despite their target being a child, the General had taken six of them with her. Nakti ranked lowest of all of them. That, at least, was something she was used to. She was a strong fighter but had joined the Legion years after her Gifts had manifested. When she was already old enough to make the decision for herself. She hadn't earned her rank yet.

The journey from their barracks took them eight days. In that time, she wasn't sure she had spoken more than a couple of sentences. She wasn't sure they would even notice if she weren't there. She would have been tempted to leave if it weren't for something at the back of her mind telling her this was exactly where she was meant to be.

The house was barely standing when they got there. Not because anything particular appeared to have happened to it, but rather that time had not been kind. There was a mismatched pattern of unfinished wood patches worn by weather and the sun. And there was life inside. Nakti could feel it thrumming through her.

"Three bodies. And something else. Something small. I'm not sure." She was the only life-Gifted among their crew. Something she had belatedly just noticed.

"Rumors place her with two parents," the General spoke. "We should expect resistance. Any force needed to subdue and restrain the child must be taken. She cannot get away."

Four soldiers broke off from the group, positioning themselves at each corner of the house, weapons drawn and prepared for the family to flee. Nakti missed when those orders had been given. Her orders had not changed, though, so when the remaining group moved towards the house, she went with them, keeping her senses open to the life inside the hut.

Her General opened the door with one well-placed kick, though it looked like even an errant wind could have knocked it ajar.

There were butterflies flittering around the family, wings flinching as they tried to fly away from the door. At the sight of the armed soldiers, the father pushed his wife and child behind him and pulled a small knife from the shack's table.

It was not enough of a weapon to even be considered a threat.

Still, the General didn't hesitate to run him through in front of the rest of his family. His blood soaked the floor as soon as his body landed, his eyes staring unseeing as the butterflies tried to escape the cottage.

The mother huddled around her child in the kitchen, keeping her body between the small girl and the legionnaires, the surrounding air ripe with tension.

Through tears, the mother spoke. "You cannot have my child. I will not let you take her."

The General finally spoke the words that would damn them. The words she should have said *before* opening the door, *before* spilling blood and irreparably breaking this family. "You are charged with the ultimate treason for harboring an abomination to the gods. You and your family will be sentenced to execution, and should you resist, I have been authorized to dole out sentencing here."

The woman's cry interrupted the charges. "She's my daughter. Not an abomination. You can't do this."

The child didn't cry. She just watched her mother and watched the guards. "I'm sorry, mama. I didn't mean to go outside."

Her chest ached as she watched the two cling to each other, the child's small hand resting against her mother's cheek.

The General motioned two of the soldiers forward to rip the child from her mother. They knocked the two apart without care for injuring either, and the power tethering Nakti to their life forces flickered.

"No, you can't take her from me." Even without the rudimentary weapon her husband reached for, the mother managed to throw one of her captors from her. The second guard lifted his weapon and hit her on the back of his head with the hilt. The life inside her flickered, but Nakti couldn't focus on it, refusing to feel another of this small child's parents die.

The child was braver than most would be at her age, holding her ground as the General approached her, weapons forward as if the child were a true threat.

Nakti barely processed what was happening before she was pulling her own weapons free and stepping between them, the child at her back.

As her General moved to strike, Nakti committed her first act of treason. She protected the Blood-Cursed child. "Stop!"

Her voice temporarily silenced the cottage.

"Move, or I will run you through just as easily as any other enemy."

"Look at the child. A six-year-old would never be able to control that power. If she were cursed, why wouldn't she move to defend herself? She's not a danger to anyone."

The General stepped up to Nakti. "You bring dishonor on yourself and no one else with this choice. Should you make it, the consequences will be yours until the end of your days."

"Then I will bear it."

The General didn't answer. She simply nodded and motioned for her soldiers to bear the little girl's mother out of the shack.

Once her weapons were sheathed, Nakti turned and knelt down in front of her new charge. "What's your name?"

"I'm Saiden." Her voice was small, but the fierceness was still hidden inside.

"Let's get you home."

Saiden had been missing for the past twelve hours, and if Nakti didn't find her soon, she was sure the General would relieve her of her position in the

Legion. Or worse. And she couldn't even ask anyone to help her. Not without them reporting back to the General.

Bringing back the Blood-Cursed girl had been the right choice. Nakti felt it deep within her bones, but that didn't mean anyone else had agreed with her. The other soldiers had shunned her, and her commanders had made it even more difficult by assigning her the most menial grunt labor.

She was already unprepared to be raising a small child, but raising one while still honoring her duties was far more difficult than she had expected. Not to mention that the child kept trying to run away.

There was nowhere left on the grounds she could think of for a small child to hide.

Nakti was going to have to widen her search.

Running wasn't exactly great for staying under the radar, but she needed to get to the stables. She needed to find this child, hopefully before she got too far or anyone else found her. There were still plenty of people who would see her hair and kill her on sight for it.

She prepared to saddle her own horse, grabbing the supplies before anyone even had a chance to ask to assist her. There were no assigned horses, so she simply went to the first stabled horse, pushed the gate open, and then froze.

Saiden was huddled up with the horse, running her fingers over the fur on its back. She was shivering, despite the animal's body heat, to the point that Nakti was sure she must've been here all morning.

"What are you doing in here?"

"The horses don't hate me. The people all do. You think I am blind because I am small, but I'm not. I'm just weak."

"Come with me." She saw Saiden flinch as she reached a hand out to her. Inside, her heart chipped just a little more.

Even after saving her from death, the girl was still afraid.

"Where are we going?"

"You're going to train."

"Are we training in your bedroom?" Saiden asked as Nakti pulled her into the small room she shared with her fight partner and two others.

"If you want to train, the first thing you need to do is remove obvious weakness. Your hair is an obstacle to your protection."

Saiden pulled her hair to one side, grabbing it as if trying to keep the locks safe.

"We aren't going to cut it," Nakti explained, trying to comfort her. "You see my hair?" She bent to the floor and turned so that Saiden could see the neat rows of braids that kept her coiled hair out of her face and out of reach of her opponent. "It keeps it tamed and out of the way. You need something to do the same."

She turned the girl around so that Nakti was standing behind her in the mirror and started sectioning her hair. She walked her through what she was doing, and for the first time since bringing Saiden with her, the child was completely still.

Nakti put four braids in her hair, careful not to pull on her scalp as tightly as she would on her own, and tied them off with little ponytails at the back.

Saiden's smile in the mirror was a hesitant one, but Nakti relished it all the same.

She took the child to one of the smaller private training rooms to avoid interruptions or and the girl feeling threatened by other people training around her. Then Nakti reached her powers out and attached herself to the girl's life force, reading for any signs of panic.

Though a usual training session might start with a bo, Saiden was still too small to hold one. So, she started with the basics, teaching Saiden powerful stances. She encouraged her to move her body and to see where she felt strongest.

"That's the thing, little one. You think you're weak because you don't have Gifts. But the opposite of weakness isn't power. It is strength. You don't need to be powerful. You need to be strong. If people are going to see you as a threat, you need to be able to back up their assumptions. You don't let anyone hurt you ever."

The words sounded harsh to her ears, but it was a reality Saiden needed to hear. "Every time you pick up a weapon, you expect someone to be coming at you with their own already drawn. You do not waver. Strike first, and put your body behind everything you do."

"When do I get a weapon of my own?" There was steel behind Saiden's voice again.

"You can have a blade when you wipe the floor with me."

ACKNOWLEDGMENTS

I dreamed of this day for half of my life. I understand that I'm young so that's not a lot of time in years but perspective is everything. This is the culmination of my dreams. Thank you to everyone who helped me get to this point. And thank you Zara for taking a risk on my baby.

Thank you Mom for never making me get a "real job" and for letting me pursue this dream. Your belief in me made it possible all those times I doubted I would make it here.

Thank you Dad for promising to buy multiple copies of my books, your support means the world.

To my twin, thanks for always having my back. That's it. Want to get Taco Bell?

Jennie, Andy and Mary thank you for being as excited for this book as I am. Your constant reminders that I'm an author has made this feel real.

To Kay— For reading this book and loving these characters as much as I did I will be forever grateful. Your faith in them made this book possible.

To Catie— I would never have gotten the timeline straight if it wasn't for your help. Thank you for taking the time to help me figure it out.

To Jesse— You helped me fix the last pieces of this book, and it makes a lot more sense because of it. I guess brothers can be useful, occasionally.

Kelli, I'm so glad that signing with Inimitable Books brought you into my life, and that we get to share this wonderful step in our journey. I couldn't have asked for a better debut sister.

To my writing friends Jessi, Aly, Ashley, Stephanie, Kate, Kayla and so many more, your community made this solitary task feel less lonely. Thank you for checking in on me during the progress, and for all encouragement given.

ABOUT THE AUTHOR

S amantha Traunfeld's love of stories began when she was about 12—back when she could read a whole book in a day and wrote lots of stories featuring cute ghosts. Now she writes stories about badass women, sharp weapons, and banter-y relationships. *The Legionnaire* is her first novel.

When she isn't writing, she's usually cuddling her dog, starting a new craft project she might not finish, or tryin to figure out how video games work. there's a 94.6% chance you can find her curled up in a bookstore somewhere (math is not her strong suit), but if you don't, you can find more information at samanthtraunfeld.com.

NORTHERN

ERAST

TAEZHALI